SKULLS OF ATLANTIS

EDWIN MCRAE

Editor: Rachel Rees
Cover art: Rusharil Hutangkabodee
Typography: Kim Dingwall

1

LAND HO

"LAND HO!" be the call from the crow's nest.

I look up and shield me eyes against the sun so I can see the woman in the roost. It be Rumguts on duty today, a chubby Irishwoman with a permanently red face due to her nasty habit of drinking on the job. I've warned her three times and confiscated her grog twice. Hasn't worked. Rumguts and the bottle are practically married so I've let her have her self-destructive relationship. After the third warning, where I threatened to maroon her, she at least curbed her drinking enough to fulfill her work around the ship. And despite them being permanently bloodshot, the woman still has the sharpest eyes among me crew.

Mary "Rumguts" O'Malley
Level 5 Sailor
Perception: 11 (17)

Apart from me, that be. I have a Perception score of 13 (19). That's why they call me Deadeye. Me real name's Grace Cortez, but no one calls me that except for magistrates and me mother. She's

1

back in Mindanao, Southern Philippines, running her fishing fleet. I send her letters when I can, but there's usually a lot of water between me and the Sulu Sea.

"What do you see, Rumguts?" I shout up to her.

"Best I can make out, captain, be a small island, but it's got a mighty big structure on it. Took it for a mountain at first, but I reckon it's a building of a sort. Tower, maybe."

"Alright, keep them bleary eyes of yours peeled. And not another sip until we make landfall, you hear me? Then you can go blind as a bat for all I care."

"Aye, Captain Deadeye, ma'am. Not a drop until me feet touch the sand." And to punctuate her promise she bellows, "Look alive below!" and drops her silver flask off the side of the nest.

I wince, imagining that flask cracking the skull of an unwitting sailor, but Inkman's there to catch it. For a big man, he moves freakishly fast.

Tamaki "Inkman" McKenzie
Level 6 Marine
Quickness: 13 (16)

I reckon I could out-duel him with a pistol on account of me Flashfire skill, but I'd not fancy me chances with a blade. I've seen Inkman slice an English marine to pieces in less time than it takes me to say "Jolly Roger".

"Good hands, Inkman, as always."

Inkman winks at me, a gleaming white grin breaking his dark, tattooed face. He's a Māori warrior from a place called Ōtākou, a settlement in southern New Zealand the local Scottish colonists then anglicized to Otago. He tried his hand at whaling for a bit before turning to piracy as the more lucrative occupation. Also, he likes whales more than he likes people, and I think I'm one of the few exceptions to that rule.

"Would that be the lighthouse, captain?" Inkman asks me this as he climbs the steps to the quarterdeck.

"Aye, according to me chart."

"You should get that map copied sometime, captain. Could be some important bits under those bloodstains."

"One day soon," I promise. "For now they remind me of how hard it was to get the bloody thing."

"Yellowteeth sure put up a fight that day," agrees Inkman. "And even in death, he wasn't letting go of that precious paper."

"Good thing I waited a day before cutting his fingers off, otherwise I'd have drowned Atlantis in pirate claret."

Inkman chuckles. It be a mirthful rumbling like thunder in his throat. "Ain't that the truth."

"Sail ho! Off the port bow!" This from Rumguts again, a shrill edge of excitement to her voice. Or be it fear?

"What colors she be flying?"

Rumguts squints and I hold back a smile. Her face looks like a red-skinned potato when she does that.

"Union bloody Jack, captain! Limey bastards looking to steal the treasures of Atlantis out from under our noses."

I take me spyglass from its loop on me belt, extend it and have a gander at these trespassers on our course. This spyglass be me most precious possession, aside from me musket.

Squintlock's Peeper

Perception + 2

Enables the viewer to see the core stats of any vessel.

"Peer into the gizzards of your prize and see if you have the guts to take it!" - Captain Squintlock

That's what it says on one of the thing's polished brass barrels. Well, not *on* it as such, more like hovering in the air above it. I always find the otherwords strange in style. Stiff as a schoolma'am and twice as aloof.

"God writes in mysterious ways," me mother would say to me when she helped me interpret it all, "but She just wants to make good characters of us all. That's why She gives us the otherwords, so She can read the stuff of our souls."

Right now I'm seeing the 'stuff' of this sleek, freshly-painted sloop. Looks like a maiden voyager to me.

Sea Stallion
Hull Defense: 100
Sail Defense: 50
Agility: 100
Speed: 100
Guns: 10
Crew: 60

"She's a sloop. Standard outfitting," I tell Inkman, "probably some lordling out to make their fortune since they're too far down the bloodline to inherit anything."

"Pretty, aye?"

"Like a toy ship at Christmas."

"We're running low on supplies, too. It's been a long trip."

Inkman's right. We were hiding out in Tasmania before we got wind of Atlantis. Rumors had it that the ancient city rose out of the sea soon after the Mighty Shake. We heard that tidal waves made a mess of every port from Brazil to Greenland in the west, from Liberia to Ireland in the east. But London would've been sheltered from all that. Me guess be the limeys are some of the first to get out here for a bit of exploration and exploitation.

"Then let's be having some of their supplies, then." I squish me spyglass back down to size and stow it on me belt. "They're likely full to the gunnels with grub and grog."

Me mouth waters at the thought of a cool lemon juice and sugar, the standard remedy for staving off scurvy. Bleeding gums and bulging eyes are the first signs of that malaise. Just as well Doc the Croc, so-named for his cold-blooded approach to anything medical, urged me to make regular stops to pick up fresh fruit along the way. We did so in Argentina, just after coming around Cape Horn, but we've since run out again. I sure as hell be hoping that sloop be laden with more than Englishmen. I'd take lemon over an Englishman any day.

"Set course to intercept, Jonesy," I order me helmswoman.

"With pleasure, captain."

THE SEA STALLION

Cedella "Jonesy" Jones
Level 4 Pilot
Wit: 12 (15)
Navigator: 1st Class

OUR HELMSWOMAN BE JAMAICAN, a veteran of the Caribbean, and easily the best looker on me ship. Best singing voice too. Easily half the lads have an eye for her, and a few of the ladies, Rumguts included. Hell, even I would try to sweet-talk her into me cabin if I was that way inclined. Captain's advantage and all. But I'm not one to make that mistake, with neither man nor woman in this company. Unlike most on me boat, I don't screw the crew, as it were. I have a hard enough job maintaining order and discipline without seasoning the stew with me personal affairs.

I feel the Albatross shift gracefully under me boots as Jonesy turns the wheel and aims our bow ahead of the other sloop. As long as the wind holds, we'll cut her off before that lighthouse up ahead.

I take a gander at the gizzards of me own ship, just to be sure we be ready for the battle ahead.

The Albatross
Hull Defense: 101/120 (131/150)
+30 Defense from Iron Scantlings
Sail Defense: 31/50 (51/70)
+20 Defense and +25% Fire Resistance from Sails of the Salamander
Agility: 100 (130)
+20 Agility from Copper Plating of the Bow
+10 Agility from Navigator: 1st Class at the helm
Speed: 110 (120)
+10 Speed from Sails of the Salamander
+10 Speed from Navigator: 1st Class at the helm
Guns: 14
12 Seaworth Culverins
Base Damage per Gun: 10 (15)
+5 Damage from Gunner: 1st Class
2 Seaworth Falconets
Base Damage per Gun: 5
Crew: 99

This time I let meself smile. She needs a few repairs, but the Albatross still be in fair fighting shape. Time to go teach this English lordling who the true upper classes of the sea be.

Since we're faster by a good twenty points, we reel the Sea Stallion in like a fishy on a line. She fires a warning shot from one of her swivel cannons as we draw close, but that's all the protest she can offer us. Jonesy has brought us in on the prey's stern to avoid the build of the Stallion's cannons. Coming in on a broadside, that's just asking to get peppered like a steak on a plate.

"Hard to starboard, Jonesy! Let's answer her squeak with a roar of our own."

That gets a holler of approval from any crew within earshot. They look a motley lot, not a uniform style among them, clothes cobbled together from a dozen or more nationalities. Some have bits of armor, pikeman's chest plates, conquistador's greaves and gorgets, the odd dented helmet here and there. All have boots though, purchased with doubloons from the ship's treasury when we was anchored in Wellington. I've insisted on me crew wearing boots, during a battle at least. Ran into a cunning French merchant captain who sprinkled his deck with broken glass and tacks before we boarded his ship. I lost too many good sailors that day.

The Albatross responds smoothly to Jonesy's gentle touch, coming about to put us broadside to the fleeing Englishman. I move to me gunner's position at the port corner of the quarterdeck. There's a pull cord there that I've had installed. It runs to bells on the main deck and the gundeck below. Me gunners know to be ready to fire when they hear that death knell.

I pull the cord once we're turning on the right line but still be well shy of the target. There'll be a delay of three seconds before me gunners can light the fuses and another five seconds as the fuses burn down. We're also tilting to starboard now, which helps with the elevation of our shots. I'm aiming for the sails with this volley. Me gunners know to load the cannons with chain shot for the first blast. A ship full of holes can still flee on a full set of sails, especially in the time it will take us to turn back on course now that we're broadside to the Sea Stallion. But with tears in her sails and a few broken yards, she'll be going nowhere fast.

The thunder of our cannons sends a delightful tremor through the deck beneath me. It warms me heart to hear me Albatross give her battle cry. Spinning chain shot blurs out towards the Stallion's fresh white sails, shredding them like paper and splintering a good portion of rigging. Four of me six shots hit, and I watch with grim satisfaction as a few of their crew fall like snowflakes to the deck. One or two are more like rain, having been torn apart like the sails.

The otherwords appear in the corner of me eye, as they always do in these circumstances, letting me know how we're faring.

Sea Stallion
Speed: 40/100
Crew: 55/60

Now there's no hope of retreat, the English captain brings his boat about, aiming to return a broadside of his own. Little does he know that he's playing right into me hands. There's a funnel next to me pull cord, the opening to a brass tube that also leads to me gunners on the main and gun decks. Battle be fearful noisy and me voice would be lost in the din otherwise. And the crew be fond of using me hollering tube for their drinking games, pouring ale down at this end for some hapless guzzler at the other end trying to open-throat the flow. At least it ain't far for them to go to the gunwale or a gun port where they can puke their guts out into the sea. I tried it once meself, on a dare from Rumguts. Damned experience made me cry. Never been so drunk nor sick in all of me days. Never again, I told her.

This time it ain't ale that be pouring out of the spout below. It be me orders.

"Heavy shot, ladies and lads! Let's be having their cannons!"

The Sea Stallion gets the drop on us this time as I quietly wagered she would, but it be a stuttering speech, barely heard and leaving little impression. One shot manages to put a hole in me bow, another one blasts the port bow gunwale.

The Albatross
Hull Defense: 129/150

A scratch, nothing more. But that second shot takes out two of me sailors who be standing too close to the impact. Leblanc and Roberts. We'll drink to them and likely many more when the fray be done.

The Albatross
Crew: 97/99

I wait until we're bang-on broadside and we're in the gutter of the sea swell before unleashing all hell against the Stallion's belly. Four cannons only as I don't want to sink the English sloop outright. All four guns hit their marks and our heavy shot eviscerates the poor vessel, wiping out most of its starboard cannons and gunners in one fell swoop.

Sea Stallion
Hull Defense: 40/100
Sail Defense: 40/100
Agility: 50/100
Speed: 40/100
Guns: 6
Crew: 50

One of their swivel cannons barks at us. The shot smashes the rail behind me, showering both me and Jonesy with splinters. I feel the sting of jagged wood pierce through me coat on me left arm and shoulder. I look to Jonesy and see that her smooth caramel skin be unblemished, unlike Inkman who's now bleeding from a cut on his chin and his bare left arm. A few scratches on his conquistador's breastplate show where more timber shrapnel would've pierced his chest. He's clearly spotted the enemy gunner's aim and has put himself between the impact and our helmswoman. Clever lad.

Captain Grace "Deadeye" Cortez
HP: 153/166

Tamaki "Inkman" MacKenzie
HP: 202/224

The Albatross
Hull Defense: 128/150

"Grapeshot!" I bellow into me speaking horn, and once again I wait until we're tilted upwards to port. We're rocking in the swell now so it's just a matter of timing to get the right elevation for this volley. I be aiming for the decks where most of the surviving Englishmen are crowded, including that bastard marksman with his swivel cannon.

When I believe the time be nigh, I yank on the pull cord and am rewarded with a thunderous report that sprays the Stallion's aft decks with black death. The cheer from me crew be cruelly echoed by the cries of the wounded on the other ship. I note with grim satisfaction that their swivel cannon be unmanned.

Sea Stallion
Crew: 36

"Bring us into boarding range!" I shout to Jonesy.
"Aye, captain!"
This be the bit where things get really hairy. Me Albatross be the tougher, more heavily armed ship so the Stallion's defeat was pretty much inevitable, as long as we didn't do anything stupid. But boarding. That be a different matter entirely. Aye, we outnumber them almost two to one, but many a brave ship has repelled borders with worse odds than that. If this goes pear-shaped, I could be losing many a fine matey today.

I offer a quick prayer to Bathala and fetch me musket. Time for me to add a few more notches on the old Deadeye belt.

3

QUEEN OF THE WAVES

SOME WOULD CRITICIZE me for not being the sort of captain who swings like a shrieking monkey onto the enemy's deck to wreak bloody havoc with her crewmates. But a smart woman plays to her strengths and dodges her weaknesses. That's what me mother taught me right from the cradle to the captain's hat. Aye, it's good to make sure them weaknesses aren't too damned weak, but no point in bailing out a sinking ship either.

I wait until we're alongside and me crew have launched their grappling hooks before taking up me firing position. Inkman's at the top of the steps, his taiaha clutched tightly in his big, scarred hands. I've never seen another man bear its like. Best described as a warstaff of solid hardwood, pointed like a spear at one end, flat-bladed like an oar at the other. Inkman has made a few piratical adjustments to the traditional Māori weapon, cladding its blade and point in razor-sharp steel.

Ngāi Tahu Taiaha
Base Damage - Point: 30
Base Damage - Blade: 50
Steel Edging: +20 Damage
Kaumātua Blessing: +2 Agility

"Give them hell, matey!"

He responds with what he calls a pūkana, widening his eyes and sticking his tongue out at me. I'd laugh if it weren't such a bloody frightening sight. Had I not known better, I'd have thought he was about to chop me up and eat me.

I wave him away. "Save it for the English ladies, you ugly blighter."

He gives me a sailor's salute and then he's off down the steps to lead the boarding party. I'd hate to be on the receiving end of one of Inkman's battle charges, that's for damned sure.

Me crew fires their grappling hooks at the enemy ship and soon the winches are singing as our two vessels are joined in what will be volatile and violent matrimony. On the Stallion, a couple of the Englishmen start hacking away at the grapples with boarding axes, desperate to free their vessel from our tentacles. I line one up, a red-headed giant of a man, breathe out slowly, and put a bullet right between his ginger eyebrows.

Critical Hit!
Shot Damage Inflicted = 300
Level 2 English Marine
HP = -150/150
You have killed a Level 2 English Marine.
XP reward = 200 XP
Progress to Pirate Captain Level 7 = 21200/30000

Yes, the otherwords have spoken true. I've got a wee way to go yet before me next level-up. Me last one was when we captured a fat sealer in the Tasman Sea. I was tempted to dump both cargo and captives overboard. Inkman and I see eye to eye on that matter of animal butchery. Neither of us can stand to see the slaughter of defenseless beasties. And for what? So some fancy-man can have himself a plush coat? Don't seem right at all to me. But I have a crew to feed and a ship to maintain, so I dumped the furs and sold the sealers to the slave mines of Broken Hill. A girl has to set her course and stick to it, no matter how murky the skies be getting.

Now I be out with fresh powder and shot, loaded and cocked in a shade over ten seconds. It'd normally take an experienced musketeer fifteen seconds to reload, but I've got a couple of nifty advantages on your average rifleman.

Rumpus Musket

Base Damage: 100

+1 Quickness

Built for faster reloading than standard muskets.

-2 seconds to loading speed.

"Be quick or be dead." - Happytrigger Hakura

Hasty Hands

This ability enables increased fine motor skills.

-20% reduction in the time it takes to perform manual tasks involving hands.

This be no time for dwelling on what else these quick hands of mine can be doing. There be a sea battle to win.

I poke me head over the gunwale and see the flash of a musket on the opposite quarterdeck. One of me sailors, a blondie Swede named Icepick, spins and falls into the frothy water below.

The Albatross
Crew: 96/99

Me guts twist at the sight, but I know it's just part of the pirate life. I'll be losing some more of me crew before this battle be done, especially now that Inkman's boarding party has jumped over to the Stallion and be engaging the English in hand to hand.

I wait until the English musketeer has reloaded and popped her head up to take her next shot. Aye, she's lining up Inkman no less, having recognized him as the leader of the boarding party. Can't be having that. I don't have time for careful aiming so trigger me Flashfire skill. Won't be able to use it again for a bit. It has a one-minute cooldown. The battle might be over in half that. But it's well worth it to save Inkman's skin. I know he's a tough bugger, capable of taking a bullet or two to the body, but the musketeer be at close range. If she scores a critical as I did with that ginger giant, Inkman will be a deadman.

Quick as a striking adder, I aim and fire. By the spray of blood from the Englishwoman's neck, I can tell I've hit me mark, and the otherwords soon confirm it.

Damage inflicted by shot = 150
Level 2 English Musketeer
HP: -50/100
You have killed a Level 2 English Musketeer.
XP reward = 200 XP
Progress to Pirate Captain Level 7 = 21400/30000

Inkman looks in me direction and snaps off a quick salute before engaging his next foe, a saber-wielding officer. I feel a little warm inside at the acknowledgment, a tad bit proud of protecting me friend.

Then I set to loading again while I cast me gaze over the enemy ship, searching for their captain. I spot him on the steps of his quarterdeck, well-turned-out in his smart red officer's coat and captain's hat. He's fending off a couple of me crew with his rapier and doing a damned fine job of it. He's got that prim and proper style of a private school fencing champ, but he's doing a right number on me own fighters. Before I can bring me musket to bear, he's skewered the German, Bratwurst, neatly through the throat. Yet he still be quick enough to parry a brutal cutlass slice from the lanky Zulu lad, Shaka.

The Albatross
Crew: 93/99

I can't tell where but seems I've lost a couple more of me crewmates somewhere in the fray. The English are falling like flies, but not fast enough for me liking. There's only so many in me social circle I feel I can afford to lose on any given day, and today I'm feeling a might miserly on the matter.

I line the lordling up, ready to put a shot through his temple, but can't seem to pull me trigger. He's a handsome lad, all clear blue eyes and soft brown curly locks beneath his hat. And there's a grace about the lad that makes him seem like some delicate artwork. A stained glass window. I just don't have the heart to shatter him. I sigh, curse me own squishy innards, drop me aim and wait a moment while Shaka drives the nobleman up the steps. As soon as I see the white of the bugger's clean pants, I put a shot through his thigh.

Damage inflicted by shot = 50
Level 3 English Captain
HP: 70/120

He stumbles backwards and falls onto the quarterdeck while I stand and holler at the Zulu.

"Shaka! Take him alive!"

The lad hesitates for a moment and glances back at Bratwurst's corpse. I know the two of them been bunkmates off and on, and I can see the lustre of vengeance in Shaka's eyes. I bark at him again.

"Shaka! Think of the ransom, lad!"

Nothing like the mention of money to snap a pirate out of his sensitivities. He nods, knocks the captain's rapier aside and hogties him with some nearby rope. I reload and cover Shaka while he's about his business, making sure he doesn't get stabbed in the back for his troubles. And I'm impressed to note that Shaka takes the time to slice a strip from the captain's coat and tie it around his gunshot. Don't want the bugger bleeding to death before we get a chance to ransom him.

Out of the corner of me eye, I can see that the Englishmen are faltering now that their captain's out of the action. Shaka's done his job and is now guarding the nobleman, cutlass at the ready, so I drive a nail into the coffin of defeat by shooting the Stallion's quartermaster through the heart.

Damage inflicted by shot = 150
Level 3 English Officer
HP: 0/150
You have killed a Level 3 English Officer and incapacitated a Level 3 English Captain.
XP reward = 450 XP
Progress to Pirate Captain Level 7 = 21850/30000

With both captain and quartermaster at Level 3, it's as I reckoned it. This be an inexperienced crew with a relatively green captain too full of his own well-bred self-importance to know he be sailing into hostile waters. He's completely underprepared. I'll quietly enjoy rubbing some salt in his wounded pride. Can't stand toffs of any color or creed. Me mother took over our family's fishing boat after me father drowned and now she has a dozen trawlers in her fleet. But she weren't about to treat me like some little new-rich princess. Sent me off with a packed lunch and the clothes on me back, and told me to put what she'd taught me to good use.

Turned out her lessons were more valuable than any amount of gold she might've handed me. I worked me way up from powder monkey to head gunner, led a mutiny to unseat the whip-happy tyrant of a captain, and had me own pirate ship by the tender age of twenty-three years. This very ship, in fact. The Albatross. Inkman was quartermaster and didn't much like the captain either. But he's never wanted the burden of captaincy so was happy to let me shoulder the charge while he stayed on as quartermaster. We was only Level 3s back then, like these green limeys, and four years of piracy soon put scars on our skin and experience in our gizzards.

Speaking of the tattooed devil, Inkman waves at me from the Stallion's lower deck. The remaining Brits have surrendered under orders of their only surviving officer, the sailmaster. I'm quietly hoping she can be persuaded to join our crew. I lost me last sailmaster in the tussle with Yellowteeth, and one of me boatswains, Jerry "Hyena" Mugabi, has been filling in. He does a fair enough job of it, but I'd prefer to have a specialist on deck again.

I wave back and then order a couple of me sailors to lower the gangplank so I can saunter across to the English ship like a conquering Queen of the Waves. Can't put me finger on why, but I want to make an impression on this English captain. Frighten the bejesus out of him? Aye, that'd be nice.

4

STAR OF ATLANTIS

I GREET the captain with a smile and ask after his name. His pretty face be tense and flushed with the pain from his leg, but he makes a good fist of being dignified as he responds.

"Captain James Montagu of Sandwich, and my father, the earl, shall have you hunted down like the-"

"Sandwich?" I interrupt him. I have no patience for empty threats. "Your father be famous for ordering roast beef between two slices of bread so he could hold it in one hand while gambling with the other. Sorry, matey, but I doubt he'll be lifting a finger for his fourth spawnling in the line of succession."

Sandwich looks suitably startled at that. "Fifth actually, but how did you-"

"I hear them toffs be all the same. One to succeed, one for the military, one for the clergy, and if there's more, send them packing to make their own fortunes. If number one and two cark it, there's always the one wrapped up in lamb's wool in the church to take over."

He eyes me for a moment, weighing his options. He knows I'm right. Then he makes a brave move, one that catches me off guard.

"I care not what you do with me. Ransom me if you like, but do not make it too large. My father will likely pay up just to seem magnanimous in the company of his fellow nobles. But please allow my crew to return to England. They are good people and I will not see them butchered due to my own ridiculous ambitions."

I do a quick headcount of the Stallion's remaining crew.

Sea Stallion
Crew: 31

I lost a few more of me own crew before the fracas ended. Croc is already having the injured shifted back to our ship to be seen to. Five in total, but two of them look like they won't survive to see the sunrise.

The Albatross
Crew: 90

Shaka still has that glint of vengeance in his eyes. Likely enough, there's a few other ladies and lads with their blood up still, wanting to avenge their shipmates. But I'm just not that kind of pirate.

"Give me one good reason why I shouldn't feed you all to the sharks? And don't be trying to play on me kind heart. I left that in the pants of me other life."

That gets a chuckle from me crew and a few finger their cutlasses in bloodthirsty anticipation. Even though I have no intention of murdering these poor buggers, it's always good practice to improve to me reputation with me fellow pirates. Some of them ain't as nice as me.

"The Star of Atlantis," he offers with a faint smile like I'm some fishy he's trying to bait. I resist the urge to slap that stupid smirk off his face.

"No such bloody thing," scoffs Inkman beside me.

"Oh, I assure you," Sandwich persists, "the finest scholars in London have confirmed its actuality. Imagine that, captain, a jewel with the power to take you wherever you wish in the blink of an eye."

I reckon he's just playing me, bluffing on a dud hand, so I press him a little bit.

"Tell it to me straight, Sandwich. Be the Star of Atlantis real or are you pulling this all out of your backside."

He looks me in the eyes with those baby blues of his. "The Star is real and I know where it is."

I feel a warming in the cockles of me heart. We've all heard the legend of the Star, how a ship bearing that jewel could vanish from one spot and reappear one hundred leagues away. Bloody dangerous tool in the hands of a pirate. It could make me the richest and most feared buccaneer in all the seven seas. It'd be nice to knock a few of them Caribbean corsairs off their pedestals.

"I think you best be giving me that map, lordling."

"There is no map." He taps the side of his head with his index finger. "It is all up here."

I find that hard to believe. "You mean to say you've all the coordinates and specifics in that noggin of yours? Must be quite some grey matter in that skull."

"The blessings of a Cambridge education. Rote learning under threat of the cane. Does wonders for one's memory."

"Wouldn't know," I admit. "Tend to do most of me learning on the job."

Me mother taught me all the basics but I've never been one to sit still long enough to jam schooling down me throat. Too busy seeing what life has to teach me. I draw me rapier and press the point gently to the neck of the boatswain alongside his lordship. She's a tawny-haired lass with a few streaks of grey in her hair.

"Then you'll be drawing me a map else I'll be adding a little sauce to your sandwich."

Another chuckle from me crew and a pleasing note from the otherwords.

Your shipmates are clearly enjoying the show.
+1% to crew morale
Morale: 86%
Please note that, upon taking the Sea Stallion, your crew's morale increased by 10% from 75% to 85%

"That would be an experienced sailmaster you are threatening to dispatch. Abigail North, meet Captain…"

He trails off, leaving me to fill in the blanks. I have to give it to this toff. He's cool as a cucumber under pressure, and I quite like cucumber in me sandwiches.

"Captain Grace Deadeye Cortez and this be the fine and fearsome crew of the Albatross." Me crew give a rousing cheer. "Assuming I do come over with a bout of mercy," I tell the English sailors, "you best be sharing the story far and wide that it was the hungry Albatross that plucked your Stallion's gizzards."

A few of the Brits are smart enough to eagerly nod their agreement. I turn back to Sandwich and fix him with me most magnanimous smile.

"It be your crew's lucky day then. Looks to me there's enough sails left on this tub to limp her as far as the Azores archipelago, as long as those poor Portuguese bastards haven't been swept away in the tidal waves. We'll leave your lot enough supplies so they don't starve or die of thirst before they get there."

"I appreciate your mercy, Captain Cortez," says Sandwich. "In return, I shall be your guide on a quest to find the Star of Atlantis."

You have been offered a quest!
Star of Atlantis
At the height of the Atlantean Empire, its ships were said to be able to travel vast distances in mere moments, thanks to enchanted jewels affixed to their helms.
During the Fall of Atlantis, most of the minor jewels were lost, but the largest and most powerful, the Star of Atlantis, was embedded in the helm of the Emperor's Dragon, the flagship of the Atlantean fleet.
The Dragon is thought to have been docked at Atlantis during the Great Submergence, but its exact whereabouts have been veiled by the mists of time and rumor.
Do you wish to accept the Star of Atlantis quest?
Aye or Nay?

"I can tell by that faraway look that you are at least considering my offer," remarks Sandwich with that faint smile of his again.

"It'd still be easier if you drew me a map."

"Then you would have no use for me, other than the meagre sum you will gain in ransom." He inclines his head toward Boatswain North. "I will throw Abigail in to sweeten the deal. We shall willingly assist you in this quest. In return, I simply ask for our freedom once the quest is complete."

The boatswain fixes him with a filthy glare but she's smart enough to keep her mouth shut. After all, she's about to have the adventure of her life, and aiding pirates is generally preferable to being torn apart by the sharks that I can now see circling our two ships. Nilsson and a few of the English casualties fell into the sea during our battle, offering plenty of blood for the sharks to get a whiff of.

I have to admit that this whole Atlantis Star thingy be a turn up for the journals. I will the quest text over to Inkman to get his opinion. His dark eyes flick back and forth as he reads. Then he looks to me and nods his assent.

"Agreed," I tell the toff.

Congratulations!
You have accepted the Star of Atlantis quest.
Please confer with James Montagu of Sandwich for further details.

I sheath me rapier and turn to me crew. "Ladies and lads, gut this ship like a fish, but leave enough supplies for these English folk to make their way to Azore."

Me crew gives a hearty cheer and sets about ransacking the Stallion, under Inkman's watchful gaze, of course. Pirates aren't renowned for their impulse control.

I motion for the *former* Captain Sandwich and Ms North to follow me back to The Albatross. Yes, this be quite an unexpected eventuality, and me mouth fare waters at the prospect of it. This trip to Atlantis is already looking up in me eyes. No doubt about it.

5

AN IMPRESSIVE SANDWICH

I PUT me boots up on me desk because...hell...it's me desk until the crew vote otherwise. But with crew morale at 85 percent, I can't see that happening anytime soon. Still, we're sailing into the unknown waters of a legendary city that's been drowned for one thousand years. Who knows where I'll be putting me boots in a few days.

Sandwich be seated opposite on one of me three padded swivel chairs that I nabbed from a plush French merchantman in the Pacific. You can trust the French to add a touch of luxury and style to their tubs.

"We'll be in among the Atlantean Isles by nightfall," I tell him. "Then we'll find a quiet bay, do some repairs for a couple of days, then head out in search of this Atlantis Star of yours." I be slicing and eating an apple from the Stallion with me dagger which I now point at him to make me point extra clear. "I know there be a quest, but only a fool trust them otherwords without checking a few things with their own peepers first. If this turns out to be a wild goose chase then your goose be well and truly cooked."

"Aptly put," agrees Sandwich. "And on my honor as a

gentleman, I can assure you that the Star of Atlantis is real, at least to the best of my knowledge."

"Any idea what we're up against in salvaging the damned thing?"

"Only theories and pure speculation."

"Try me, Sandwich. You'll find me powers of speculation more than up to the task. Imagining the worst be what's kept me and me crew alive this long."

Sandwich smiles, and it really is a handsome smile. I do me best not to match it. Damned thing's contagious as the pox.

"Well, legend has it that the Atlanteans were masters of necromancy, among other dark arcane arts. Some say they could summon the very denizens of hell."

I laugh. "We be the only denizens of hell you'll ever meet, m'lord."

"Please, no need for that. I'm fifth in line. I have no title."

"And I was pulling your leg."

He's suitably abashed. "Oh."

I slice another bit of apple, pop it into me mouth, and chew as I talk. "Let's get this crystal clear, Sandwich. Blood be blood to me. I don't believe in all that inheritance bilge. No one has the 'right' to lord it over anyone else. They need to earn that right."

"Ah yes, the rough and ready democracy of pirates."

"Mark me words, our rough and ready democracy will unseat all you privileged bastards one day. But I'm not here to argue politics with you. I'm here to get rich and infamous."

"At least you're honest about it."

"Aye, you can rely on that with me, Sandwich. I'll bash you in the moosh with honesty if I believe you to be thinking under false pretenses."

"There is a fine line between honesty and ignorant opinion, captain."

"I be as informed as I can." I point me dagger at him again and add a little steel to me eyes for good measure. "Just as you best be well-informed, or you be having your next meeting with sharks."

"On that pleasant note," he says, gesturing at me bookshelf, "thank you for allowing me to retrieve my reference materials."

"Knowledge be money. A saying me mother be fond of."

"Shouldn't that be power?"

"You ever met a powerless rich person?"

"Can't say that I have, no."

"There you have it then. And don't be questioning me mother again or you be-"

"Having my next meeting with the sharks. Yes, I understand."

"Quick learner. Good. You might even live to see the sun bless these merry isles in the morning."

"I shall take each day as it comes. I assure you."

I'm impressed, I really am. Sandwich be a more adaptable sort than I would expect from an English toff. Rather than be filled with a sense of self-importance, he's got the air of a survivor about him. Probably why he's here, making his fortune, and not drinking and whoring away his generous allowance in the seedier end of London.

"I hope so. I be looking forward to learning more about this Atlantean necromancy and such, but me grey matter's feeling a might weary from all the excitement today, so I'll bid you adieu, for now, Sandwich."

"One last thing, captain."

"Aye?"

"Sandwich. Is that really what you are going to call me from now on?"

"What would you prefer. 'Your lordship', perhaps?"

"James will be fine."

"Afraid not, Sandwich. First names be for me friends, and I can count them on one hand. You be me captive, remember?" I point at the door. "Rumguts be waiting to escort you to your cabin."

I enjoy his look of genuine surprise. "A cabin? I thank you for your hospitality, captain."

I swat his gratitude out of the air. "It's just so you don't get stabbed in the middle of the night. Some of me crew ain't as tolerant of their 'betters'. There's a bar on the back of the door. Use it."

"Indeed I shall, captain."

I whistle for Rumguts who strides in and waves for Sandwich to follow her out. I note with approval that her gait be good and steady. She be keeping to her word so far.

"Make sure Sandwich and our new sailmaster are fed and grogged. And ask Croc to see to Sandwich's leg. They be our valued guests. Best be spreading that among the crew tonight over your dicing and yammering. Any harm comes to our guests and the offenders will be answering directly to me. Got that?"

"Aye, captain. Touch the toffs and we're for it."

Rumguts leads Sandwich out, allowing me to eye his physique. Trim and strong he be. And a cute, taut pair of buttocks he has too. Reminds me that it's been some time since I've had me some decent loving. Perhaps there's a good whorehouse been set up in Atlantis already, a place to scratch me itches, as it were. Rumor has it that a few enterprising folks from the New World have set up a town in there. Freebooters from the Caribbean mostly, hoping to make themselves a new Nassau. Freeport it's called, and long may it stay free as far as I'm concerned. We're in unclaimed waters out here. No empire to tell us where we should be setting our knives and forks. One of them imperial bastards will try to plant their flag in Atlantis before the year be out, but we've got a bit of time up our sleeves thanks to the tidal wave. They'll be concentrating on rebuilding their ports before they turn their attention to these here isles in the middle of nowhere. That said, we'll likely see plenty more expeditionary forces, probably better equipped and armed than Sandwich's little outfit. Yes, interesting times ahead.

But those musings can all wait. Time for me to do some navel-gazing, prepare meself for the adventures ahead. Me mother raised me to be a girl of good Character.

6

A WOMAN OF CHARACTER

Grace "Deadeye" Cortez

Level 6 Pirate Captain

Progress to Pirate Captain Level 7 = 21850/30000

Core Attributes

Perception: 13 (19)

+1 Musketeer: 1st Class

+1 Pistoleer: 1st Class

+1 Gunner: 1st Class

+1 Calligrapher: 1st Class

+2 Squintlock's Peeper

Quickness: 11 (14)

+1 Musketeer: 1st Class

+1 Pistoleer: 1st Class

+1 Rumpus Musket

Wit: 14 (17)
+1 for Leader: 1st Class
+1 for Calligrapher: 1st Class
+1 for Gunner: 1st Class

Sand: 15 (17)
+1 Free Diver: 1st Class
+1 for Leader: 1st Class

Brawn: 9 (11)
+1 Athlete: 1st Class
+1 Coat of the Salt

Stamina: 13 (16)
+1 Free Diver: 1st Class
+1 Athlete: 1st Class
+1 Coat of the Salt

Health Points: 153/176
HP = Brawn x Stamina

Advanced Core Skills
None

Base Core Skills
1st Class
Musketeer
Pistoleer
Free Diver
Leader
Gunner
Calligrapher
Athlete

2nd Class
Fencer
Merchant
Chess Player
Angler

3rd Class
Navigator
Violinist
Croupier

Special Skills
Earned from 1st Class Base Skill Achievement
Flashfire (Required: Musketeer 1st Class)
Hasty Hands (Required: Pistoleer 1st Class)
Lungfish (Required: Free Diver 1st Class)
Stirring Words (Required: Leader 1st Class)
Applied Physics (Required: Gunner 1st Class)
Decipher Script (Required: Calligrapher 1st Class)
Daring Dash (Required: Athlete 1st Class)

Kit
Squintlock's Peeper
+2 Perception
Rumpus Musket
+1 Quickness, -2 Reload
Coat of the Salt
+1 Brawn, +1 Stamina

I PULL up them otherwords I received shortly after negotiating Sandwich's surrender. They make for some right satisfying reading.

You have negotiated the surrender of the Sea Stallion and gained both a noble captive and a sailmaster.

Surrender = 1000 XP

Noble Captive = 500 XP

Sailmaster = 300 XP

Total XP Reward = 1800 XP

Progress to Pirate Captain Level 7 = 23650/30000

Under your captaincy, the Albatross has captured the Sea Stallion, a Standard English Sloop.

XP Reward = 23000 XP

Less 100 XP for each crew member lost in battle.

XP Loss = -900 XP

Total XP Reward = 22100XP

As captain, you receive a double share of XP

Your reward = 500 XP

Progress to Pirate Captain Level 7 = 24150/30000

I let out a long sigh. Such is the cost of the pirate captain's life. I've given up counting the dead, and I sleep easier than most on account of knowing I treated them deceased well while they was under me command.

Now I has to weigh up the trials and tribulations this Star of Atlantis quest will no doubt toss in me path. It still be a wee way to Level 7 and I don't feel like lurking about out here in the surrounding waters so we can pick off another hapless adventurer. I'm fair itching to get amongst them wonders of Atlantis. The riches in that city will far outweigh anything that can be plundered on the open sea.

Then again, I could be a right sneaky bugger. Just wait for all them adventurers to do their dangerous salvaging and then pick them off on their way home. I've no doubt there'll be other pirates thinking like that, so we best be careful when we finally leave Atlantis.

It's tempting, but I shrug it off. I ain't that kind of buccaneer, skulking about, ambushing those what have worked hard for their wealth. Actually, I be happy to admit the hypocrisy of that thought. Too much grey in that stretch of moral sea. So here be the practical consideration what comes to mind. By surviving the dangers of Atlantis, said adventurers will accumulate themselves some tidy sums of XP and a fair few levels. Chances are, they'll have exceeded our own Characters and will thereby mop the proverbial deck with us.

No, if I have me way, me and me crew will be the most experienced seadogs in these here isles before we leave off to enjoy our riches in calmer waters. To be otherwise would be to chart ourselves a one-way voyage to Davy Jones' Locker.

With that in mind, I take another look at me skills and decide it's time to trim the fat. There's a few there I haven't used in years, and some I never really enjoyed the use of anyways. It was me mother's idea to take up the violin. Even made me join the Dapitan City Orchestra at one point. I can get a decent enough sound out of them F-holes, but up against committed musicians, I'm just a hack with some horsehair. Same with Croupier for that matter. Got that job at House of Cards in Dapitan under similar orders from me mother. She wanted me to learn the value of money by seeing firsthand how easy it can be taken from you by the silken hands of Lady Luck. She were right too. I swore off gambling for good after seeing one too many poor fools tumble from riches to rags, like the double sixes to snake eyes on their dice.

According to the rules laid down by the otherwords, I can trade in two skills of a particular class to upgrade one skill of the same class. Me mother will likely kill me if she finds out since she paid a hefty sum for them violin lessons, but I figure she'd rather I was alive and uncultured than a dead woman able to mix in polite society. And as for Croupier? She won't mind that. Lesson learned.

I trade in Violinist 3rd Class and Croupier 3rd Class so I can boost Navigator up to 2nd Class. Means I'll be able to take the wheel and sail the Albatross through treacherous waters if I have to. Jonesy would be a bloody tragic loss to me crew, but someone has to be ready to take the helm in that awful eventuality. Also, I'm thinking there'll be plenty of pathfinding to be done once we delve into them Atlantean ruins, and I ain't risking Jonesy's pretty hide on them endeavors.

By sacrificing Violinist 3rd Class and Croupier 3rd Class, Navigator 3rd Class will be upgraded to Navigator 2nd Class after 8 hours of sleep.

Aye, that's usually how it happens. Me grey matter needs bunk time to get its affairs in order. I've only done it once before, cashing in Lockpicker 2nd Class and Pickpocket 2nd Class to take Pistoleer from 2nd Class to 1st Class. Figured I should put the wayward youth in me to bed for good. Me mother never knew about any of me after hours pursuits in the mean streets of Dapitan. At least, she pretended not to know.

I cast me beady eyes over me other skills to see if there's anything else I can spare. I enjoy a game of chess too damned much to give that away. Most of me other skills come in mighty handy during me life at sea, though I'm keen to take me rifle skills up a notch. Reckon there'll be plenty of shooting to be done in Atlantis, and the more foes I can drop at a distance, the fewer crewmates I'll likely lose.

I bring up the advanced skill that leads on from Musketeer.

Sharpshooter: 3rd Class
Advanced Skill
Maintains all of the skills of a Musketeer 1st Class while adding +2 to
Perception and Quickness, reducing reload speed by -3 seconds,
along with increasing the Damage by 100% and the likelihood of a
Critical Hit by 50%
At 3rd Class, Sharpshooter unlocks the Special Skill of Anticipation,
the ability to predict the movement of objects and living creatures up
to 3 seconds in advance of the target's motion.

I simply can't resist that offer. Though I'll miss +1 Perception and +1 Wit from Calligrapher 1st Class, Sharpshooter more than makes up for it. Now here's the really tough choice. Which 1st Class skill to pair up with Calligrapher for this sacrifice? For a moment I consider Free Diving, but its bonuses to Sand and Stamina are just too valuable. And there's bound to be some fierce swimming to be done in a place like Atlantis. Likewise with Athlete. Got plenty of on-land time coming up so I don't want to be caught weak-kneed at any point. Leader, that's non-negotiable too. I'm a bloody captain, after all.

With gritted teeth, I eye up me Gunner skill. The lower deck gunner chief, Viktor "Powderfinger" Tchaikovsky, be at 2nd Class and damn near to topping 1st Class. Just needs one more sea battle under that wide Russian belt of his. It's tempting to hang off until he's reached 1st Class, but I just know I'll be needing that Sharpshooter skill sooner than I'll need me Gunner skill. I sigh and bite the proverbial bullet.

I select Calligraphy 1st Class and Gunner 1st Class and cash them in for Sharpshooter 3rd Class. Plenty of room for improvement in Sharpshooter too, whereas I've reached me cap with Calligraphy and Gunner. Hell, I can always relearn that Gunner skill at some point and have Powderfinger as me mentor. He'd have a bloody good laugh about that.

By sacrificing Calligraphy 1st Class and Gunner 1st Class, Musketeer 1st Class will be upgraded to Sharpshooter 3rd Class after 8 hours of sleep.

Which means it be bedtime for me! I strip off to me underclothes, climb into me bunk and fancy meself in the Freeport whorehouse with three sleek and skillful lads as I drift off to la-la land.

7

BEACON OF HOPE

ME MORNING COFFEE be more than just a ritual. "Me magic beans", I call them, like I be Jane in "Jane and the Beanstalk". Truth be told, they might not be magical, but they certainly be alchemical. +1 Wits for three hours ain't nothing to be sneezed at.

Grace "Deadeye" Cortez
Wits: 14 (18)

I found me special coffee beans during our stopover in Argentina, and after sampling its enlightening effects, bought enough to last me three months. With careful rationing. I'll be fine for me twice-daily brew for a while yet.

From the quarterdeck, I survey me busy crew. Our new sailmaster, Abigail North, be out on the main deck giving orders in a voice that sounds like a roaring sea lion to me ears. It's having the desired effect though. Them sailors in the rigging are moving fast and crisp, better than I've seen them work in weeks. They're finishing the repairs to our sails with cloth taken from the Sea Stallion, and doing a fine job of it.

Sail Defense: 44/50 (64/70)

I'll not even have finished me coffee before Boatswain North has us back up to full speed.

The Albatross
Agility: 100 (140)
+20 for Copper Plating of the Bow
+10 for Navigator: 1st Class
+10 for Sailmaster: 1st Class
Speed: 100 (130)
+10 for Sails of the Salamander
+10 for Navigator: 1st Class
+10 for Sailmaster: 1st Class

Hyena's standing beside her, arms folded, grinning like a happy dog. He never much enjoyed the role of sailmaster, and he's a dab hand with cutlass and pistol, so I'd much rather have him in Inkman's boarding party anyways. Only trouble be, he has an unnerving tendency to cackle with delight in the middle of a slaughter. Hence the name, Hyena. Then again, if we was all sensible and hinged we'd be a hallway of doors, not a shipload of pirates.

But we ain't going nowhere just yet. We're moored in the lee of the lighthouse, a magnificent structure by all accounts, even though its beacon's been dead for over a thousand years. Looks like the top's been knocked off by whatever cataclysm sank the old city into the sea, but I'd still wager on it being at least three hundred feet tall. I be mighty keen to explore the thing, see if there be any plunder to be had. Seems Sandwich be in agreeance with me.

"As chance would have it, captain, that lighthouse was to be my first port of call. It contains certain-"

I stop him in his tracks at the top of the stairs. "Is that me coffee you be swilling?"

He blinks at me for a moment and raises his mug in a toast. "And a finer brew have I never tasted. It is also doing marvellous things to my cognitive processes."

"Who the bloody hell made you a coffee from me personal stock?!"

At least he has the good manners to look embarrassed. "Mister McKenzie?"

Hearing his name from down on the deck, Inkman salutes me with his coffee mug, a wry grin on his moko-bedecked moosh. I send him a withering glare in return, one that he simply shrugs off as he returns to his duties, supervising the hull repairs.

The Albatross
Hull Defense: 141/150

To be honest, I'm acting more surprised than I actually am. I been sharing me stash with Inkman since Argentina. Being me quartermaster, he needs to stay at least as sharp as me. Yet for a big murderous bastard, he's got a soft heart when it comes to hospitality, hence extending the coffee invitation to our new lordling captive. Inkman and me are going to have quiet words about rationing the coffee supplies. He of all people knows how I get without me morning brew.

"I suppose that be alright. But don't be making a habit of it. I've made blighters walk the plank for less."

"Duly noted, captain."

He moves to the gunwale and starts to tip his mug.

"What the bloody hell you be doing now?"

"Well, since it was not mine to-"

"You be wasting that coffee and you be surely walking the

plank, me lad. In fact, I'll tip you over that gunwale meself, right this moment."

He steps back from the edge and presses the mug to his lips instead, takes a sip and sighs. "Much preferable to a shark-infested dip."

I shake me head. These noble types be hard to get one's head around. "Just tell me what you know about that there lighthouse."

He brightens, glad to be back on comfortable ground. "The Atlantean lighthouse is constructed of whitestone, a form of limestone found only in-"

"Hell, man. You fixing to bore me to death out of revenge for me taking your ship?"

"Ah, I see. Straight to the point?"

"If you please. I ain't getting any younger and the pirate life be a notoriously short one."

"Perhaps if they refrained from taking what's not theirs? Law and longevity are rather complementary."

"By taking, are you including the lives of English toffs what annoy me?"

His Adam's apple works up and down in his slender throat as he gulps down a wee draught of fear.

"Point taken, captain."

"Not yet it ain't. You'll feel it when I makes a point." I gesture at the lighthouse. Its whitestone sides glow rather fetchingly in the golden morning light. "You think it be worth our time to take a gander inside?"

"By worth are we talking in material bounties?"

"Aye. Ain't risking lives for the sake of arche-bloody-ology."

"The lighthouse had to finance its own maintenance, and it kept a small fleet of boats for use in rescues, therefore it requested levies from any ships passing this way. It stands to reason that there should be some form of small treasury within. But the Gleams might be of more interest to you. They would be awfully useful in our search for the Star of Atlantis."

"Gleams?"

"The Atlantean version of a lantern. Quartz treated with an alchemical formula so that it converts biological energy into illumination."

"What? Makes light by sucking the life out of you? Sounds bloody horrible."

"From what I have read, the energy drain is slight, perhaps a health point per hour of continual use. Natural healing processes are more than enough to counter its effects. However, if you wish to place your Gleam as some sort of fixed lighting, you can invest health points upfront to the measure of the hours you wish to illuminate."

"Sounds promising. How many Gleams you reckon be in there?"

"They were carried by the lighthouse keepers and by the crews of rescue boats. Assuming they have not been stolen already by a… one of your colleagues… there should be thirty, at least."

He's right. Mighty handy for underground expeditions, and we could sell a few of them afters for a pretty sum. It be a curse to have to illuminate a wooden vessel with oil-burning lanterns. Many a ship has met its end over a single broken lantern.

"Inkman!" I holler.

"Aye, captain?" he calls back from the main deck.

"Quit your lollygagging with the carpenters and form a landing party."

"Right you are. As long as you know that it'll slow the repairs by a good thirty per cent."

Being a Carpenter 1st Class and Quartermaster 1st Class, Inkman's presence buffs any repair crew by almost a third. Handy when we're out at sea and need to get ship-shape before some storm or warship catches up with us. But we'll be moored here all day.

Plenty of time for the repairs to be completed, even without Inkman's bolstering effect.

"The Albatross ain't going nowhere today. We've a lighthouse to be plundering!"

While Inkman makes preparations for our expedition, I put me hardest stare on Sandwich. We're enemies, of that there be no doubt, but I need to know we're enemies what can work together for a spell.

"You're coming along. If I be relying on your advice, it's only good sense you be risking your neck along with the rest of us."

"I would have chosen the same, captain."

There's no malice in those baby blues of his. If anything, I see excitement. "You don't seem all that cut up about the loss of your ship and freedom. Something you're not telling me?"

He takes another sip of me coffee as he considers his answer. "Though I was raised in luxury, I consider myself a practical man at heart. I came to Atlantis to do two things. To make my fortune and to test my mettle. The latter is more important, to be frank. One cannot sharpen a blade on a velvet cushion."

I laugh. "Wise words, Sandwich."

"Now I find myself on a well-equipped pirate ship with a crew that bested my own like we were mere children playing at war. What better circumstances under which to carve away the softness of gentility and discover what lies underneath?"

I wink at him and offer me most predatory grin. "Well, if it be carving up you be wanting, you've come to the right place."

He pales, but not as much as I would've thought. Perhaps there's indeed some iron to be found inside this silver spoon. I leave him to his anxious musings and head down to me cabin to prepare for our foray to the lighthouse.

On me way to don me brace of pistols, I stop at me violin. Picking it up, I try a few experimental bows and attempt to finger a gavotte from memory. Nothing but cat mewling and fumbling. I smile and pop the violin back into its case. That bit of me life be gone. It's a funny thing though. I can still remember playing that gavotte with the speed and fluency of a practiced fiddler. I recall the childhood concerts me mother made me put on for me aunties. But now it's like they was just dreams with no say in how reality be. Aye, the Character be a wily thing, not to be dallied with. Drive you mad if you're not careful with it.

I buckle on me saber, slip me Coat of Salt on, load me pistols and stow them in a belt that I sling across me chest. Then I hook Squintlock's Peeper to me waist belt, load me Rumpus Musket, sling that over me shoulder, and tie me hair back, ready for action. Can't help but take a sneaky gander at meself in the mirror, and I'm happy with what I see. A dashing pirate captain if ever there was one. Look out, Atlantis. Deadeye be having you in her sights.

8

SQUIDBEARD

WITHIN THE HOUR me landing party has pulled our two longboats up onto the beach and we're trekking up the rocky cove to the lighthouse. We're twelve in all, including Sandwich, Inkman, Rumguts, Shaka, Hyena and Doc the Croc. Shaka's here so I can keep an eye on him. He's still understandably salty about Fritz's death at Sandwich's hands, and I don't want him stirring up resentment on me ship. There already be mutterings among the crew about me gentle treatment of the English lordling. But it's a sad fact that few of me crew can see the big picture as I can. I don't mean to sound arrogant, but it does get bloody lonely at the top.

I've brought the good doctor along in case any of us come a gutser on this adventure, a pretty likely occurrence considering we've no idea what Atlantis has in store for us. Speaking of the devil, Croc sidles up beside me for a word in me ear.

"Begging your pardon, captain."

He always starts like that, no matter how many times I tell him there be no begging nor pardoning in me company. I ain't exactly polite society. It's not like he's from polite society neither. Australia being more penal than colony, Croc was a prison doctor before signing on with us. He knows more about the insides of the human being than I'd have expected from one of his tender age. Makes me wonder if he took some medical liberties with the prisoners in his care. Exploratory surgery and such. I shudder at the thought and stow it back in me mind. Croc's cold-blooded all right, but I ain't exactly one to be casting judgements about.

"Aye, Croc? What be on your mind?"

"This toff. You sure we can trust him?"

"You think I'd bring ten of me finest pirates along if I thought this be plain sailing?"

Croc smiles, and it ain't a pretty sight. "Point taken. It's just that I've seen his like many times, the prisoner putting on a show for his captors, all helpful and polite until he stabs you in the eye with a sharpened spoon."

"A silver spoon in Sandwich's case."

"You'd be right there."

"Well, Croc, all I can say is that I hope you been brewing up some of them foul remedies of yours."

Croc pats his doctor's satchel. It jingles softly. "Aye, captain. Plenty of tinctures, although I'll be needing to restock me supplies. I was quietly hoping we'd be docking at Freeport sooner rather than later. Keen to find me a half-decent apothecary there."

"After this here foray, indeed we will. And if Sandwich be speaking the truth, we'll have a few handy relics to be selling off. I'll be sure to add some of that coin to your medicinal fund."

"Much appreciated."

"Oh, and with regards to Sandwich," I say, lowering me voice, "if he betrays us like you suspect, I'd consider giving him to you for a bit of experimentation before we throw his remains to the sharks."

Croc's pale blue eyes take on a cold light, like that of a full moon. "Aye, captain. I'd like that."

I bet you would you creepy son-of-bitch, I think to meself.

Instead, I say, "I'll mention as much to Sandwich, to offer him a bit more incentive for fair play."

The fact is I've no intention of handing Sandwich over to the tender mercies of Doc the Croc. I just want him to see that icy hunger in Croc's eyes when the time be right to make me threat. It'll add nicely to the whole effect.

It ain't long before we be standing before a mighty pair of copper gates. They've turned deep green during their time under the ocean. This be the main entrance to the lighthouse and it be pretty clear that someone's had a go at forcing entry before us. There be scorch marks and barrel splinters where some buffoon has tried to blast them gates open. There also be plenty of scratch marks around the lock mechanism, attempts to free it from corrosion enough to allow for a lockpick. Though they've clearly failed, they've at least saved us some work.

"Sandwich?"

"Yes, captain?"

"I was just having a word with Doc the Croc over there. The gist of it was that if you don't prove yourself useful, he'll be finding a use for you... of a medical nature."

With some small satisfaction, I see a sheen of sweat break out on the toff's forehead, and it beads up nicely when he catches Croc's predatory stare.

"I can assure you, captain, that I shall do my utmost to ensure the success of this endeavor."

To prove his point, he walks up to the gates, studies them for a moment, traces a few of the weird Atlantean symbols with his fine fingers, and then grabs hold of the gate handles. There's a screech and a click as he turns the handle this way and that, lining the copper bar up with different symbols each time. No more than a minute later, there's a loud 'clunk' from inside the mechanism and Sandwich turns to us, a small smile on his handsome lips.

"A little assistance, if you will?"

I motion for Hyena and Lena Longshanks, a mountain of Dutch muscle, to help Sandwich haul the gates open. As the sunshine lights up the lighthouse's entranceway, I murmur a soft prayer of thanks to Amin Sinaya, God of the Sea. I be a Catholic by christening, at me departed father's insistence, but me mother and I have always kept to the old ways, favoring Bathala and his lot over all them saints. I thank Amin Sinaya for sending me this bookish lord and all his Atlantean learnings.

Then I look to Inkman. "Care to lead the way, quartermaster?"

"Aye, captain," he agrees as he unlimbers his taiaha and makes his way into the ancient building.

When he waves for us to enter, having not been eaten by anything mythical, I let out the breath I didn't know I was holding and lead me party inside. There's not much to be seen in this lowest level, apart from carvings and statues, all of which have a disturbing number of tentacles. There be a mosaic on the floor as well. A bit of a dust off reveals the great face of a man with tentacles for his beard. His sea-blue eyes glare up at me like a pair of sapphires and his claws are held in a way that reminds me of them Buddhist hand symbols. The whole thing gives me the shudders, and I can tell me crew feel similarly unnerved.

"Don't mind this ugly bugger," I tell them. "Those who worshipped him be long dead and eaten by the crabs."

Most murmur their agreement but it don't take the otherwords to tell me that morale has just taken a knock.

Landing Party Morale -15%
Morale = 70%

I'm taken aback by the size of the drop. Aye, feels like snakes be slithering in me belly, but I figured that was just me own nerves. Clearly not. There be something about this place that gets under your skin and gnaws at you. It worries me. If we drop to 50 percent

Morale then we start to suffer combat penalties and I can't be having that.

"Rumguts?"

"Aye, captain?"

"Methinks we need a tipple to ease our humor. This place makes the heart go clammy if you catch me meaning."

"I do indeed, captain."

With a grin, she shares out a couple of hipflasks of rum and takes a healthy swig herself once everyone's had a draught.

A wee dram to soothe the nerves.
Landing Party Morale +5%
Morale = 75%

Aye, it may seem unwise to have our rum stocks be cared for by a raving soak like Rumguts, but there ain't no one thinks booze be more precious than our Rumguts. She'd defend them bottles with her life, she would.

"Shaka and Longshanks, you're on point. Up those stairs with you."

They're a good fighting pair those two. Shaka has the speed and Longshanks has the reach. I'll be right behind them with me musket and pistols to make sure they don't get overwhelmed. Also, I don't want Shaka feeling tempted to shove a dagger into Sandwich's back when no one be looking.

"Aye, captain," they respond in unison, although there's a tremor in Shaka's voice that I find more unnerving than the damned mosaic beneath our boots. There's a man not easily shaken, but this place is clearly getting to him.

"Sandwich and Croc, you stay right behind me. The rest of you fall in while Inkman and Hyena bring up the rear." I see Croc give Sandwich a leery wink and I chuckle as Sandwich noticeably tenses, putting distance between himself and the 'good' doctor.

The rest of our party be a pair of sisters we call Black Russian and White Russian on account of one being swarthy and one being fair. And they're both Russian. Aye, we pirates be a subtle lot. Then there's Odin, the one-eyed Norwegian, and Silverback, a bizarrely hairy Turkish bruiser. A motley lot, to be sure, but not to be trifled with neither.

We're up the steps in a jiffy and out onto the next floor. Must've been a storeroom once, filled with maintenance gear for the lighthouse. Though it's been kept airtight, the tower seemingly sealed against the sea all these years, there's nothing valuable to be had. Just a lot of cogs, brass bits and pieces, and a whole lot of glass panes. The next floor be slightly more fruitful. Looks to have been sleeping quarters for the lighthouse keepers. By smashing open some of the footlockers we manage to salvage a few hundred Atlantean silver coins. At least that's what Sandwich says they are. Old tentacle-face scowls at us from one side while the other has some weird geometric patterns what make me cross-eyed just trying to make sense of them.

Party Haul = 321 Atlantean Crowns

"Who be Squidbeard then?" I ask Sandwich, holding up one of the coins.

Sandwich hesitates for a moment, and something passes across his eyes before he says, "Neptune, the god of the sea."

"Strangest depiction of Neptune I've ever seen," remarks Croc.

I'm inclined to agree, but then this be Atlantis. I reckon we be seeing many a 'strange' thing, and far worse before this adventure be done.

We head up to the next floor and that be where things get… interesting. So far our oil lamps be doing a fair job of lighting our way, though they make the lighthouse's grotesque decorations dance like demons under a harvest moon. Now our lamps are swamped and our eyes blasted by an unholy glare. While we're blinking away the color blotches in our peepers, out of the light scampers a half dozen misshapen figures. They be screeching at the top of their lungs like a pod of harpooned dolphins, and each bears a saber made of what looks to be glass.

"Look lively, mateys!" I shout as I raise me musket and take a bead on the leading monstrosity.

9

MISTRESS OF LIGHT

"Shaka! Duck!"

The Zulu does as he's told and I blast the first screecher right in its ugly face. Before the thing explodes in a shower of blood, I note with fascination that its moosh reminds me of an anglerfish crossed with a bulldog. A fierce light be coming from a glowing orb suspended above its nasty visage by a writhing appendage of sinew and scales. It's like a mini elephant's trunk with a white-hot ember shoved in its snout.

Shot Damage Inflicted = 200
Level 3 Lightkeeper
HP = 0/200
Your XP Reward = 300 XP
Progress to Captain Level 7 = 24450/30000

Blimey, they be tough buggers! It's a good thing I upgraded to me Sharpshooter skill and got the 100 percent Damage bonus.

I set to reloading me musket and hear me fellow pirates charge into the fray. There be enough room on this floor to overwhelm the enemy with our numbers, though I bark at Sandwich and Croc to stay their swords. Don't want to lose me scholar and me doctor in the first foray.

Inkman's already battling the fishman closest to me, parrying its glass saber with the flat end of his weapon while jabbing holes in its scaly hide with the pointy end.

To me right I see Silverback stumble, a glass blade shoved clean through his thigh. I line up his assailant, this time aiming for the soft, slimy bit of skin under its jutting jaw. Me musket roars and the fishman goes down.

Critical Hit!
Shot Damage Inflicted = 400
Level 3 Lightkeeper
HP = -200/200
Your XP Reward = 300 XP
Progress to Captain Level 7 = 24750/30000

Now that be more like it! I survey the battle and see that the Russian sisters have double-skewered themselves a fishman. Hyena's helping Inkman finish his opponent off. Longshanks and Shaka are getting the better of theirs, the Dutchy keeping the thing distracted with her long-handled boarding axe, while the Zulu ducks in and slices away at the creature's belly and legs. Rumguts and Odin are struggling a bit with theirs, but before I can reload and help them out, the lightkeeper knocks Odin's cutlass aside and drives its blade into the Norwegian's good eye. Odin shivers for a moment, stuck on the end of the blade, then drops like a stone as the lightkeeper withdraws.

Landing Party: 11/12

I know Rumguts won't last long on her own, so I draw me two

pistols in one move and fire them at the fishman. Both shots impact it in the chest, sending it reeling backwards.

Shot Damage Inflicted = 100
Level 3 Lightkeeper
HP = 100/200

"Under the chin, Rumguts!" I holler.

She's got the smarts not to waste time acknowledging me advice. Instead, she thrusts forward with her cutlass and impales the fishman right in the gullet.

You and Rumguts have killed a Level 3 Lightkeeper
Your XP Reward = 150 XP
Progress to Captain Level 7 = 24900/30000

I spend me time reloading as me crewmates finish their bloody work, and Croc rushes over to see to Silverback. He's quick to get a tourniquet onto the Turk's leg to stop him from bleeding out and then hands him a vial of the sludge he brews up for such occasions. Silverback grimaces as he swallows it down, but I know it won't be long before he's up and walking again. Croc's remedies are a power of good to those willing to brave their loathsome flavors.

With the battle good and done, I kneel beside Odin and ask the valkyries to take him off to Valhalla. Then I look to Inkman.

"We'll pick him up once we're done. Take him back to the ship for a proper burial at sea."

"Aye, captain. He'd have liked that."

I stand and survey the room under the light of our lanterns. The lightkeepers' freakish blinders are all extinguished in death, but they be not the only Atlantean light makers in the room. There be the Gleams that Sandwich was talking about, polished and pristine, thanks to their fishy caretakers.

"Looks like we be in the booty today, ladies and gents. But there be more floors above us, holding who knows what treasures. Who's up for pressing our luck?"

The resounding "Aye!" puts a grin on me face that near breaks me cheeks. The next few floors give us a wee bit of trouble. Having heard the kerfuffle below, the lightkeepers start dimming their lanterns and ambush us in pairs and trios. Thing is, I'm always expecting to be jumped, so I order me surviving fighters to form a circle around meself, Croc and Sandwich as soon as we enter a room. Seven fishmen in all pay the price for our complete lack of surprise when they attack.

You have slain three Level 3 Lightkeepers with Silverback, Longshanks and Shaka.
Your XP reward = 450
You have killed a Level 3 Lightkeeper.
Your XP reward = 300
Your progress to Captain Level 7 = 25650 XP

The fourth lot, they're a bit trickier.

Two of them come charging out of the dark and flash their lanterns just like the others done, hoping to blind us. But we're ready for that sort of carry on, our hands be guarding our eyes even as we enter the floor. Inkman and the sisters hold their positions and meet their new foes, while we watch the rest the chamber, covering all angles with our keen peepers. All angles except straight up.

Down tumbles another slimy piranha from the roof. The bugger lands right behind Longshanks and stabs the poor Dutchy up through her back and right through her heart. The big woman just gurgles and topples like a pine tree.

Landing Party: 10/12

Howling like bloodhounds, Shaka and Hyena break formation and cut the fishmen into fish sticks in less time than it takes to say, "She sells seashells on the seashore." Turns out, that be the last of the fishmen we find in this godforsaken tower.

What we find instead, on the top floor, ain't no fishman. It's not like me to be found speechless, but this thing certainly caught me tongue for a moment or two. How best to describe it? An anglerfish made love to the Hindu death goddess, Kali, whose great-uncle turns out to be a great white shark?

And the smell, it's enough to make your eyes water. A tin of sardines left out in the tropics, three days running, and then shoved right under your nose. Me guts feels like butter in a churn but I manage to hold me breakfast down. Sandwich and Black Russian ain't so reticent, chundering their juices onto the stone floor as the monstrosity rises from its midden of fish skin and bones and takes up six glass scimitars in its six scaly claws.

Mistress of Light
Level 12
HP: 1000/1000

Aye, looks like we be in for quite the tussle.

10

BLIND FAITH

WHERE THE FISHMEN had just one fleshy lamp, this thing has three, and they be flickering like embers, ready to flare.

"Close your peepers!" I yell, taking me own advice just as the Mistress blasts the chamber with a light so fierce it feels like it burns right through me eyelids. And when I open me eyes, I'm damn near blind. All I can make out is the vague shadow of the Mistress as she lumbers forward, her blades raised and ready to cut us to ribbons.

"I'm blind!" wails Hyena but Croc is quick to shut him up.

"It'll pass, you damned fool! Hold it together and keep your eyes closed in case she does it again."

It's just as well me Sharpshooter skill ain't just about relying on me eyes. I listen for her steps, recognize the creak and pop of a knee bearing a half-ton of weight, raise me musket, and shatter her kneecap with me shot.

Shot Damage Inflicted = 200
Mistress of Light
Level 12
HP: 1000/1200

The Mistress roars like a stuck walrus and collapses to one knee. Problem is, we've only got seconds to take advantage before she recovers, and none of us can see worth a damn. But then, maybe we don't need to.

"This old monster ain't done hollering yet, lads and ladies! Raise your pistols and fire at the cacophony."

Me ears being keener than the rest, thanks to me Sharpshooter skill, I listen for the Mistress' pained breathing, draw me pistols and fire them one after the other. Me shots land true, right in her chest, and she lets out another roar of agony.

Shot Damage Inflicted = 100
Mistress of Light
Level 12
HP: 900/1000

That's all me party needs. Twelve pistols go off, riddling the Mistress of Light with hot lead. She's big enough, and we're close enough, that every one of them hits. None of them be critical, and the creature's scales are tough, but it's enough to soften her up nicely for the coup de grâce.

Shot Damage Inflicted = 600
Mistress of Light
Level 12
HP: 300/1000

I hear four of her scimitars clatter on the stone floor as the

Mistress of Light struggles to get up to launch some sort of desperate attack. If she does, me people will be slaughtered like lambs. I ain't having it.

She's snuffling and wheezing hard now, in a world of hurt, so I can pinpoint where the air be gushing in and out of her curve-toothed gob.

"Stay where you are!" I shout to me shipmates as I finish loading. I shoulder me musket, track the wheezing to where it turns to a gurgle in the thing's throat, and hope to Bathala that I've judged this true.

I pull me trigger and wait with held breath for the result. There's a slap, like a salmon being whacked down onto a chopping block, and then a thundering *thump* as the Mistress of Light crashes to the floor.

Critical Hit!
Shot Damage Inflicted = 400
Mistress of Light
Level 12
HP: -100/1000

Right through the soft fleshy bit under her jaw, just like with them fishmen.

Your party has slain the Mistress of Light!
There are no remaining enemies in the lighthouse.
It is now yours to plunder to your heart's content!

The lighthouse XP pool is as follows:
One Level 12 Mistress of Light = 1200 XP
Clearing the lighthouse = 2000 XP
Slaying the Mistress of Light without any Damage incurred = 1000 XP
Penalties for losing two party members = -200 XP
Total to be divided between surviving party members = 4200 XP

As Leader of the party, you receive a double share of XP
Your personal XP reward total = 760 XP
You receive an XP bonus for innovating the blind attack on the
Mistress = 500 XP
Progress to Pirate Captain Level 7 = 26910/30000

It only takes a few more minutes for our sight to come back, and the first thing we do is search the chamber for anything valuable. Experience tells me that where there's a big monster, there's big loot, and I ain't disappointed. Behind the stinking midden, there's a massive chest that the sisters have open quicksmart.

They told me once, over a few rums one night on the quarterdeck, that they grew up in a street gang of children in Saint Petersburg. Their main means of survival was pickpocketing and burglary. I felt a bit ashamed to know that I did those things just for fun back home when they was doing it to stay alive. I kept me trap shut about it, of course. No need to spoil me rough and ready reputation with tales of silk sheets and rich brat rebellion.

Anyway, feels like that was a different Grace in a different time. Voyaging and pirating will scrape the softness off you. Even Sandwich will learn that if he lives long enough.

In the chest, we find roughly two thousand Atlantean crowns, more of them Gleams, a few gold effigies of Mister Squidbeard, a couple of books that Sandwich scoops up and clutches to his chest like a pair of babes, and a finely-tooled pistol fashioned from silver and ebony. White Russian picks it up and gently offers it to me.

"For captain. Without her, we all be very dead."

Her words be met with a unified "Aye" so I don't put up a fight about it. I take the pistol in me hand and test the weight. Perfectly balanced, despite the screaming skull that be decorating its muzzle.

Stormshot

+2 Perception

+100 Lightning Damage to target.

+50 Lightning Damage to adjacent enemies within a six-foot radius.

I whistle, impressed, then turn to me party, me face a picture of wicked glee.

"Let's see ourselves back to the ship so we can get those layabouts to ransack this here lighthouse, eh? Then I reckon our next stop should be Freeport for a bit of well-deserved frolicking. What do you say?"

I doubt this tower has heard such a shout of raw jubilation in all its countless days.

ILL-GOTTEN GAINS

I PUT me Merchant skill to good use as me crew stores the last of the booty in the hold of the Albatross. Truth be told, it ain't exactly a trove, but then it be a lighthouse we've plundered, not the Bank of Atlantis.

2434 Atlantean Crowns

It's hard to know exactly how many doubloons each crown be worth, but me Merchant skill tells me roughly 3 doubloons per crown based on the amount of silver in them squid-faced coins. Me estimates tend to be pretty good on such matters. I been well taught by me mother.

Value of 2434 Atlantean Crowns = 7272 Doubloons

Add that to the 4310 doubloons we already have plus the 3000 we scored from the Sea Stallion, and we have a tidy little sum to go towards outfitting our endeavors here.

Treasury = 14612 doubloons

Then we have 33 Gleams, but I be thinking we'll hang onto those. Best if every member of me landing party has themselves a reliable light source since we'll no doubt be crawling into the gloomy bowels of Atlantis' ruins.

The 5 ugly effigies look to me Merchant eyes like they'll fetch about 200 doubloons each, so there's another 1000 for the coffers.

Treasury = 15612 doubloons

Aye, this be a fine start to our adventure, leaving plenty of money after outfitting to get right royally sauced up in Freeport, if the amenities allow.

Finally, there be the 22 glass sabers taken from them dead fishmen and the Mistress of Light. The sturdiest damned glass I've ever seen and it holds its edge even better than Toledo steel. I take one for meself and give the landing party first pick before divvying out the rest to me crew members what have the best Fencing skills.

Atlantean Waterblade
Base Damage = 100

A decent improvement on our cutlasses that have a base Damage of 75. Sandwich seems particularly fond of his new blade and insists on swishing it about on the main deck as he works his way through a series of lunges, slashes, guards and ripostes. I admire his movements as I sip at a well-deserved coffee. He be like a lethal ballerino.

He stops to take a breather and notices me watching him. "I am sure you are quite capable with a blade, captain, but would you like me to teach you a few moves?"

"What be your Fencing level?"

He smiles. "First Class. One hundred per cent. I keenly await my next level-up so that I can apply an upgrade and ascend to Swordmaster."

I quirk an eyebrow at that. Almost as good with a blade as I be with me musket. I could indeed learn a thing or two from this toff.

"Might take you up on that offer. We've a solid day's sailing tomorrow before we reach where Freeport is supposed to be. Seems like a good way to pass the time."

He eyes the setting sun that be painting the sky blood-red above the islands of Atlantis. "Perhaps in the morning, after breakfast?"

"Aye, and I might nab one or two other students for you, too." Silverback's nearby, splicing some rope. "Me hairy matey over there needs to learn how not to get himself skewered by the fishies."

Ayez "Silverback" Tekin
Level 4 Marine
Fencing: 3rd Class

"Aye, captain," Silverback agrees. "Can't say I enjoy being a shish kebab."

Level 4? I wonder. I try to keep track of where me crew is at and I could've sworn Silverback was Level 3 last time I checked.

"Did you level up in the lighthouse?"

"Aye, right after we did for that Mistress."

"In that case, you're absolutely joining us for fencing lessons. Don't have many level four Marines on board so you'll be a regular in me landing party if that be dandy with you?"

He grins at me, showing a mouthful of gold. Some of me pirates like to carry their wealth around in their mouths. Makes sense. Harder to filch than a purse, and withdrawals from your treasury should be as painful as possible. Me father found out the hard way there. Me mother's fishing fleet almost sank along with him, to the bottom of the Sulu, thanks to his misfortune with dice and cards. I miss him, every now and then, but me mother don't.

I point at Hyena who be mending a sail nearby, his needlework nimble and fine. "You too, Hyena. What's your Fencing skill?"

His pockmarked face crinkles and gets that faraway look as he reads his Character. "Says here I be Second Class."

"You don't know off the top of your head?"

"No, captain. Don't spend much time thinking about me Character. Prefer to keep me hands busy and me brain quiet most of the time. Otherwise I start to worry about stuff what doesn't need chewing over. Gets me guts in a twist otherwise."

I sympathize. I can get meself in a right state too if I start overthinking. There's a happy balance there though, where your brain works for you and not the other way around.

"Alright, we'll keep those hands busy with some swordplay lessons, care of Sandwich here."

Hyena gives Sandwich a suspicious look but is wise enough not to openly question his captain. It's clear that he don't think much of our captive toff and his prancing blade. I put his troubled mind at ease.

"Don't fret, Hyena. We won't have you prancing around like a fancy boy at the carnival. Just the stuff what gets the murderous job done, right Sandwich?"

"I shall do my best to pare your education back to only the most brutally effective techniques."

"Much appreciated." I jerk me thumb towards me cabin. "Now, a quick word with you about all this Atlantean guff. Don't want to bore me crew's ears off when you start reciting all that book learning at me."

Hyena and Silverback both laugh at that, appreciating me consideration. Personally, it's so I can get me head around these strange isles without being second-guessed. Me crew's good at being pirates, but they aren't the most educated and open-minded lot I've ever met. Don't want them getting all wary and superstitious on me. That's a sure way to sink your morale to the bottom of the sea. Best not to involve me crew in discussions that ain't part of their day-to-day thinking. All you get is fear and strong opinions what need to be allayed and tempered. It's bloody exhausting. Ignorance, in some ways, truly is bliss.

Doc the Croc's up on the quarterdeck and so is Jonesy. I wave for them to join us. Rumguts is doing her best to look busy while not doing a damned thing, so I beckon her over, and Inkman too. He's supervising the last of the repairs, but they can easily be finished without him.

Moments later we're all gathered in me cabin, most standing because I don't have enough chairs, and me sitting at me desk with a chart of Atlantis that I be drawing up. I've already sketched the lighthouse in. Got a good view of the small island's coastline from a porthole I was able to unshutter up in the Mistress' lair.

"Lady and gents," I begin. "In light of what we found in that tower, pun intended, me concern is that Atlantis be far more dangerous and unpredictable than we might have imagined."

"Aye, captain," agrees Inkman. "Longshanks and Odin would testify to that."

"Indeed. But I be thinking. I have a plan what might even our odds."

I stifle a smile as everyone leans a little closer, almost in unison, and not one of them realizing they be doing it.

"What do you have in mind, captain?" asks Jonesy.

I give her a smile since Jonesy be the one what me plan hinges on. "We, me dear salts, need a witch." Me Navigator's lovely jaw drops. She knows exactly who I be talking about. "And she be waiting for us in Freeport."

1 2

MAD WITCH

CROC'S the first one to speak. He does it with his mouth curled like he's just spooned something real nasty out of his chowder.

"Captain, if it's healing you have in mind, the dubious arts of Wicca are no match for-"

I raise me hand and stop him in his tracks. "I won't be letting a witch anywhere near the wounded, I promise you that, Croc. Magic's strictly for dealing with the likes of the Mistress." I fix him with me best piercing stare, summoning all the gravitas me Leader 1st Class skill can muster. "Science weren't much good to us when we was all a bunch of blind mice at the mercy of the carving knife."

His face flushes scarlet but he has the sense to stay his tongue. Me and Doc the Croc don't always see eye to eye, but at least he respects the pecking order around here.

I look to the rest of me officers and briefly wonder how Sandwich ended up in me inner circle so quickly. I convince meself that it's because of his Atlantean scholarship, not that I find him easy on the eyes and ears. Never thought I'd like an English toff accent, but you never know the flavor of something until you taste it.

67

"Glass swords, gems that suck the life out of you to make light, fish-headed freaks and monsters what can burn the sight from your peepers. I reckon we're only scratching the surface of Altantis' weird ways and I don't want to get caught by some spell-slinging squid-head with me breeches down."

Everyone nods in agreement at that. Even Croc. Jonesy clears her throat and winces in advance at what she's about to say.

"Are we talking Mad Maggie here?"

"Aye."

Jonesy and Mad Maggie have history. They met in Nassau and got up to no good together for a bit. Mad Maggie was just Maggie MacDonald at that point, a simple witch-for-hire, selling protective charms to prostitutes and love potions to privateers. It was at Jonesy's suggestion that Maggie supplement her Wicca with a bit of Voodoo. Spirit Speak and Zombie Walk, that kind of darker carry on. Maggie took to the dark arts like a fish to water. Actually, more like a barracuda to a school of herring. Rumor has it that Maggie summoned Baron Samedi himself, and asked him to give her power over the dead in return for a sliver of her soul. The way Jonesy tells it, Samedi took more than his fair share. The way others tell it, Maggie and Samedi are one and the same these days.

"But captain," continues Jonesy, "Maggie signed on with Silvernose. She's been on the Narwhal ever since."

"That's right. And I reckon Silvernose be right here, in Atlantis. He's probably in Freeport right now, drinking away the sorrow of his dearly departed brother."

I see a smile crease Inkman's tattoos. "There be two copies of Yellowteeth's map of Atlantis, and Silvernose has the other one."

"Stands to reason, don't you think?" I ask him. "It were a rare occasion for us to catch Yellowstone alone, them brothers being thick as thieves mostly."

"Apologies for being a bit of a naysayer here, captain," says Jonesy, "but Silvernose sails with a crew of one hundred and fifty, and the Narwhal's a brigantine with more guns than we got. And then there's Maggie to contend with. We ain't going to be able to take them at sea."

"And begging your pardon, captain," interjects Sandwich, "but perhaps we should focus our efforts on finding the Star? I have read extensively on the arcane hazards of Atlantis and should be able to steer us around-"

"Stow that yap, toff, or I'll be gagging you," growls Inkman. "If the captain says we need Mad Maggie, then we go get Mad Maggie."

Sandwich has the good sense to clamp his jaw and raise his palms in supplication.

"Thank you, Inkman," I say.

"Well, to be fair, captain," Inkman responds, "I still don't know how the hell we're going to pull it off. Warranted, Silvernose's bunch ain't the ablest pirates about and he's running his poor ship into the ground, but the numbers are still against us. And I don't know how you're going to talk Mad Maggie into joining us. She ain't exactly one to be reasoned with."

That gets a laugh from Jonesy and a scowl of agreement from Croc.

"Research, lads and lady," I assure them. "Research. I make it a point of finding out all I can about me rival captains, and Silvernose's quartermaster be a talkative sort when he's in his cups. Gets a bit careless with expressing his hopes and dreams, he does. Especially when he's losing in a drinking game with Rumguts here. Ain't that right, Mary?"

"Aye," she agrees. "Them Japanese should know better than to try and out-swill the Irish."

"Tell the others what you learned from Shogun that night."

Rumguts expands like a pufferfish, loving the chance to be as important as Inkman and Jonesy. It's not something she gets to be often, but she has her special talents that come in handy from time to time.

"I reckon it was about the thirteenth whisky, maybe the fourteenth. Shogun was glowing red as the setting sun and swaying like a ship in the swell. Me, I was steady as a bloody rock, sharp as a-"

I sigh and motion for Rumguts to move the story along before we all get a case of the glazed eyes.

"Right, sorry, captain. Overheard Shogun complaining to the bosun about Maggie. This was at the bar, so I bring the subject up, real subtle like, and Shogun is only happy to empty his bilge about the 'wretched witch' and the curse he thinks she's cast over Silvernose. Reckons he's gone as mad as her, especially about the whole bloody Atlantis affair. You see, Shogun's a straight and narrow pirate who don't understand anything he can't eat, drink, shag or sell for a profit. He was already right put out by this whole Atlantis buggery, and hiring Maggie was the straw that broke the camel's back. But Shogun being a samurai, his oath is his bond. He can no sooner turn against his captain than chop his own balls off."

"I see where this is going," interrupts Croc. "With Silvernose gone, Shogun will pitch Maggie off over the side and sail back to the Pacific." He looks at me with those icy orbs of his. "But how do you propose to get to Silvernose? We can't just attack the bastard in the streets of Freeport. It's against the code."

I laugh. "Like it was against the code for Yellowteeth to come after us in open water?"

Croc shrugs. "No one out there to raise the issue, I suppose. Just your word against his."

"That's right," I agree. "No one knows what went down between Yellowteeth and me. But I'd bet good money that Silvernose thinks I hunted and murdered his brother in cold blood, just for his map."

The doctor's smile is a damned creepy sight. "You mean to incite him into a challenge."

"See, Croc? This is why I keep you around because it ain't for your fair looks."

Even Croc laughs at that. "All I need do is show me face at the right time, in the right place, and me pistol will do the rest."

The worry is clear on Jonesy's face. "You know he's a First Class Pistoleer like you, Deadeye. You'll only get one shot."

I draw Stormshot from me belt and lay it on the desk. "It were Stormshot what helped me hatch this nefarious plan of mine. Assuming I'm right, that Silvernose *is* in Freeport, and that his crew haven't already thrown him overboard for being the flesh-flogging tyrant bastard that he be, then this piece should give me the edge I need to put him down.

I see in everyone's eyes that the otherwords have appeared to us all at the same time.

Subquest: The Mad Witch
Mad Maggie MacDonald is deemed vital to the Albatross' success in attaining the Star of Atlantis.
This subquest requires the elimination of Captain Silvernose so that Quartermaster Shogun may take control of the Narwhal and thereby relieve MacDonald of her post on that vessel.
Do you wish to accept the Mad Witch subquest?
Aye or Nay?

"Before you accept it, captain," urges Inkman, "the code be stating that pistol or blade be decided by a coin toss. Silvernose be also a Fencer First Class. You be Second Class, last time I checked."

"Nothing a fencing lesson with Sandwich won't fix, right lordling?"

"Of course, captain." The slight tremor in his voice belies his certainty.

I shrug. "Wouldn't be interesting if it were a foregone conclusion. What do we say, mateys?"

"Aye!" shouts Rumguts.

"Aye," follow the others a hesitant moment later.

The Mad Witch subquest has been accepted.

"Are we ready to set sail for Freeport in the morning, Inkman?"

"Indeed, captain. We'll be shipshape by then."

"How's the weather looking, Jonesy?"

"Fair skies and a light breeze. Won't be a quick journey, but we should be there for lunch."

"Looking forward to that pint and pie already," adds Rumguts.

"Likewise," I concur. "And plenty of time for those fencing lessons in the meantime, right Sandwich?"

"Right you are, captain."

"I hope I am, Sandwich. I certainly do."

THE SIMPERING SIREN

SANDWICH WORKS us pretty damned hard. By the time we be done, me arms and legs are burning and me Fencing progress bar has crept from 60 percent to 80 percent. I know from experience that it won't budge from eighty unless I engage in a proper melee.

Sandwich gives me a crisp fencing salute and sheaths his rapier. It took me full concentration to keep the lordling from slapping me with his clothbound blade, and I doubt he was giving it his all. Bugger's hardly broken a sweat while I be glowing like a rutted pig.

"I say," he remarks, "for being self-taught, you really do have fine form, Captain Cortez."

Hyena snickers beside me. "Shall I tell him what happened to the last man who eyed your form too closely, captain?"

I knew that would come up sooner or later. "Leerballs was marooned for theft."

"Aye. For stealing too many glances at a certain pair of buttocks, if I recall rightly."

"You've got the memory of a sprat," quips Silverback. "A dead sprat, pickled in rum."

I roll me eyes at the bemused lordling. "Don't mind them, Sandwich. Leerballs was what we call in the pirate business, a bit grabby. Didn't have much respect for personal possessions, whether they be attached to a person or otherwise." I give Hyena a hard look. "He was warned plenty of times."

"Aye, not the sharpest cutlass in the armory was our Leerballs," Hyena wisely agrees. "It were nice of you to leave him a packed lunch and a loaded pistol."

"I just hope you lot offer me the same courtesy," I finish with a wink. I turn back to Sandwich. "Your Cambridge style might look a bit poncy, but it'll be bloody effective in a pinch. Thanks for the pointers."

Hyena and Silverback grunt their agreement while Sandwich blushes. Makes me wonder how lonely it was for him back home. No one to give him the time of day without first wanting something from him. Aye, he's only on me tub because of his knowledge of Atlantis and potential worth in ransom, but he somehow already feels like he belongs here. Strange, I reckon. Didn't expect that.

I take me leave and head up to the quarterdeck where Jonesy is steering our final approach to Freeport. The town's up ahead now, tucked into a half-moon bay at the foot of a towering mountain. There be Atlantean ruins dotted all the way up them craggy slopes, and I've no doubt it's a rabbit warren of tunnels and passages. It must've been impressive in its day. A city-clad mount teeming with hustle and bustle. Now it's a looming graveyard, and we be the graverobbers coming to pick it clean.

There be other rugged islands scattered about this main isle, all boasting jagged hills of varying heights, all encrusted with ancient Atlantean structures. Feels like an eerie place, that be for sure, especially after me encounters in the lighthouse. These islands are bound to be infested with aquatic horrors that make them fishmen look like harmless kippers. A wealth of experience to be had along with all the gold, jewels and magic items. Those who survive will sail away with many a pretty level and special ability under their belts. I aim to be one of them.

As we pull into Freeport Harbor, I see Silvernose's brigantine among the few other ships clustered in port. His silver skull flaps lazily in the breeze atop the Narwhal's mainmast. I point it out to Jonesy.

"You be alright with this plan of ours?"

"Aye, captain. Of course."

There's a tightness around her deep brown eyes that clues me into her lie. "Weren't your fault, you know."

She winces. "It was me what introduced her to Voodoo."

I wave that notion away with a flutter of me right hand. "Maggie's as curious as she be fearless. She'd have found her way there eventually. In love with the darkness, that one be."

There's more than enough worry for both of us in Jonesy's eyes. "Makes me question why we need her. When she was just playing with Wicca, I could see the help in it. Charms to make your skin a bit tougher, your aim a bit truer, that sort of carry on. But zombies and Voodoo dolls?"

"Look about you, Jonesy. This city's been dead for a thousand years, and what's living looks like it's swum here from the straits of Hell. We need someone what can peer into them tombs and dark corners and make sense of what she sees without losing her mind."

Jonesy laughs. "Maggie lost that a long time ago."

"Exactly me point. It takes a beggar to keep an eye on the thieves."

In just under an hour we're moored and ready to go ashore. I sincerely doubt there be any kind of law here, so I split me crew into two shifts, forty-four apiece. The first shift be on shore leave with me for the day, once this nasty business with Silvernose and Mad Maggie be done. The other half be staying on the ship to deter any what thinks they might like to procure it for themselves. I put Hyena and Barber in charge of that second lot. Hyena's fierce enough to knock sense into any malcontents and Barber's got a cool head on her shoulders for any problem-solving what needs doing in me absence. Barbara Broome be her real name, a sturdy lass from Yorkshire. We call her Barber on account of her being the only one what can give a decent haircut on me whole ship. Means she's mighty nimble with her blades too.

I've me usual suspects along, including Sandwich, and I be keeping Shaka close too. As we was getting ready, I noticed him having a chat with two of his closest mates, and the three was glaring at Sandwich something wicked. Shaka won't dare have a go at Sandwich in the open, but I know the lordling will be fish food if I turn me back on the situation. And it worries me that Shaka's now seeking solace and support among me crew. It's little quarrels like this what can turn into a full-scale mutiny.

Me dark thoughts be driven off by a gaggle of strumpets, lads and ladies decked out in paint, perfume and not much else, all touting their own bare wares along with whatever house of ill repute they be aligned with. I see some of me crew eyeing them with longing, and I can't say I blame them. We've been a long time at sea. Aye, many of me crew have each other for company. There've even been a few marriages onboard, presided over by me as their celebrant. But even when we're at full strength of one hundred, there be plenty within that number what find themselves detached or in need of pleasures me small community ain't willing or able to provide.

"Plenty of this to be had this evening," I announce to me crew, "once our dirty dealings be done for the day."

I offer a doubloon to the strumpet what can tell us where Silvernose be wetting his whistle. A lanky Morrocan lad comes forward and whispers in me ear about a certain tavern called the Simpering Siren. He asks for another doubloon to take us there. I hand over the cash and order me party to spread out so that we're harder to ambush.

As we follow our guide through the streets, I marvel out how quickly this town has grown. It's only been a few months since Atlantis poked its head above the water, but already Freeport looks big enough to rival the rough and ready colonial towns of Australia. Most buildings look to be made out of cannibalized ships, rickety structures of salvaged hull and sail. Others have made the most of Atantis' existing buildings. These be strange and unsettling in their architecture, like the shells of sea life what Neptune might've dreamed up during his most stormy nightmares. We humans have crawled into them like hermit crabs and made ourselves at home.

Along our path, I see plenty of opportunities to exchange our treasures for coin, and a place called Carruthers Cannoneers what looks to have some fine upgrades for the Albatross' artillery. I point it out to Inkman.

"Aye, captain. We be needing more firepower, for sure. This be the legendary Atlantis, and where I be from, legendary places come with legendary dangers."

"Spoken like a true worryguts, Inkman."

He pats his belly. "Listening to me puku has kept me alive so far, Grace."

"Even when it be full of grog?"

"*Especially* when it be full of grog."

I laugh as we round the corner and lay eyes on the Simpering Siren for the first time. Turns out it's an overturned Spanish galleon with windows cut in the hull and balconies nailed to the outside so the strumpets can give potential customers a fair eyeful as they prance and preen. I suspect that many a seaside den of debauchery was wreckage from the waves what followed the Big Shake. The survivors figuring they'd come to Atlantis to try their luck rather than rebuild where they was. Fair enough too. No taxes to be paid out here.

I deal out ten doubloons each to twenty of me entourage, order them to grab some grub and grog and to stay close on the off chance that there be trouble. They gladly take up their posts as me and me remaining company enter the smoky confines of the Simpering Siren.

SILVERNOSE

I HEAR Captain Silvernose before I see him. He has a braying nasal laugh that's like a saw across me skull. He's a hulking chap, like his brother, the former Yellowteeth. Long hair and beard, tied up in braids like a Viking, his coat and breeches bulging with Scandinavian muscle.

And there be his signature metal honker, freshly polished and gleaming. It be strapped to his face as a replacement for the real nose he lost in some fracas at sea. The way he tells the tale, it was a Kraken what took his nose before he sank his cutlass into its eye. Don't make no sense to me, that story. A Kraken's sucker would pluck your whole head off. More likely he was drunk and tried picking his nose with his cutlass.

Mad Maggie's there with him at the bar, stooped over a pint of ale, seeming none-too-amused by her captain's boasts as he regales his captive audience of crew members with some hogwash about how he was once captured by mermaids, but such was his sexual prowess that he was able to shag them all silly enough to allow his escape.

This be where me Leader 1st Class skill comes into play. I read the body language of Silvernose's assembled shipmates, looking for signs of interest and favor. I count how many be looking straight at him, body posture open, versus how many be turned away, have one leg up on the other in a defensive pose, or have their arms folded. I check their eyes to see how many are bright with engagement and how many are glazed over, pretending to listen while mulling over their own thoughts.

Me observations confirm the rumors I've heard about Captain Silvernose. He be competent enough to keep his crew satisfied with the prizes they take, but he ain't got their loyalty. Judging by the apathy written in their body language, they be surrounding him out of self-interest, nothing more.

I take a closer look at Shogun, noting with satisfaction that his body language mirrors the rest. He's sitting on a barstool next to Silvernose, but he's eased himself as far away as possible without seeming like he's shunning his captain. He's leaning back against the bar, his arms crossed, only parting them to take a swig from his tankard. There be a scowl on his face that tells me he's weathered this tale before and didn't think much of it the first time.

Having made me observations, the otherwords be kind enough to summarize me findings.

The morale of the Narwhal crew under Captain Silvernose is 51%

Just shy of mutinous murmurings and a long way from fraternal flattery. This be all the confirmation I need for me plan.

While Silvernose be finishing his tall tale, I hand out coin enough for me crew to settle in and watch the show. Then I collar Sandwich for a quiet word.

"You be new to this, so sit tight and keep your wits about you. If this goes well, it'll be Silvernose's blood draining into the sands. If not, we'll have ourselves a proper brawl. If that happens, go with Jonesy back to the Albatross, quicksmart."

"To summon the rest of the crew?"

"Hell no! They need to stay put and guard me ship in case our trickle of trouble turns into a flood."

"I shall tell Abigail to ready the sails for a quick departure."

I give him an appraising look. He be taking to this pirate life like Rumguts to a bottle of brandy. "Aye, not a bad idea, that. But leave the rest of the orders to Inkman. And if something happens to me, it be Jonesy's ship, you understand?"

"And I trust we will still go after the Star of Atlantis?" There's an eagerness in his eyes that be almost endearing.

"Aye. Inkman ain't come all this way for nothing. Now grab yourself a drink and stay out of the fray. Me crew knows how this type of fracas plays out. You, me bit of green seaweed, would get yourself killed."

He blushes a little at that. "I am touched by your concern, Captain Deadeye."

That makes me snort. "I be concerned by that Atlantean knowledge you got tucked in that snooty head of yours. Don't be having any notions otherwise."

He looks suitably chastened as he forces a smile and heads to the bar.

Silvernose has been too busy yapping on about himself to notice me, so I sidle over to Inkman and tap him on the shoulder.

"You ready for this?"

"Aye. I hear Silvernose be slick with a blade, but couldn't hit a pregnant whale with his pistol."

"That's why he has that there blunderbuss at his hip." I point out the hefty, funnel-barrelled pistol the pirate keeps slung on his right leg. "At close range, damn thing will cut me in half."

"Not if you're faster, captain."

"Aye, there be that. And what if the coin toss comes down tails? It'll be blades then."

"Just as well you got a few pointers from your fine young lad then."

I look suitably aghast at that. 'Me fine young lad? Whatever the bloody hell do you mean by that?"

Inkman holds his poker face, but I can see the smile in his dark eyes. "Ain't seen you look at any of the crew like you do at Sandwich."

"Ain't never had the chance to converse with an English toff, that's all. He be a curiosity, nothing more." Me excuse be delivered with too much haste and Inkman knows it.

"Of course. A true tale spoken like it were from the very lips of Captain Silvernose."

I shake me head. "You be a right brutal bastard sometimes, Inkman."

"Aye. Someone has to be, captain."

I'm about to respond with something terse when I'm interrupted by a roar from down the bar.

"Deadeye, you murdering bitch!" It seems Silvernose has finally pulled his head out of his ass long enough to notice me.

I wink at Inkman. "Shall we?"

Inkman's grin has more than a little bite to it. "Would be rude not to, captain."

Silvernose being the predictable sort, it don't take long for him to lay down his challenge. I did kill his little brother, after all. He'd never be able to look his crew in the eyes if he didn't call me out there and then. So after a fierce moment of face to face posturing and cursing each other's mother, we head outside for the business proper.

The sun beats down on us, setting the shiny doubloon alight as it tumbles into Shogun's palm.

"Tails!" he calls out and gets a roar of approval from Silvernose's assembled buccaneers.

I stifle a wince and exchange a grim glance with Inkman. He

knows, understanding the risk I be about to take. Silvernose be a Fencer 1st Class, at least. Me Fencer 2nd Class skill may not cut it, pun intended. If I go down in a shower of me own blood, he'll turn this duel into an all-out melee between our crew and his. If he then makes fish food out of Inkman and captures Sandwich, he'll take me precious Albatross and continue the Star of Atlantis quest.

There be a storm of fear brewing in me guts, but I know it'll only fuel me fervor in the battle ahead. I haven't got to where I am without taking risks.

I take a step back so I'm beside Doc the Croc and whisper in his ear. "Have one of your remedies at the ready to pour down me throat... if I'm still breathing. Then you, Jonesy and Sandwich get me back to the ship while Inkman raises some merry hell."

"Aye, captain," he murmurs.

I then place me hand on the pommel of me cutlass and stride toward Silvernose like I got no care in the world.

"Let's be having you, Metalmoosh! I be looking forward to hanging that nose of yours around me neck as a souvenir!"

Me crew hollers their approval while Silvernose scowls and draws his cutlass. "It'll be your head on me cabin door more likely, Deadeye." And with that, he charges at me, sword swinging.

15

DUEL FOR JUSTICE

I FIRE up Hasty Hands to give me a little extra speed, then draw me glass saber and parry Silvernose's first blow. His powerful strike sends a jolt of pain down me arm, teaching me that I won't be able to slug it out with this bugger. His Brawn score be a lot higher than mine. I'm going to have to play it smart. Thankfully, me Sharpshooter skill be about to come in handy, even in this here meat-chopping melee.

I pull the trigger on me Anticipation skill and am rewarded with double vision. What I mean is, there be two Silvernoses now. The stinky, sweaty real one and his ghost twin what be like a future reflection. I watch the ghost like a hawk each time, ducking and weaving away from his spectral blade. Silvernose moves mighty quick, thanks to his Fencer 1st Class ability, so I don't have anywhere near the three seconds Anticipation would offer were I facing an equal opponent. A split second, that's all I get, but it's just enough to keep me out of harm's way, as long as I stay sharp and focused.

After half a dozen near misses, Silvernose lets out a roar of frustration. "Stay bloody still you slippery wench!"

I don't bother answering. You see, his bellowing has given me an opening. He's over-committed his strike, thrown himself off-kilter, so I reward him with a slash across his right flank.

Hit Damage Inflicted = 30
Captain Rollo "Silvernose" Jergen
Level 6 Pirate Captain
HP: 170/200

Shiver me bloody timbers. It's going to be a long fight if I have to slice him down piece by piece.

Silvernose grunts with pain and redoubles his efforts, nearly closing the gap between his flesh self and his ghost self. I be hard-pressed to keep up, and such be the ferocity of his assault, he soon has me backed up against one of the Simpering Siren's outdoor swilling benches.

Though it seems at first I might be cornered, this turns out to be a blessing in disguise. Out of the corner of me eye, I spot an empty pewter tankard. I parry his next blow with me saber while grabbing the tankard with me right hand. Then I slam the vessel into the side of his head. It don't do no damage, Silvernose being a thick-skulled sort, but it's enough of a distraction for me to duck under his sword arm and bring me saber sweeping into the small of his back. The blade goes through his sturdy woolen coat and digs deep into his back.

Hit Damage Inflicted = 60
Captain Rollo "Silvernose" Jergen
Level 6 Pirate Captain
HP: 110/200
Back wound = -3 Quickness

I hoped the blow might sever his spine, but seems the big lad be made of sterner stuff than that. He bellows with fury and suddenly he's all red and glowing, like a piratical bloody demon. Then he spins about far faster than a back wound like that should allow him. He blasts right through me parry and lands a blow on me left shoulder. Though it hurts something fierce, I go with the force and turn me fall into a roll. I'm back on me feet in a jiffy, saber at the ready, but now me sword arm's screaming at me every time I move it.

Hit Damage Received = 50
Captain Grace "Deadeye" Cortez
HP: 100/150
Shoulder wound = -2 Quickness

There be a number above Silvernose's ugly noggin now, and that clues me in on the ability he's activated. Reaver Rage, a piratical Fencer 1st Class thing. The floating number drops from nine to eight as he launches his next barrage of attacks. Thanks to Hasty Hands and Silvernose's more severe injuries looks like we're on par for quickness. Then there's me Anticipation skill what be enabling me to hang on for grim death as I dodge his strikes.

00:06

00:05

It takes me full concentration. Can't even think beyond the next parry or sidestep. But I know, at the back of me mind, all I have to do is wait out that countdown.

00:02

00:01

Me whole body's burning with the effort by the time that counter hits zero and Silvernose loses his ruddy sheen. Like a sail what's lost its wind, his face sags and his body slumps a little as the post-rage lull sets in. I've got a three-second window before the brute recovers and I aim to make the most of it. Now's the time to pull me last trick out of me sleeve. *Daring Dash.*

It's an ability meant for getting out of trouble, not into it, but I've no time for quibbling over semantics. The Siren and all its jeering harlots and pirates are a blur about me as I charge at Silvernose. Me muscles howl their defiance and the fire in me left shoulder is enough to bring tears to me eyes, but I do me best to shove it all aside as I lower me saber point and plough straight into me opponent.

He's a foot taller than me, so me face ends up banging into his chest. We go down together in a tumble of meat and murder. The world comes back to me in a jolt of clarity and agony, and it's all I can do to roll off Silvernose to take a deep, shuddering breath. I taste the warm tang of blood in me mouth, streaming from me nose which has gone totally numb. Looks like I banged me moosh pretty hard against the big lug's ribs.

Impact Damage = 20
Captain Grace "Deadeye" Cortez
HP: 80/150
Shoulder wound = -2 Quickness
Post Daring Dash lull = -3 Quickness

I feel like a three-limbed sea slug as I struggle to me feet and reach for me saber. It's only when I've wrapped me fingers around the handle and try to tug it free do I notice that it's stuck fast in Silvernose's sternum. I blink away me tears and look at his face. His eyes are wide and blank, his mouth gaping in a silent scream.

The roaring of me triumphant crew finally reaches me ears and the otherwords appear in me bleary eyes.

Critical Hit!
Hit Damage = 150
Captain Rollo "Silvernose" Jergen
Level 6 Pirate Captain
HP: -40/200
You have slain Captain Rollo "Silvernose" Jergen in a Duel for Justice.
Your XP reward for defeating a Level 6 Pirate Captain = 600 XP
Your XP bonus for winning a Duel of Justice = 1000 XP
Your XP bonus for defeating a Fencer one Class higher = 500 XP
Progress to Pirate Captain Level 7 = 29010/30000

A grinning Inkman presses a tankard into me hands. I be shaking, and I spill some of the ale as I lift it to me lips. The cool, nutty brew washes away the blood and some of the pain. I sigh with relief and raise me drink to me assembled pirates.

"In honor of brave Captain Silvernose, the crew of the Narwhal drink for free today. Grog be on the Albatross, ladies and lads!"

That gets me a cheer all around, even from the likes of Shogun and Mad Maggie. I take another healthy swig of me ale to hide me smug smile. Aye, bloody fine work, even if I do say so meself.

16

INTO THE MAW

THE SIMPERING Siren be ahum with piratical debauchery. Figuring I well deserve it, I be fresh from a hot bath with a pair of lithe lads what "freshened me up from top to bottom", you might say. And having swilled one of Doc's concoctions to heal up me wounds, I be feeling right as rain. With a pint in me hand and the last of a seared tuna steak disappearing down me gullet, I take a quick gander of me latest otherwords.

Fencer: 2nd Class skill progress at 100%
Your Fencer skill has increased to 1st Class
You have unlocked the Special Ability, "Reaver Rage" and your Quickness is now +1
Due to your triumph over Captain Rollo "Silvernose" Jerge and your generosity towards the subsequent celebrations, your overall crew morale has increased to 91%

On that note, I wave a barmaid over and ask her to send a couple of kegs and some floosies of every persuasion down to the Albatross. Not enough to distract me guards too much from their duties, but a decent token to make them feel part of the celebration. They'll get to do some proper reveling, like us, on the morrow. The rest of us will be ship-ridden anyway, getting over our hangovers.

I blink me otherwords away and then turn back to matters more material; drinking, and getting what I want out of Shogun and Mad Maggie. Jonesy's on me left, deep in a whispered conversation with the witch, doing me spadework for me in that regard. They make a striking pair do Jonesy and Maggie. Caramel skin and short black dreadlocks against porcelain skin and a wild mane of curly red. I reckon they be chewing over the past so I leave them to it, holding back me offer of recruitment until Jonesy and Maggie have made their peace. Having a friendly face on board will go a long way toward enticing Maggie to sign up.

Inkman's on me right, and a rosy-cheeked Sandwich be opposite, alongside Shogun. The toff's on his fourth Siren Sauce and I'd wager we be carrying him back to the ship before the evening be done.

I wave me tankard at Shogun. His face be almost as red and shiny as Sandwich's.

"I suppose we need to be calling you Captain Shogun now, eh?"

Shogun offers me a gap-toothed grin. He be missing his front teeth, top and bottom.

"Got a nice ring to it, don't it?"

"Aye, it does," I agree, touching the silver nose that now be hanging from a leather cord around me neck. "Nicer than the last one."

Shogun leans forward on the table top, fixing me a shrewd look with those almond eyes of his. "You were playing a risky game there, Deadeye. Aye, Silvernose had a reputation for being a loud-mouthed bully boy, but that don't mean his crew were going to take kindly to you sticking a blade between his ribs."

I tap me cheekbone with me forefinger, just below me left eye.

"I've never had much time for books, but people, now them I can read all day long. Your crew had themselves a gutsful of Captain Blabbermouth, and it was only the steady trickle of booty what was stopping them from pitching him overboard and naming you captain."

Shogun bridles at that. "I'd never betray a superior officer like that. Honor forbids it."

"Aye, and that's why you be making a finer captain than Silvernose could ever be. You've more integrity in your little finger than he had in his entire, stinking body."

That puffs Shogun's chest up a little bit. "Kind of you to say so, Deadeye." And then his eyes widen and he cottons on to me plan. "Which be why you just strolled in, plain as day, and allowed him to challenge you like that. By killing Silvernose in an honorable duel, you cleared me conscience and me way to captaincy." He raises his tankard in salute, takes a sip, then fixes me with another shrewd look. "Now I know you didn't do it out of pure philanthropy, so what is it you want from the Narwhal, Captain Deadeye?"

"I don't imagine you'll be staying in Atlantis long. All them fat tobacco plantations in the Caribbean be more your style."

"Bloody hell, Deadeye!" laughs Shogun. "Am I really that easy to read?"

"If it be any consolation, Shogun, you're up against a Leader 1st Class. It be part of the package."

"I best be leveling up me own Leader skill then. Can't be having you predict me every move now, can I?"

"I don't know. Means I can stay out of your way, don't it?"

"Aye, that it does. And you be reading me right. This place gets under me skin worse than a case of ringworm. I be itching to get someplace what behaves like it should." He leans forward again, and this time there be a hint of fear in his eyes. "Have you seen what lurks in the shadows here, captain?"

"We got a taste of it as we sailed in. A lighthouse full of things what were more fish than man."

"Oh, you'll be seeing far worse than that, I guarantee it. Hold onto your mind as tight as your pistol."

Now it's me own turn to feel a jab of fear. "What you be meaning by that?"

"You know of the Tasmanian Devil?"

"Captain Bluegums' ship?"

"Aye."

"Of course. We did a plum raid together off New Caledonia. Last time I saw, he had a French warship on his tail, but he had the wind on them too. Figured they'd shake them Frenchies off, so I left them to it. We had our own pursuer to contend with anyway." I look around the bar to see if I recognize any of his crew. "Bluegums make it to Atlantis, did he?"

"Aye. Don't look like he'll be leaving any time soon." Shogun's tone be low and ominous. "We found the Tasmanian Devil burned out on a cove, two islands away to the north. There be a bloody great temple there what Bluegums had his eye on. Said to be quite the hoard of treasure in that there edifice."

"Someone blew them all to hell?"

Shogun shakes his head, releasing a few drops of sweat from his brow in the process. I ain't never seen the samurai this scared. It puts the willies right up me.

"No sign of cannon fire that I could make out. Looked to me like the ship were burned from the inside out. We found bodies on the beach. Some burned, having washed up from the Devil. The rest had their throats cut. They was piled up for the seagulls to have their fill. Single big bloodstain on the sand where they was executed and a few right ugly artifacts be lying about. Must've been brought down from the temple."

I take a swig from me tankard and note, with a bit of a start, that me hand be trembling. I look to Inkman to see what he makes of this tale so far. His painted lips be clenched tight and his eyes be almost black. Aye, he's feeling it too.

"Was Bluegums among the dead?"

"Nay. All told there was sixty-three corpses on that beach. We built a pyre out of what timber we could salvage from the ship. Gave them a proper sendoff."

"Inkman? What was Bluegums' complement in New Caledonia?"

"Same as us, captain. As many as he could fit in that sloop of his. Ninety-nine."

"That be thirty-six unaccounted for then." I look back to Shogun. "You see where they went?"

"Aye, plenty of tracks leading up to that eyesore of a temple. None coming back. Bloody strange if you ask me."

"Bloody strange indeed! Bluegums struck me as a reasonably sensible sort. Can't imagine he'd persist after losing most of his crew at first landing."

"I say, Captain Shogun," interrupts Sandwich, his eyes now keen with interest. "Are you able to describe this temple for me?"

Shogun visibly shudders as he tries to recall the look of the thing. I know Shogun ain't no admirer of the supernatural, but I've never seen him quite so spooked as this.

"That be the strangest bit," he says, his voice now low like he's telling us some dark secret. "The damned building changed every time I looked at it. One moment it was a face, a woman screaming, her wide mouth being the beshadowed entrance. Next moment it was the head of a shark, a great white, its tooth-rimmed jaws gaping like it was about to swallow us whole. Never the same thing twice, but each face as nasty as the next. Only that yawning, black gateway remained the same, all inky no matter the angle of the sun."

Sandwich slams down his tankard, making us all damn near soil our breeches.

"Hells bells, Sandwich," I scold him, "what be getting into you?"

"Pher'gorth'mha Agha'dath," the toff gurgles.

"You got a fishbone stuck in your throat?" I ask him.

"No, captain. That is the language of Atlantis. It means the Maw of a Thousand Deaths."

"Sounds cheerful," grunts Inkman.

"It was a place of great power and sacrifice," continues Sandwich, his beer shine now taking on a more fevered sheen. "Apparently, the more lives you feed the Maw, the more power it regurgitates."

I feel a chill across me shoulders and pull me jacket closer, even though it be hot from all the carousing bodies in here. "Are you saying that them sailors of Bluegums' was sacrificed?"

"Ceremonial artifacts and corpses piled high for the gulls? Yes, stands to reason."

"Ain't nothing reasonable about it," I counter. "Sounds like madness to me." I catch meself and offer the witch an apologetic look. "No offense, Maggie."

Both she and Jonesy are keyed into our conversation now. Jonesy looks as pallid as Inkman, Shogun, and likely meself, if I was to look in a mirror. But Maggie's green eyes shine like polished jade.

"None taken, captain." She turns those emerald peepers on Sandwich. "What sort of power are we talking about, sassenach?" She uses the Gaelic term for 'lowlander' and the connotations ain't complimentary.

Sandwich seems not to notice, so caught up is he in his creepy Atlantean fancies. "The power to peer into the hearts of humanity, pluck forth their darkest fears, and manifest those terrors from the flesh and bone of the Maw's victims." He leans forward, taking on a more conspiratorial tone. "It is also the key location we should be visiting in light of our current aspiration in these here isles."

I'm not happy about him raising our quest in front of Shogun, but at least he's circumspect about it.

"Then it seems we best be following in Bluegums' wake," I suppose. "Best go see what's happened to the poor bugger."

"Right, that's it!" concludes Shogun. He slaps his hands on the table and pushes his chair back. "Good luck to you, Captain Deadeye, but me and the Narwhal are off to the Caribbean first thing on the morrow. I ain't mixing meself up with all this ancient bloody Voodoo. Me and me crew have good, honest prizes to be taking from them fat tobacco farmers."

I recognize his sharp mention of Voodoo as a deliberate slight against Maggie, which means he knows what I'm about where the witch be concerned and is thankfully all for it.

I look to the witch and do me best to lock me gaze with those sharp emeralds of hers. It be like staring into the jellies of a rabid dog, but I can still see the intelligence behind the lunacy. Maggie can be managed, especially with Jonesy there to dampen her fires.

"What about you, Ms MacDonald? Would this Maw of a Thousand Deaths be of interest considering your current 'line of studies'? As long as Captain Shogun don't mind me stealing his witch away, of course."

Shogun shrugs. "Don't make no difference to me. MacDonald's her own woman. She can do what she likes."

Maggie's smile ain't what I'd call warm or friendly. Reminds me of Croc's smile, actually.

"If you be willing to have me, Deadeye, then I be happy to lend me arts to your cause for a time."

She clicks her fingers to punctuate her offer. Smoke puffs up from them long, black nails of hers and forms into the very skull and crossbones what flutters above the Albatross.

Congratulations!
You have completed the subquest: The Mad Witch
Your XP reward = 1500 XP
Progress to Pirate Captain Level 7 = 30510/30000
You be a salty seadog at the crest your wave!
A Level 7 Pirate Captain!
You receive 7 points to apply to your core attributes.
You receive 2 free skill upgrades.

Though it be mighty fine news, I ain't got the time nor inclination right now to be tending to me Character. That can wait for a more private moment.

I watch Shogun eyeball Maggie's little magic trick with open suspicion. Then he grunts with disgust before adopting a cool and professional tone. "I thank you for your services, MacDonald. I'll be sure to send your share of the treasury over to the Albatross." Then he gives me a sailor's salute and he's off to wrest his crew from their revelings and shepherd them back to his ship.

The otherwords, being polite sorts, have waited until me conversation with Shogun be finished before popping up over our table.

The subquest: Into the Maw is now available
Delve into the Maw of a Thousand Deaths, find out what happened to Captain Bluegums, and recover the key required to locate and secure the Star of Atlantis.
Do you accept this subquest?
Aye or Nay?

I lean back in me chair and fix Sandwich with a no-nonsense glare. "There best be more than beasties and black magic in that temple, Sandwich."

"Fear not in that regard, captain," he assures me. "All of

Atlantis paid tribute to the Maw, as much in wealth as in sacrifice. It was said to be the richest cult in all these isles."

"Bluegums probably heard the same about them riches," ventures Inkman. "Made it his first port of call."

"In that case, quartermaster, let's be dragging our motley lot out of here by the scruffs. We have ourselves a temple to plunder!"

I select *Yay* and hope to Bathala that I'm not leading us all to our dooms.

17

DAMNED FOOLS

THE NEXT DAY, half me crew be recovering from their hangover. Even I have a bit of a headache for me trouble. So I lie in me bunk a bit longer than usual and set to applying me level up bonuses.

I like to sort me skill upgrades first and build me core attributes around me favored occupations. I be tempted to put both points into Sharpshooter, but then me mother taught me never to put all me eggs in one basket. Ain't much use being a legendary crack shot when you've been relieved of your musket or you're in a tight space and there be no room for wrangling such a large weapon. There also be plenty of scope for natural improvement with Sharpshooter whereas a few of me other skills have topped out at 1st Class and won't be budging without a boost of some upgrade points. And then there's this new pistol, Stormshot, to be considering. Would be sensible to be making the most of it.

With those thoughts in mind, I steer meself away from the Sharpshooter shortcut, and put an upgrade point in Pistoleer 1st Class, thereby unlocking Gunslinger 3rd Class.

Gunslinger: 3rd Class
Advanced Skill
Maintains all the skills of a Pistoleer: 1st Class whilst adding +2 to
Perception and Quickness.
Reduces pistol reload speed by -3 seconds along with increasing
pistol Damage by 100% and the likelihood of a Critical Hit by 50%
At 3rd Class, Gunslinger unlocks the Special Skill of Quickdraw, the
ability to draw a pistol, aim, and fire in under a second without any
reduction in accuracy.

A mighty handy skill when we be delving into the ruins of
Atlantis, not knowing what horror be popping its slavering head
around the next corner.

The next upgrade be a toss-up between Leader and Fencer. The
latter be giving me some fine bonuses to me Quickness and
Stamina, along with a special skill called Slice and Dice where I
effectively chop an opponent into bits with a blinding flurry of
blows. But Leadership boosts me Wit and Sand and offers me the
Special Skill of Rallying Cry that adds a tidy fighting bonus to all
me crew within earshot.

I decide to remain true to me title, Captain Deadeye, and apply
the upgrade to Leader, unlocking the Hero skill for me troubles.

Hero: 3rd Class
Advanced Skill
Maintains all the skills of a Leader: 1st Class whilst adding +2 to Wit
and Sand, and improving your ship's Agility and Speed by +10 whilst
you are onboard.
At 3rd Class, Hero unlocks the special skill of Rallying Cry, the ability
to shout words of encouragement to your crew, thereby improving
their Stamina and Damage Dealing by 10%

Now that I've sorted out me skill upgrades, I build me core

attribute points in around those favored skills of Sharpshooter, Gunslinger and Hero, boosting me Perception, Quickness and Wit by two points each. Then I drop a point into Brawn, just to bring it into double figures and to give meself a wee health boost.

Of course, none of it will take effect until I've had me a good night's sleep, so I don't bother looking over me Character just now. Besides, it be time to get up, have me coffee and some breakfast, and head into town to spend some money.

I give the other half of me crew twenty doubloons each for a day of shore leave and a night of carousing. Once I include all one hundred and twenty of Shogun's crew into the celebrations, Silvernose's wake cost me a pretty penny indeed.

Treasury
Doubloons = 7310
Less Strumpet Guide cost = 2
Less Albatross crew carousing costs = 880
Less Narwhal crew carousing costs = 1200
Total Doubloons = 5228

Ah well, it ain't pirating without the partying to go with it, and me crew have had a long and dull journey to get here. They deserve a good blowout.

Me and Inkman find a buyer for our gold effigies and an exchanger for our Atlantean crowns. Turns out to be the same wizened old Italian, Onesto Medici. He offers us two hundred doubloons per effigy and a one for two exchange on our crowns. Thanks to me Merchant 2nd Class skill, I know we could get one for three or better in any major European port, but we're a long way from any of them places so I console meself by talking him up 20 percent on both the effigies and the crowns. By the end, the old dealer's face takes on the aspect of sundried tomato, but he accepts me terms.

Treasury

Doubloons = 5228

Plus 200 per gold effigy and 20% haggling bonus = 1200

Plus one for two on 2434 Atlantean crowns and 20% haggling bonus

(rounded up) = 5355

Total Doubloons = 11783

No point in having all that cash sitting around doing nothing, especially with far greater plunder on the Atlantean horizon, so I take Powderfinger and Inkman cannon shopping. Carruthers Cannoneers proves to be the only decent gun merchant in town, stocking even the famous Thunder God Culverins from Sweden.

Thunder God Culverins

Base Damage per Gun: 30

Allows Chief Gunner to shoot one Class higher than normal.

Reload and firing times reduced by 50%

"None fully appreciated Thor's might until the invention of the

cannon." - Admiral Bjorn Sigurdson

A broadside of six of those buggers would turn the likes of the Stallion to kindling and even blow the spleen out of a reinforced frigate. But they're ten thousand doubloons apiece. Too rich for our blood just yet, so I take a look at some nice Barking Mastiff Culverins at eight hundred apiece.

Barking Mastiff Culverins

Base Damage per Gun: 12

Reload and firing times reduced by 20%

"The seadog's bark be worse than her bite." - Captain "Mastiff"

O'Brien

Instead of going for me usual 20 percent discount, I talk

Carruthers into throwing in a couple of Barking Mastiff falconets, the swivel guns what we use sometimes for surgical shooting. Carruthers be willing to take our old culverins off our hands for two hundred apiece, so the hit to the treasury ain't too bad, all things considered.

Treasury
Doubloons = 11783
Less the cost of 12 Barking Mastiff culverins at 800 apiece = 9600
Plus sale of 12 Standard culverins at 200 apiece = 2400
Total Doubloons = 4583

While Powderfinger's organizing the shifting and installing of our new artillery, Inkman stocks up on our provisions of food, water and rum. In the end, we're still left with a healthy kitty for emergencies.

Total Doubloons = 3000

Me final stop be a quick trip back to the Simpering Siren where I get up on a table, fire me pistol in the air to get everyone's attention, and announce that I have eleven berths available on me ship for experienced sailors what can swing a cutlass and shoot a pistol straight. Seems that Bluegums' ship ain't the only one to have run into dire trouble of late. About thirty Spanish sailors offer themselves up, formerly of the Santa Lucia under Captain Delgado. Taken by a ghost ship, they tell me in fearful whispers, a great black warship with skeletons at the oars and ghouls at the gunnels. I'd have not believed a word of it before encountering those fishmen in the lighthouse. Now I'll be sure to double the watch during the witching hour when the Santa Lucia met its grisly end while moored off an island on the outskirts of Atlantis. A place these sailors have dubbed Hellmouth

Harbor on account of it being an old naval port of some description.

I use me Leadership skill to pick out the best from the bunch and escort me new recruits down to the Albatross where they be met by a mixture of good cheer and suspicion from the rest of me crew. We've become a tightly woven lot over our voyage so far. A little bit of wariness towards strangers be understandable, but I be quick to remind me crew that everyone be fair and equal on me boat, no matter how long they've sailed with me.

Then I be up on the quarterdeck with Inkman, Sandwich, Jonesy and Mad Maggie. First things first, I take a gander at me Albatross' gizzards to make sure we're ship-shape and ready to depart first thing on the morrow.

The Albatross

Hull Defense: 120/120 (150/150)
+30 Defense from Iron Scantlings

Sail Defense: 50/50 (70/70)
+20 Defense and +25% Fire Resistance from Sails of the Salamander

Agility: 100 (150)
+20 Agility from Copper Plating of the Bow
+10 Agility from Navigator: 1st Class at the helm
+10 Agility from Sailmaster: 1st Class at the rigging
+10 Agility from Hero: 3rd Class on deck

Speed: 110 (150)
+10 Speed from Sails of the Salamander
+10 Speed from Navigator: 1st Class at the helm
+10 Speed from Sailmaster: 1st Class at the rigging
+10 Speed from Hero: 3rd Class on deck

Guns: 14

12 Barking Mastiff Culverins

Base Damage per Gun: 12

+5 Damage per cannon from Gunner: 1st Class on the gun deck

2 Barking Mastiff Falconets

Base Damage per Gun: 8

Crew: 99

Me chest swells with pride at the sight of me beautiful boat in full health. Inkman notices and offers a small smile of agreement.

"Aye, captain. We be ready for anything Atlantis be throwing at us."

"The horrors of Atlantis be foul and deep, and seawolves be circling in wait for the sheep." This from Mad Maggie, her tone deadpan, a faint smile on her lips.

Jonesy rolls her eyes and laughs, though the show of humor be a little forced. She be used to hearing bilge like that from Mad Maggie, but familiarity don't make it any less unsettling. Maggie's green eyes be seeing in darker shadows than most can penetrate.

"Right cheerful that, Maggie. I'd be appreciative of you keeping your macabre murmurings to the present company," I ask her, keeping me voice low. "Don't want me crew jumping at their own shadows."

"Shadows fall where they are cast, captain," be Maggie's answer. "But I be doing as you ask."

"Much appreciated."

I look to Sandwich now, hoping he might be able to shed some light on the gloom that no doubt awaits us tomorrow.

"Anything from your readings you can enlighten us with on the subject of the Maw of a Thousand Deaths?"

He clears his throat and stands a little straighter, clearly happy to be of service. "It is said that the Maw was attended to by the Sanguine Cult, a collective of blood-drinking fanatics. Some accounts depict them as, how should I say this, somewhat *less* than human."

"How much *less than human* are we talking about? More light-headed fishmen like in the lighthouse?"

"No. The descriptions were a little vague on the exact visage of the cultists, but their focus of worship has been depicted in quite vivid detail. The Bloodwyrm. Imagine a lamprey eel the size of an Amazonian anaconda."

"Taniwha!" growls Inkman, who then spits over the railing, into the sea, as if to rid himself of the foul taste of the word.

Sandwich quirks an eyebrow at Inkman. "I am not familiar with that term. Is it some sort of mythical Māori beast?"

"Ain't nothing mythical about it, Englishman," retorts Inkman. "Taniwha be both the guardians and terrors of river, lake and sea. They come in all shapes and sizes, but the giant eel be one of the more common ones."

The lordling's eyes go wide with astonishment. "I would surely love to see a taniwha someday."

"A taniwha be the *last* thing someone usually sees," answers Inkman.

"Then we need to be making sure that this taniwha be the exception to the rule." I point at the falconet next to Inkman. It be on its swivel now, ready for firing at another ship's decks, but it can be detached and carried about easily enough. "We'll take them guns along with us, and the small harpoons we use for catching tuna and sharks. Once we meet this slimy goddess, we don't want her slithering away on us."

Inkman casts a suspicious glance at Sandwich before fixing me with them dark eyes of his. There be worry lines etched into the corners what I ain't noticed before. "If the Star of Atlantis were as important to this city as Sandwich says it were, and the key be under the personal guardianship of a taniwha, makes a man wonder what they was so keen to protect the key *from*."

I give Inkman what I hope be a reassuring pat on the shoulder. "Why, from scurrilous sea scum like us, matey. The first ever seafarer were a fisherman. The second were a pirate itching to plunder his catch. I be sure, a thousand years ago, Atlantis had as many corsairs plaguing its shores as it does right now."

He don't look totally convinced, but his faint shrug tells me I've managed to at least dilute his concerns. I give him a hearty slap on the back to punctuate me encouragement then look with him out at the surrounding isles. The island of our destination be just where Shogun said she would be, a few hours sail to the west. The sun be going down behind it now, casting its ragged profile in a hue of red that be disturbingly close to freshly spilt blood.

"Right then. Come first light, we be going after Bluegums, and hopefully, we be rescuing the poor bugger and whoever's left, assuming they ain't all had their juices sucked out by a bloody great lamprey. Either way, we need to be killing that slippery Bloodwyrm bitch. I reckon we'll have ourselves a proper fight on our hands, and I hope you lot be ready for that."

"Aye!" be the unanimous answer from Inkman, Sandwich, Jonesy and Mad Maggie alike.

I can't help but smile. We be damned fools, the lot of us.

18

MOUTH OF THE LAMPREY

I BE ON THE QUARTERDECK, taking a quick gander at me updated Character as we drop anchor next to the burned-out husk of the Tasmanian Devil.

Grace "Deadeye" Cortez
Level 7 Pirate Captain
Progress to Pirate Captain Level 8 = 30510/40000

Core Attributes

Perception: 15 (25)
+2 Sharpshooter: 3rd Class
+2 Gunslinger: 3rd Class
+2 Squintlock's Peeper
+2 Stormshot
+1 Pistoleer: 1st Class
+1 Musketeer: 1st Class

Quickness: 13 (21)

+2 Sharpshooter: 3rd Class

+2 Gunslinger: 3rd Class

+1 Rumpus Musket

+1 Pistoleer: 1st Class

+1 Musketeer: 1st Class

+1 Fencer: 1st Class

Wit: 16 (19)

+2 Hero: 3rd Class

+1 Fencer: 1st Class

Sand: 15 (19)

+1 Free Diver: 1st Class

+2 Hero: 3rd Class

+1 Leader: 1st Class

Brawn: 10 (13)

+1 Athlete: 1st Class

+1 Fencer: 1st Class

+1 Coat of the Salt

Stamina: 13 (16)

+1 Free Diver: 1st Class

+1 Athlete: 1st Class

+1 Coat of the Salt

Health Points: 208/208

HP = Brawn x Stamina

Advanced Core Skills
3rd Class
Sharpshooter
Gunslinger
Hero

Base Core Skills
1st Class
Free Diver
Athlete
Fencer

2nd Class
Merchant
Chess Player
Angler
Navigator

Special Skills
Flashfire (Required: Musketeer 1st Class)
Anticipation (Required: Sharpshooter 3rd Class)
Hasty Hands (Required: Pistoleer 1st Class)
Quickdraw (Required: Gunslinger 3rd Class)
Stirring Words (Required: Leader 1st Class)
Rallying Cry (Required: Hero 3rd Class)
Lungfish (Required: Free Diver 1st Class)
Daring Dash (Required: Athlete 1st Class)
Reaver Rage (Required: Fencer 1st Class)

Kit

Squintlock's Peeper

+2 Perception

Rumpus Musket

+1 Quickness, -2 Reload

Coat of the Salt

+1 Brawn, +1 Stamina

Stormshot Pistol +2 Perception

Only the charred bow of Bluegums' ship be sticking up out of the water now. This time we take all four longboats, forty-four of us in total. Best we not take any chances with the Bloodwyrm and her freakish attendants. For them to have all survived in the deep for so long, them cultists will likely be of a fierce and fishy nature. I've no doubt in me mind that we'll lose a few good skulls today. How many be down to seven pieces good management and one piece dumb luck.

I look up at the Maw of a Thousand Deaths as we touch sand on the shore. It be built into the face of a looming cliff, and it's as Shogun described it. The first time I look, it's a screaming woman, and the face be awfully similar to me own mug. Next time I look, it's a gaping shark.

Mad Maggie's beside me, so I give her a nudge. "You seeing what I see right now, Maggie?"

"Depends if you be seeing a big screaming portrait of me, Deadeye."

Just as I thought. "This maw be picking things out of our brains. I be seeing me own face."

"Psychotropic Illusion," explains the witch. "Pulls your own fears out through your eyeballs."

I shudder. Aye, it be a chilly morning, but there be a cold sweat on me back about now. "Probably hiding all sorts of bedamned traps too. Reckon you can dispel the thing?"

"I'll give it a try."

She leads us up the beach. In her sleek black leathers and faded white woolen coat, she looks all the world like a predatory gull stalking a fluffy penguin chick. She stops a dozen feet before the Maw and sets to drawing some intricate symbols in the sand with her skull-topped cane. Jonesy tells me there's a silver rapier tucked inside the thing, the blade specially treated with enchantments what can do for zombies, ghouls and other undead nasties. I look to me crew and note with satisfaction that they be carrying the glass sabers what we took from the lighthouse. It stands to reason that Atlantean weapons are going to be more effective against Altantean denizens, especially the supernatural sort. I'm sure we'll get plenty of opportunities to put that theory to the test on this sojourn.

Maggie's sand sketch looks like a swirling mess of intestines and maggots to me untrained eyes, and the magical mumbo jumbo she be muttering sounds altogether too slimy to be coming out of a human mouth. Sounds like them ugly words Sandwich uttered back at the Simpering Siren.

I wave him over and whisper in his ear so that Maggie can't hear me. Up this close, I see that he's freshly shaven and smells of expensive cologne. It be rather fetching. Makes me glad I let him rescue more than just his books from his cabin on the Sea Stallion before we plundered it.

"Be that the same language you spoke? All that guff what sounded like you had a throatful of snot?"

"Yes, Captain Deadeye. That is indeed the language of Atlantis."

"How do you reckon Maggie knows it?"

"Clearly she and I have been reading the same books, although I am rather surprised to see that she has mastered the Atlantean arcanities so well. She must be quite the magical talent indeed."

"If she weren't, I'd have never stuck me neck out to be chopped through by Silvernose, would I?"

"Quite so, captain. Quite so."

Maggie finishes with an ungodly scream that gives all assembled a right start.

Warning!
Your landing party's morale has dropped by 3% to 87%

"Jesus and Mary, Maggie!" I shout at her. "Was that bloody necessary?"

Her wild cackle says it all. No, she be winding us all up like a fishing line. A magical talent Maggie might be, but her sense of humor leaves a bit to be desired.

At least the spell seems to work. I look up at the temple entrance to see me contorted visage fade away. In its wake, there be a grand and gloomy edifice, its unnatural lines mercifully masked by the heavy encrustation of limpets it be gathering over its many centuries beneath the waves. I can make out the rusted remains of mechanisms what must've once guarded this archway. Pendulum blades long ago seized by corruption and colonized by shellfish.

I hear a collective sigh of relief from me crew, and let out an involuntary one meself.

"Silverback! A light, if you please!"

The Turk's at me side a moment later, a Gleam in his left hand, glass saber in his right. I unlimber me Rumpus Musket and hold it at the ready as I address the rest of me landing party.

"Inkman and Shaka, you bring up the rear. Sandwich, Maggie, and those bearing the falconets, I want you lot squarely in the middle where we can best protect you. The rest, keep your eyes peeled and what Wits you have focused on every nook and cranny. Nightmares be awaiting us, so this ain't the time for daydreaming!"

I lead me motley marauders the last dozen paces to the Maw and delve into the dark beyond, trying as I go not to show any of the tingling anxiety that be prickling me skin from scalp to sole. Even without that mind-twisting illusion, this temple has the ambience of a crypt during the witching hour, and I be hard-pressed not to let me imagination turn the encroaching shadows into the stuff of me own girlish terrors.

The Maw be true to its name, filled with water-smoothed stalactites and stalagmites aplenty so the whole affair looks like the toothy mouth of a lamprey. Seems this temple has been built into a natural cave, as we don't encounter any signs of habitation until we're deep into the thing. Then the horrifying carvings and mosaics begin. A myriad of spirals and swirls that crawl up the walls like swarms of eels or perhaps the twisted intestines of a sacrifice's innards.

Whatever the case, the aesthetics are what I'd call 'slithery' at best and 'nauseating' at worst. More than a few of me crew have to excuse themselves to go chunder behind collections of grotesque statuary after they been appreciating the artwork for too long.

We round a corner and encounter the first of Bluegums' crew. She be impaled on a stalagmite what has been carved with twisting and turning symbols. Doc the Croc hurries forward to take a look while we encircle and guard the spot.

"There's no blood on this stalagmite," he observes in a hushed tone. "She were exsanguinated before being skewered." He peers closely at the woman's neck with a magnifying glass and offers a "hmmm" of interest.

"What you be finding there, Croc?" I ask him.

"She been sucked dry by a lamprey of some sort."

"The Bloodwyrm herself?"

"Nay. She'll be too big to make marks like this. Judging by these circular tooth marks, whatever did this has a mouth about the same size as you or I."

"One of them cultists, perhaps?"

"Only if they have the face of a lamprey eel."

"After seeing them fish-headed freaks at the lighthouse, I wouldn't find meself surprised by that."

Those who were with me on that sojourn, Hyena and the likes, be nodding their agreement.

"Alright, we'll collect the poor lass on the way out and burn her on the beach. Onwards for now, and be staying lively you lot. You can see what fate awaits you if you don't."

We encounter several more of Bluegums' crew, skewered and drained like the first one, before coming out into a large and ornate chamber. It be dominated by an immense statue of what I first assume to be Naga, one of them Hindu creatures what be half woman and half serpent. This one be all serpent from the waist down, her snake body coiled like a cobra on the floor. Her torso be that of a young woman, and her beautiful eyes be a pair of gigantic gleaming rubies. But her mouth be that of a lamprey. Circles of teeth in an orifice good for one thing only. The sucking of blood.

The floor beneath us be a swirling mosaic fashioned out of paua and polished lobster shell what has been sealed over with some sort of resin. And only when we're all in the chamber does the artwork reveal its treacherous nature. The statue's ruby eyes flare bright red and the tiles beneath us begin to fall away.

Three of me crew vanish through the floor. Three screams that be silenced all too quickly by whatever awaits us beneath.

19

TAKING THE PLUNGE

Landing Party: 41

INKMAN BE next to one of the holes and peers into it. He grimaces and looks me way.

"Me Gleam barely reaches the bottom. Something be moving down there."

"Our crewmates?" For the others' sake, I inject a little hope in me tone that I definitely don't feel.

"Nay, captain. No sign of them."

"Then what be making the movement?"

He leans further into the hole, making me skin prickle with sympathetic vertigo. His lips curl back from his teeth with open disgust. "Lamprey," he growls. "Juveniles. Bloody thousands of them. Must be breeding-"

To me left and right, two more sailors lose what's beneath their boots and fall to their spiky deaths.

Landing Party: 39

Another breaks for the tunnel what be lying just beyond the statue, bellowing in a wild panic.

"Stay put, you daft bugger," I yell at him, but it does no good. He's not gone but a few paces before plunging through the floor.

Landing Parting: 38

But at least his demise allows me to bring me Wits and Perception into play. I can feel the challenge slow everything else around me, placing me within an hourglass where the sands be running slower within than without. I've experienced this many times before. The otherwords be pitting me abilities against fortune to see what's what.

The Bloodwyrm's Mosaic Challenge threshold is set to 50

Perception 25 plus Wits 19 equals 44. With the challenge being worth 50, I have an 88 percent chance of working out what's going on here. That be pretty fair odds, made even better by me Chess Player: 2nd Class skill what gives me a 10 percent bonus to pattern recognition, giving me a total of 97%. Piece of fish pie.

I imagine I hear the rattling of dice in me ears as Fate casts me lot.

The Bloodwyrm's Mosaic Challenge has rolled 51 against your 97
You have earned a revelation!
"Red is the hue of love and life. Blue is the shade of decay and death."

I look to me boots, see that I be standing on paua shell, and quickly jump to the nearest patch of lobster. Then just as time be returning to normal about me, I shout me warning to me crew.

"Stand on the lobster shells, mateys! They be safe and sound!"

Me crew reacts quicksmart, huddling together on the patches of lobster. Sadly though, it be a game of musical chairs, with not enough room to offer safe harbor to all thirty-eight players. The spaces are soon full, leaving half a dozen poor bastards behind. It's likely them stragglers will panic and try to force their way into safety, and that be like a drowning lass clasping her would-be rescuer in a death grip, drowning them both.

One of the stragglers be a big Greek marine, his bald and tattooed head now shiny with the sweat of terror. To his right, another of the stragglers goes down through the floor with a shriek.

Landing Parting: 37

It be the last straw for Tabouli. He lines up one of the safest clusters and readies himself to charge. He'll be like a bowling ball to a bunch of skittles if I don't put a stop to this.

I raise me musket and take a bead on his smooth head. "Don't you be moving, Tabouli!" That's not his real name. He's earned that culinary moniker on account of his bullish physique and his massive appetite.

Tabouli glowers at me, his eyes bloodshot with fear-driven rage. "You expect me to hug death like an old friend, captain?"

"I expect you to take stock of the numbers, matey. You charge that group, knock them off balance, and half a dozen will die."

Me statement be punctuated by a scream as the second to last straggler makes a break for the closest group. I switch me aim to her, but I be saved from pulling the trigger. She plunges through the floor instead. We all hear the splash below, and the splashing of a thousand baby lamprey as they swarm her.

"That's assuming you even make it that far, sailor," I shout over the doomed woman's dying screams.

"I'll take me chances!" he roars and charges forward.

I give him a second, hoping the floor will do me dirty job for me. No such luck. So I breathe out, nice and slow. If I miss this shot, people will die. I pull the trigger.

Critical Hit!
Shot Damage Inflicted = 600
Level 3 Pirate Marine
HP = -400/200

Tabouli's head shatters like a pumpkin. His hefty body crashes to the floor, crunches through the blue tiles, and be gone.

You've killed a Level 3 Pirate Marine.
XP reward = 300 XP
Progress to Pirate Captain Level 8 = 30810/40000

Landing Parting: 36
Crew: 91

The grateful looks from the huddled survivors go a long way to assuaging me guilt. Not that I have any time for remorse right now. We all be stuck on these red tiles. Marooned. That ain't the sort of vulnerable position you want to be in while in hostile territory.

"Captain! Look to the statue!"

It be Mad Maggie, and I do as I be told. What I see be them red rubies glowing in the Bloodwyrm's face, all lit up by the devil knows what.

"Them eyes, Maggie. Be they doing this?"

"Aye. Me Arcane Acuity skill tells me so. The eyes be the window to a churning soul of blood and rage. Pluck out them peepers and the fury will leak away like the tears of a stilted lover."

I look about and see that I be the closest to the statue. Hyena be the next one.

"Hyena?"

"Aye, captain?"

"You have an Athlete skill or some such?"

"The closest be Wrestler, 2nd Class."

Dammit. Looks like it's up to me then.

"Alright, throw me that rope and grapple you got hanging about you."

He does as he be bade. It's a good throw, landing right at me feet. I sling the coil over meself and make ready to jump to the next patch of lobster.

"Stay where you be, me scurvy dogs," I order me crew. "I'll have you all marching out of here in a jiffy or two."

To the cheers of me shipmates, I make the first leap, counting on me Athlete 1st Class skill to sort out the details. I land well, crouching to absorb the impact. I can see through one of them gaps in the floor, where one of me sailors fell through to their death, and there be a big empty space beneath the tiles upon which Maggie's group be huddled. Must be the same with the other red patches too. Ain't nothing but magic holding them up. I best be careful not to put too much strain on the spell else I might just plough through the lobstershell and find meself bled dry by them nasty baby eels.

I size up the next jump, this one a little farther than the first, and make me leap. This time I land just on the edge and have to swing me arms forward to correct me balance, else I'd tumble onto the paua behind me and be gone, just like that. Me antics get a hiss of fearful anticipation from me crew. A warm fuzzy takes the edge off me own pang of fear. It be nice to know they care, even if it just be born of a fervent wish to not be dying.

Three more hops and I'm next to the great serpentine coil of the Bloodwyrm statue. I unlimber me rope, twirl the grapple until I got me some good momentum built up, then fling the thing upwards. It bounces off one of them great stone boobs she's got, and topples back towards me. I have to dodge aside so it don't scone me on the head.

"Don't be shy, captain!" hollers Hyena. "Fondling her tits be all very well, but I reckon your lady love's ready to be boarded!"

This gets a burst of laughter from me crew, and I be grateful to the man for breaking the tension. Still, can't have me mateys laughing at me expense without an answer. Wouldn't be captainly.

"At least I be woman enough to climb this great beauty, Hyena. She'd take one look at your tackle and wonder why you're bringing a needle to a harpoon party."

More laughter, Hyena's cackling the loudest of the lot. And before it dies down, I've swung again and found me mark, the grappling hook catching neatly into the Bloodwyrm's maw.

Then I brace me boots against the smooth stone and climb up to them radiant rubies, hand over hand, step by treacherous step. Me crew cheers me on, adding some vigor to me climb and soothing me nerves.

Me muscles be burning something fierce by the time I climb atop the ugly wench's snout. I draw me knife and pry the first gem from its socket. There be some form of magical fire burning away inside the statue's skull, though it gives off no heat. As I watch, it dulls a little, just as the ruby in me palm loses its own radiance.

I tuck the ruby into the leather satchel I carry with me on such excursions and set to work on the second eye. It comes out just as easy, and this time the fire within the skull dies away completely. I put the jewel in me satchel and look down at me crew.

"Inkman?"

"Aye, captain?"

"The woman or man who volunteers to walk out onto them blue tiles with a rope around them gets one of these bloody great rubies."

About thirty hands shoot up all at once, and there be a chorus of hoots and whistles. Inkman sensibly picks out the smallest sailor in his own huddle, an Indonesian lass who be about a foot shorter and a stone lighter than meself. Tarsi we call her, after the Tarsius monkeys from around her home village, and the fact that she can climb the rigging better than just about anyone else on the Albatross.

"Good lass, Tarsi!" I call out.

Then I take one of the rubies and hold it up for her to see, offering a little extra motivation. This one gem would be worth enough to buy her home village and set herself up as mayor.

Tarsi flashes me a pearly-white grin and then secures the offered rope around her petite waist. On the other end, Inkman and a couple of burly lads take the strain as Tarsi steps gingerly out onto the closest blue tile. We all hold our breath as she places one foot, then the next, and stands there for a moment.

The tile holds. She tries the next one, this time making her footfalls a little heavier. Nothing happens, and we all heave a collective sigh of relief.

Congratulations!
You have solved the Bloodwyrm's 'Red and Blue Seas' Puzzle and saved the lives of the majority or your crew.
Your XP reward = 2000 XP
Progress to Pirate Captain Level 8 = 32810/40000

Maggie and Tarsi are both smiling as well. They too have received some XP for the parts they've played.

Me crew spreads out across the blue tiles while I descend the statue. Once I reach the floor, I give Tarsi her prize. Then I order me crew to the grisly task of retrieving the bodies from the lamprey juveniles, using our ropes and grapples to fish the poor devils out. They all be dead, utterly drained of blood. We lay them along one wall of the chamber. I offer them a prayer and promise to pick them up on the way back out. They'll have themselves a funeral pyre, just like those sorry bastards from Bluegums' ship.

We scour the chamber for anything else of value but don't find anything. I gather me crew into our original formation, hold up a Gleam to light the damp, dark tunnel ahead, and lead me fellow corsairs into the gloom.

20

SIP OF FINE CLARET

WE FOLLOW the twists and turns, feeling like morsels passed down some great, slimy esophagus, and come out into another chamber what been carved out of the naked rock.

It be here that we find Bluegums and the rest of his crew, drained of blood, skewered upon stalagmites like the victims we found in the entrance tunnel. The floor beneath them be carved with more of them slithering maggot symbols, the grooves of which be stained with dried blood.

I pick up Bluegums' sword what be lying just out of reach of his stiffened fingers. The handle be the finely-tooled head of a bird of prey, and the blue-steel blade be cold and radiant in the light of our Gleams.

Seahawk Saber
Base Damage: 100
+1 to Stamina
+1 to Sand
+20% chance of Critical Hit
"The seahawk only strikes when the prize be sure. The rest be
watching and waiting." - Captain Bluegums

I remember him saying that too, during one of our many grog-
fueled instructionals where he lectured me on the ways of piracy.
Aye, he waxed lyrical on many an occasion, but I listened to every
crumb, me young brain eager to chew over whatever wisdom came
me way. He were a fine mentor, and I bloody miss him already.

"He'd have wanted you to have that, captain," rumbles Inkman.

The rest of the landing party murmur their agreement, all except
Sandwich what be peering at the skeletons and assorted bones lying
here and there.

"What's so interesting about them old bones, Sandwich?" I ask
as I slide the Seahawk Saber into me sheath. The question be a
diversion, giving me a chance to wipe a couple of tears from me
eyes while me party's attention be directed at the toff.

"Exactly that, Captain Deadeye. They are yellowed with the
significant passing of years."

"This ain't the time for riddles, lordling. What's it matter that
the bones be old?"

"This island has only recently been raised above the waves.
Perhaps the inhabitants have been preying on passing ships over the
centuries, or even raiding shoreside settlements along the coasts of
Africa and the Americas. I would certainly like to hear the sinister
folktales that might corroborate such-"

Sandwich's musings be interrupted by them very inhabitants,
a scampering mass of hissing, be-shadowed monstrosities.
Though these creatures run on two legs, and their five-fingered

hands clutch curved daggers of gleaming steel, that be where the resemblance to humanity ends. Cold eyes of black and silver regard us impassively over circular mouths ringed with teeth.

"To arms, mateys!" I shout as I bring me Rumpus Musket to bear. "This lot be out for blood, and I ain't speaking in no metaphors."

I take a bead on the nearest cultist as me crewmates roar with gusto and meet these eely beasties with pistols firing and cutlasses swinging.

A small pack of the buggers be trying to charge me as one and the quarters be too close for me musket, so I Quickdraw me Stormshot pistol and fire upon the foremost monster. It be the first time I've used Stormshot and the effect be gratifying indeed. The ball itself plugs a hole in the leader's chest. Then from that wound erupts a miniature storm of lightning that engulfs the fiend's entire body.

Shot Damage inflicted = 150
Level 4 Lamprey Cultist
HP: 0/150
Your XP reward = 400
Your progress to Pirate Captain Level 8 = 33210/40000

It goes down, twitching and steaming while the lightning arcs across to its four closest chums. They too stiffen and go all twitchy, their grey skin reddening as it scorches.

Shock Damage inflicted = 50
Level 4 Lamprey Cultists x4
HP: 100/150

The delay gives me time to holster Stormshot and then

Quickdraw me two remaining pistols. I fire them both at the cultist to me left. Both shots land, finishing the beastie off nicely.

Shot Damage inflicted = 100
Level 4 Lamprey Cultist
HP: 0/150
Your XP reward = 400
Your progress to Pirate Captain Level 8 = 33610/40000

To me right, one of me sailors be struggling against her cultist opponent. Loretta, one of the Spaniards I enlisted from the survivors of the Santa Lucia. She be sporting a nasty belly wound. Her parries are growing weak and unsteady as she desperately fends off her enemy's flashing blade.

It's like me own opponents can smell her blood, even though they still be twitching and smouldering after me shocking surprise. Almost as one, the three of them get to their feet and charge at the poor Spaniard. And that's when the horror starts. One cultist stands guard, watching me with dagger brandished, while its brethren tear at the woman's clothes until they have themselves some bare skin to latch onto with their nasty suckers.

Now that I have a little more room about me, I bring me musket to be on the guarding monstrosity. Seeing what I'm about to do, the thing throws itself at me, hissing with eely fury. I fire me Rumpus from the hip and blow the creature's guts all over its feasting friends.

Shot Damage inflicted = 200
Level 4 Lamprey Cultist
HP: -100/150
Your XP reward = 400
Your progress to Pirate Captain Level 8 = 33610/40000

I then set to reloading me pistols, hoping I can drive them monsters away from the stricken sailor. But I've no sooner reloaded Stomshot when I get a bit of a shock meself.

Your current opponents, x2 Lamprey Cultists, have applied their Blood Drain special skill to Sailor Loretta Sanchez and thereby replenished their health to full.

Level 4 Lamprey Cultists x2
HP: 150/150

Them otherwords send a shiver down me spine. That be why these buggers are Level 4, despite being a tad weaker in the health points than the fishmen of the lighthouse. They can bloody heal themselves by sucking me crewmates dry!

Me two remaining enemies be reinforced by a third, and seems the trio be ready to try me on for size. I've had time to reload all me pistols now, so I blast the middle cultist with Stormshot, then drop the weakened one to me left with me standard pistols. I use me Anticipate skill to dodge the dagger thrust of the third one while I draw me Seahawk Saber. The cultist has another go, stabbing at me throat, but I sidestep the attempt and amputate the thing's arm at the elbow. Me opponent stares dumbly for a moment at its shortened limb, giving me plenty of time to remove its stunned head with a brutal backhander.

Level 4 Lamprey Cultists x3
HP: 0/150
Your XP reward = 1200
Your progress to Pirate Captain Level 8 = 35210/40000

I pause to catch me breath and survey the battle. Me landing party has suffered a fair few casualties and still there be a sight too many cultists left for me liking.

Landing Parting: 27
Lamprey Cultists: 20/39

I see three different huddles of injured cultists, busy sucking me fallen pirates dry so they can bolster their health. Me party needs to be breaking those huddles up or we're done for. And there be only one way I can shout over this violent din to let them know.

I take a deep breath and power me words with Rallying Cry. "Stop them bloodsuckers from healing off our fallen crewmates! For grog and getting rich, lads and lassie!"

Me words ring out across the melee, cutting through the cacophony like a knife through lard. Right across the battle, I witness a surge of energy and ferocity from me pirates. Those what ain't immediately engaged with a foe charge at the little huddles of cultists, disrupting their feeding.

Your Landing Party has received a 10% bonus to Stamina and Damage Dealt.

Straight away, three cultists fall to me crew's renewed enthusiasm.

Lamprey Cultists: 17/39

But we ain't out of the proverbial woods yet. I reload me musket and pistols, me fingers flying with the help of Hasty Hands, while me eyes search for prime targets.

To one side of the chamber, I see that Mad Maggie's raised some sort of shadowy shield around herself and three wounded pirates. One of the injured be Rumguts. Two cultists are stabbing at her barrier and I can see it weakening, growing more transparent with every strike. I don't know how long she can hold the thing, and I be reluctant to find out. If Maggie falters, there goes me hard-earned witch and three of me crew.

On the other side of the chamber, I see Sandwich and Shaka battling another couple of cultists. It's funny to see the two fighting side by side, especially knowing how Shaka feels about Sandwich. It's less funny to see that Shaka's injured, bleeding from a nasty gash on his leg, and Sandwich be looking dog tired. He still be putting up a good fight though. More Sand than I figured for a toff like him.

Looks like I have to flip a coin. Me witch or me Star of Atlantis expert. I can't shoot two cultists and reload fast enough to knock over the other two, not before they claim their victims.

Or hang on. Maybe I can…

I use me Rumpus Musket to blast a hole in the first of Sandwich's opponents, spraying lamprey blood and slime all over him and Shaka. Not that they have any right to complain since I be saving their sorry behinds.

Shot Damage inflicted = 200
Level 4 Lamprey Cultist
HP: -50/150
Your XP reward = 400
Your progress to Pirate Captain Level 8 = 35610/40000

Then I draw and fire me two mundane pistols at the remaining cultist, dropping its HP from 150 HP to 50 HP, enabling Sandwich to finish the bugger off with a rapier-thrust through the chest.

You and James Montagu of Sandwich have killed a Level 4 Lamprey Cultist.
Your XP reward = 200
Your progress to Pirate Captain Level 8 = 35810/40000

Then I spin and fire Stormshot at the cultist closest to Maggie, just as her weakened shadow-shield shatters under a powerful strike from the creature's dagger. Me shot drills into the cultist's side and the thing stiffens as lightning rakes its body.

Shot Damage inflicted = 150
Level 4 Lamprey Cultist
HP: -0/150
Your XP reward = 400
Your progress to Pirate Captain Level 8 = 36210/40000

Bolts of lightning arc over to the other cultist, scorching and stunning it for a precious moment.

I make the most of that involuntary hesitation, draw me Seahawk, and use Daring Dash to streak across the blood-stained floor. The cultist already be driving forward with its dagger, the point aimed at Maggie's belly. I push the witch out of the way and take the hit in me flank. The blade bites deep into me side, sending a searing swathe of pain through me innards.

Damage received from Bloodforged Dagger = 75
Captain Grace "Deadeye" Cortez
HP: 146/221

I grit me teeth against the agony and chop down onto the cultist's shoulder with me saber before the beastie can yank its weapon from me flesh. Me blade slices through the joint, cleanly parting arm from body. I scream as the weight of the severed arm pulls on the dagger and widens the hole in me side as it drops out.

Damage received from Bloodforged Dagger = 25
Captain Grace "Deadeye" Cortez
HP: 121/221

I lift me saber again, this time hoping to chop the bloody critter's head off, but it catches me sword-arm in a vice-like claw, and pulls me forward. I lose me balance for a moment and end up with me head pressed against the thing's clammy chest. Before I can haul meself free, I feel a slimy kiss caress me neck.

The strength goes out of me, and me heartbeat be a panicked tattoo inside me chest. I feel a bizarre tingling across me breasts and back as all me blood rushes to me neck and out into the cultist's slurping maw.

Damage received from Lamprey Bloodsuck = 40
All attributes are dulled by 5 points while feeding is in process.
Captain Grace "Deadeye" Cortez
HP: 81/221

Out of the corner of me tear-filled eyes, I see the cultist's burns fade away. Then, to me blunted horror, I see the damned thing's arm start to regrow. Sinew and bone poke like the bud of a bloody flower from the earth of its shoulder. It thickens, stretches and then blooms.

Damage received from Lamprey Bloodsuck = 40
Captain Grace "Deadeye" Cortez
HP: 41/221

As the lamprey sips of me fine claret, I feel me mind start to drift away from me body, like a ship what's bust its moorings. I have two words left to say to that kind of tomfoolery.

"Reaver Rage."

It comes out as a hoarse whisper. Yes, I could've just said it in me head, but such be the swimmy nature of me thoughts right now, I can't be sure I'd think it clear and strong enough. By saying it out loud, I know it's so. It ain't a moment too soon neither.

Damage received from Lamprey Bloodsuck = 40
Captain Grace "Deadeye" Cortez
HP: 01/221

This be what I get for not investing more in me Stamina and Brawn scores, and then running into battle like some burly bruiser with a great, bulging… HP score.

Up from me guts comes a fracas of fury the likes of which me mild-mannered soul has never witnessed before. The strength surges back into me limbs as the mist be blown from me mind. Me white-hot brain tells me I ain't got enough room to swing me Seahawk. And the monster's still holding me sword-arm tight anyways. With me rage-improved strength, I could probably haul meself free, but I'd do meself a serious mischief as I wrenched the cultist's mouth from me neck. Probably exsanguinate on the spot. Instead, I drop me saber, curl me right leg so me boot touches me bum, and use me right hand to draw the knife I keep tucked away in a hidden boot sheath.

I thrust that dagger up into the cultist's throat and feel the sickening warmth of me own freshly sucked blood pour down me hand and forearm.

Critical Hit!
Damage dealt by your Boot Knife = 60

The beastie shudders. Pain burns across me neck as it withdraws its maw. I leave me knife where it's stuck in the cultist's neck, take a step back, pick up me Seahawk with two hands, and swing it with all me angry might.

It be right satisfying when the bastard's foulsome head comes clean off its shoulders. The cultist's cranium hits the ground at the same time me bum does. Reaver Rage be a flash in the pan, and this here egg be going sunny side up.

You have killed a Level 4 Lamprey Cultist.
Your XP reward = 400
Your progress to Pirate Captain Level 8 = 36610/40000

I let go of me saber, lie flat on the ground, and close me eyes. I hope to Bathala that I ain't going to feel one of them lamprey suckers latching onto me face any moment soon, but even that nasty thought ain't enough to stop me from sinking into a warm, dark oblivion.

21

BLOOD, OFFAL AND EXCREMENT

THE FIRST SLAP sets me cheek on fire. I sense movement and intercept the second slap by grabbing me assailant's wrist.

"What the bloody h-" Me words are drowned in something viscous and sour.

I wince, gurgle, cough, and then sit bolt upright. Me eyes are filled with tears and now me belly feels like it's full of lead shot. I try to get up, but a wave of pain washes me back down to the floor.

"Now for the rest of it, captain, or you'll be carried out on a stretcher. Not the best look for our daring leader."

Even in me befuddled state, I recognize the hoarfrost in that thin voice. Doc the Croc. Knowing it be good for me, no matter the foulness of the flavor, I push meself up on one elbow, take the proffered bottle, and gulp the goop down as fast as I can.

Once the vessel be empty, Croc takes it from me hand, and replaces it with a bottle of a warmly familiar shape. Rum. This time there be no hesitation as I put it to me lips and glug it down. It be a blessed relief as the nasty medicinal aftertaste be washed away in a few sweet draughts.

A few moments later, I be sitting up and sipping at me rum, eyes bright and clear. Every breath still makes me wince. I ain't even half-healed yet.

Captain Grace "Deadeye" Cortez
HP: 90/221

But I feel Croc's brew working within, fixing me up real nice, so I take me time and survey the carnage of our now quiet battlefield.

Landing Party: 24
Lamprey Cultists: 0/39

The place reeks of blood, offal and excrement. That be the true smell of war. Nothing sweet about victory. Not when people, and lamprey-headed freaks, have a habit of emptying their bowels after death. Really? Couldn't everyone have gone *before* the battle?

The Zealot Sanctuary XP pool is as follows:
Clearing the Sanctuary = 6000 XP
Penalties for losing twelve party members = -1200 XP
Total to be divided between surviving party members = 4800 XP
Your personal XP reward total = 400 XP
Progress to Pirate Captain Level 8 = 37010/40000

Not a lot of XP to be almost dying for, but then it's me own daft fault for sticking me neck out to save Maggie, Rumguts and co.

For your Act of Heroism in protecting your crewmates. your personal XP reward = 100 XP
Progress to Pirate Captain Level 8 = 37110/40000

Sometimes the otherwords send the heebies right up me. It's like whatever writes them, be it Bathala, Jehova, Gaia or Neptune, be reading the very thoughts out of me head. Still, just as me mother taught me, I offer a quick prayer to Bathala, thanking him for the XP and me rather miraculous survival this time. Then I struggle to me feet and pick Inkman out from me resting and recovering pirates.

"Oi! Inkman!"

He looks up and flashes me a relieved grin. "Thought you were a goner for a bit there, captain. Was bracing meself to shoulder the burden of leadership."

"Oh, you poor bugger. I'm touched that you was all cut up over the loss of an old and dear friend."

His grin widens, crinkling his tattoos like the pattern on a lady's fan when she closes it. "Nah, pulling your leg, Deadeye. I knew you'd make it. You're like a nettle in a kumara patch."

I see where this be going, but I play along with Inkman nonetheless. Me crew needs a bit of comic relief after what they just been through.

"What? I give people a rash when I touch them?" That gets me a smattering of chuckles, but we ain't done yet.

"Nay, captain," continues Inkman, deadpan, "no matter how many times you get trampled or torn out, you just keep bloody growing back."

The punchline gets a right old laugh from me assembled crew. This ain't exactly a Shakespearean comedy, but then me crew ain't the most refined lot. They're happy to find humor wherever they can find it.

Your landing party's morale had dropped to 65% due to the heavy losses sustained in this battle.
It has now risen to 75% due to your survival and subsequent normalization of the conflict's aftermath through humorous banter.

I be glad no one else can read me otherwords. Nothing like an explanation to ruin a perfectly good joke.

A loud scrape of metal on stone brings me attention to Black and White Russian. The sisters be dragging a hefty metal chest out of an alcove. The fair-haired twin kneels by the lock and has it picked and open before I can say "Pilfering in Saint Petersburg". The lid swings wide on well-oiled hinges and the sisters' faces light up at what they see inside.

"Captain? This you should see," says Black Russian with her customary abruptness.

I be on me way, quicksmart, stepping carefully over the bodies of cultists and pirates alike. When I get there, I peer into the chest, and I too feel a smile tug at the corners of me mouth.

"I think we've just found this creepy church's collection box," I announce to me crewmates.

Each of the survivors takes a gander while I do a quick tally up. At me best guess, there be close to fifty thousand crowns in this here chest. Quite the wee haul indeed! When Sandwich sees it, he nods, a knowing smirk on his face. I decide to have him up about it.

"Oi, lordling. You knew this would be here?"

"I did not know for certain, captain, but I have read that Atlanteans would make offerings to the Bloodwyrm in return for blessings of health and vitality."

"What sort of 'blessings'?"

He gestures at a dead cultist. "As we saw firsthand, these creatures were able to metabolize blood and harness that energy for rapid and extensive healing. Although my readings did not stipulate this exactly, I would infer that the blood of a cultist retains much of that potency."

"One step ahead of you there, Sandwich," says Doc the Croc from the other side of a pile of cultist corpses.

He's got a syringe full of what looks to be blood in his hand, and he be kneeling over one of me sailors what has lost his leg below the knee. The rest of me landing party seem to be healing up nicely, thanks to Croc's concoctions. This poor fella, a lanky Egyptian lad known fondly as Camel, be looking at a pegleg for his troubles here.

"Be that lamprey blood you're about to squeeze into Camel's veins?"

"Aye, captain. I've diluted the solution with alcohol to destroy any bloodborne pathogens."

"I seen one of them cultists start growing its arm back after sucking most of me own juice out of me neck, but... you sure you're alright with this, Camel?"

The lad's big, dark eyes are wide and glistening with fear, but he nods his head nonetheless. Doc looks at me and I shiver at the cold excitement I see in them gleaming orbs. You'd not think Croc and Camel were even of the same species.

"Do I have your permission to proceed, captain?"

"Aye."

I motion for three of me burliest pirates, Hyena, Silverback and Rhino, to hold the sorry blighter down while Croc completes his experiment. They pinion his remaining limbs while Croc injects his solution into the boy's thigh, above where his leg has been sliced away. No Bloodforged Dagger could've done that, but then I spot one of our boarding axes still clutched in a lamprey's dead hand. That would explain it.

Me further musings be shattered by a scream, and by Neptune's weedy balls, what a scream it be!

22

MARCH OF THE DEAD

CAMEL'S SCREAMING forces many of us to cover our ears for fear of blowing an eardrum or two. It's all me three pirates can do to hold the young Egyptian down. Pain be giving the boy strength beyond the normal limits of his lean body.

I look to Croc to see if he's going to do anything to ease Camel's suffering, but he just be standing there, his face impassive, his glinting eyes observing with fascination. He's soaking it all in, learning all he can from his squealing guinea pig.

I stride over to the doctor and grip his arm, squeezing hard enough to hurt the bugger. He flinches and pulls away as he fires back a questioning look.

"Give him something for the pain," I growl, "or you'll be next."

I fold me arms to resist the urge to slap the look of childish disappointment off Croc's face. He takes another syringe and a small bottle of morphine from his satchel, draws up a heavy dose, and injects it into Camel's arm. The effect be immediate. The young man's thrashing weakens, his screams turn to pitiful wails, and soon he be lying there silently, sleeping like a baby.

Just in time too. I can see why the poor blighter was suffering so. The bud of the boy's new leg has burst out of his sundered thighbone. It be growing at a fair clip, and I reckon he'll be a complete man again by morning. But they ain't called 'growing pains' for nothing.

Your act of mercy has improved your landing party's morale by 5% from 75% to 80%

I be just doing the right thing as far as I'm concerned, but I be glad me crew agrees. It means I've chosen them well, with the notable exception of Doc the bloody Croc. If he weren't the best medical man I could get me hands on, I'd be running a knife across his throat to save the world a whole lot of future trouble.

"Croc, gather as much blood as you can from these lampreys. Silverback and Rumguts?"

"Aye, captain?" they answer in near unison.

"You stay here. Watch over Camel and guard our booty." Then I look to Sandwich. "Any sign of this key for the Star?"

The lordling shakes his head. "An object of such import would be guarded by the Bloodwyrm herself." He points out the darkened archway across the chamber. Our Gleams don't quite penetrate the gloom. "She has her own chamber. An underground lagoon where these followers would feed and tend to her. If the key is in this temple, it will be down there, with her."

I bite me lip and consider whether I should go back to the ship first, to fetch more of me crew. Otherwise, we'll be down to twenty-one against this monster. We laid the Mistress of Light to rest with half that, but if these tough cultist buggers be anything to go by, this Bloodwyrm's going to be a whole different kettle of nasty fish.

"I reckon we be a bit light on numbers for this final push. Inkman? What do you think?"

The quartermaster opens his mouth to reply but it's Maggie who answers for him. "I can rustle up some reinforcements for you, captain."

I know where this be going. "You ain't turning our dearly departed into zombies, Maggie."

The witch's smile be bleak as one of her Scottish winters. "I thought you might say that. There be thirty-nine reasons here why I won't be messing with your crewmates' remains."

I feel the gorge rising in me throat at the thought. "Them cultists?"

"Aye. Clear your dead into the tunnel, give me the chamber for a few minutes, and I'll give you a raiding party the likes of which you wouldn't dream about."

"You're right about that, Maggie. Not in me worst nightmares."

I look at the faces of me crew, and every one of them has grown a few shades paler.

Your crew's morale has dropped from 80% to 60%

This foray be taking a dark turn, but I ain't willing to see us all slaughtered by a bloody great eel neither.

"You heard the witch, me hearties! Gird your loins and clear the room. Better them than us, I say!"

That gets me a few nods of agreement. I'm close to where Loretta fell, so I lead by example. I grab her corpse by the wrists and drag her out into the entrance tunnel. Me landing party follows suit, and soon we have all our dead lined up along the wall. Silverback and Rumguts are the last, laying Camel further down the tunnel.

Me crew then huddles around me, even the bravest of them unnerved by what's to come.

"Rumguts, I hope you be having enough grog for everyone because I think we could all use a wee dram right now."

"Couldn't agree more, captain."

Rumguts passes around her flasks while we try to ignore the Haitian mutterings and dreadful shrieks that be part of Maggie's Voodoo ritual. We've finished off Rumguts' entire supply by the time the witch's ghastly performance be done. The warm glow of booze helps blunt the chilling sounds of thirty-nine dead lamprey freaks rising to their feet.

Thanks to the anxiety-dampening effects of rum, your landing party has resisted a further 10% drop in morale.

There be a bit of scraping and shuffling as Maggie gathers her new pets into some semblance of order. Finally, she calls out for us to come back in. I lead the way, not wanting any of me crewmates to be the first to witness the horror ahead. Rumguts and Silverback look mighty relieved to be staying with Camel.

Landing Party: 21
Zombie Horde: 39

At least Maggie's had the sensitivity to arrange her zombies with their backs to us. She's formed them in a neat column facing the Bloodwyrm's archway. Each grips a Bloodforged Dagger in its claw. With macabre fascination, I see me one-armed lamprey near the back, the stub of his new arm sticking out of his raw shoulder. It ain't grown any further. Just sticks out of its mangled flesh like an oversized wart. I suppress a shudder and address me crew.

"Alright, Maggie, you walk with me behind your… troops." I'm doing me best to keep the queasiness in me belly from putting a tremble in me voice. Fear be infectious. "Sandwich, you're two steps behind me. Sisters, you flank him. Keep him out of trouble. Inkman, bring up the rear and the rest of you fall in."

Once everyone's in place, I give Maggie the nod. She turns to her little horde of zombies, barks something in Haitian, and the column of cadavers leads us into the dark.

23

THE BLOODWYRM

THE TUNNEL SPIRALS downward like a coiled eel, at last spitting us out onto the beach of a subterranean lagoon. Collectively, our Gleams illuminate enough of the murky lagoon to make out a small island about a hundred feet offshore. The island be piled high with the bones of the Bloodwyrm's many sacrificial victims, and sticking up out of them bones be a tall pedestal upon which sits a golden sculpture. It looks like a bit of coral at first glance. A stem with five branches.

I point it out to Sandwich. "That be the key we be looking for?"

He smiles and there be a lusty glint in his baby blues. "Yes, captain. That is the Elder Sign."

"Problem be, as soon as any of us try to swim out to get it, the Bloodwyrm will no doubt feel the movement in the water and turn up to eat us."

"I'll go for a swim, captain," Inkman volunteers. "I'll draw her out so Barber can hit her with our falconets." He jerks his head in Barber's direction. Our ship's barber and finest harpooner already be loading the small cannons with rope-leashed harpoons.

144

"Kind of you to offer, matey, but what be your swimming skill?"

"Second Class."

I address the rest of me gathered landing party. "Anyone do better than that?" There's some uncomfortable shuffling but no one be putting their hands up. Just as I figured. "Maggie? What about your lamprey zombies there. Can they swim?"

"Nay, captain. They could when they was alive. No doubt there. But dead, well, they only be as good as their witch."

"And how good a swimmer be the witch?"

"Like a stone with arms and legs what waggle uselessly in a mad panic."

I heave a sigh and unbuckle me brace of pistols. "Then it be down to the First Class Freediver then. Rather wishing I'd cashed it in rather than me Croupier skill when I was upgrading to Sharpshooter. Then I could've fleeced you lot in a game of poker while Inkman went and played worm-on-a-hook for our big fishy."

That gets a chuckle from all except Inkman. "You sure about this, captain? You're going to have to swim damned fast."

"Well, here be the thing. We might as well kill two gulls with one shot. I'll tie a rope around me waist and swim it out to the island. If the Bloodwyrm ain't going to take me as bait, I'll just tie the rope around the golden key there and your lot can haul it in. Or, if I get meself into trouble, you can yank me out of the water. Make sense?"

"About as much sense as that Jonah and the Whale story what the missioners used to spin for us 'noble savages', you know? Thought we might identify with the whale bit, forgetting that anyone what gets swallowed by a whale just gets turned into whale crap."

I shrug with bravado that I don't feel. "I ain't planning to get turned into eel crap today. Fear will give me the flippers of a dolphin, I reckon." I point at Barber. "You just be ready with those harpoons so you don't have to see your dear captain get turned into a bloodless Filipina raisin."

Barber grins at that. "Rest assured, captain. We'll haul this fish in before it takes the bait." Without waiting for me response, she turns to the landing party. "Get them falconets set up, mateys. Captain's putting her ass on the line here so the least we can do is make sure it don't get bit!"

Me crew hop to it, placing the falconets at the lagoon's edge while I finish removing everything except me shirt and breeches. I load me musket and pistols and set them a little bit back from the shore so I can snipe the Bloodwyrm during the upcoming fracas. While I be about it, Croc sidles over and presents me with a leatherbound capsule from his doctor's bag. I quirk me eyebrow, wondering what he be about, but he just stares at me in that impassive way of his. I sigh and pop the top off the thing. Inside be a large syringe of brass and glass, and it be full of lamprey blood.

"In case you run into trouble, captain." He jerks his head in the direction of the island. "But try to be onshore when you use it. Bit hard to swim while you be spasming and screaming."

"Your bedside manner be as sweet as always, Croc."

"I prefer to save folks with science, not kill them with kindness, Deadeye."

And with that he heads for the gun crews, ready to play the part of field surgeon if he has to. I seal the capsule, clip it to me belt, and then make a beeline for Mad Maggie.

"Reckon these zombie friends of yours can still do their blood-sucking routine?"

She eyes her horde like a mother admiring her children. "Those what were shot or hacked in the throat and face won't be much good for anything but stabbing and clawing, but there be at least thirty able blood-suckers among them."

"Then have those what can latch onto the Bloodwyrm as soon as she rears her ugly head. I be knowing what it's like to have your lifeblood drained out by them uglies and methinks thirty should weaken our queen lamprey a fair bit."

"Aye, captain. Then that's what I'll do."

By now the gun crews be all set up so it's time for me to take a dip. I give me mateys a wave and then plunge into the water. The chill sends a jolt through me whole body. It be fiercely cold, but I suppose this be where me Sand score of twenty comes into play.

Sand: 15 (20)
+1 from Freediver 1st Class
+1 from Leader 1st Class
+2 from Hero 3rd Class
+1 from Seahawk Saber

Sand: 20 + 20 percent peer pressure bonus since me crew be watching. The total be 24.

The challenge be worth 30 so I have an 80 percent chance of making this swim without having a panic attack.

I hear Fate rattle them dotted bone cubes it loves so much. I hear the tap of bone against wood as the die skitters across the fortune god's tabletop. It occurs to me that I don't know this god's name. Sure as hell ain't Bathala. I just think of her as Fate, or Lady Fortune, when I think of her at all. And it's not until occasions like this that she even crosses me mind.

The Bloodwym's Lagoon Challenge has rolled 71 to your 80
In quelling the rising tide of anxiety you have prevented such symptoms as hyperventilation and temporary paralysis.

With a surge of vigor and confidence, I strike out for the island, and it feels like I be wading up its gentle beach before I know it. I untie the rope from around me waist and loop it around the stem of the Elder Sign. Then I turn to me crew and give them a wave.

"Haul away, mateys!"

Inkman and the heftier of me pirates heave to and drag the Elder Sign into the water. Judging by the sand on the shore of the island, and on the beach I've just come from, the bottom of this lagoon should also be sandy smooth. At least, I hope so. I don't fancy diving down to unhook that Elder Sign from the rocks while some great bloody lamprey be hunting me. And speaking of the she-devil, I hear a splash in the water behind me. Spinning about, I'm in time to catch the shimmer of a grey, slimy portion of back as it slides under the surface.

I dive into the water and swim for me damned life. There be a shard of fear shoved in me guts this time, and me bare feet be tingling with the anticipation of feeling them circles of teeth close around them. As I draw close to the beach, I hear the shouts of me crew, muffled to incoherence by the water. But I know what it means, well enough. The Bloodwyrm has taken the bait and be moving in fast.

It be a blessed relief when me fingertips brush the bottom. I thrust me legs down, sink me naked toes into the sand, push meself up out of the water and wade as fast as I can. Now I hear me crew loud and clear, a ragged chorus of, "Leg it, captain!"

I don't bother looking back. I just do as I be told. Just as well too. No sooner have me feet reached dry land, I hear a resounding crash and we all be doused in a downpour of seawater. Only then do I turn and see just how close I came to being wormfood. The great maw of the Bloodwyrm be resting there on the beach, but a scant yard or two away, gaping like some great, fleshy cavern.

"Falconets fire!" I roar at me crew. "The rest of you, shoot her right down the kisser!"

To their credit, me crew responds quicksmart. Our two cannons thunder and harpoons plunge into the Bloodwyrm's glistening flanks. Before she can jerk herself free, the gun crews have tethered the ropes to a stout pair of stalagmites. Meanwhile, the rest of me pirates raise their pistols and fire, peppering the great beastie with hot, leaden shot.

Harpoon Damage Inflicted = 400
Pistol Volley Damage = 750
Total Damage = 1150
The Bloodwyrm
Level 25
HP: 3850/5000

Bloody hell! I think to meself as I scoop up Rumpus Musket. We've certainly got our work cut out for us this time!

24

THE LAST LAUGH

"ATTACK, ME BEAUTIES!" screams Maggie at the top of her lungs.

Twenty-one pairs of eyes glance in her direction, such be the naked hysteria in her voice. Even the Bloodwyrm seems to pause to consider the raw madness it has just witnessed. But the zombie lampreys don't hesitate. They swarm over their former goddess like crabs over a whale carcass. The Bloodwyrm thrashes about, trying to rid herself of this undead pestilence, but the harpoons and straining ropes hold her fast.

The lampreys make small impressions on the Bloodwyrm's thick hide with their daggers, barely a scratch per strike, but they make up for their impotence with morbid vigor and stamina.

Stabbing Damage x52 strikes = 520
The Bloodwyrm
Level 25
HP: 3330/5000

The Bloodwyrm tries one more violent thrash. Finding herself still caught, she crashes to the sand, seemingly defeated. Me crew lets out a cheer, but I know it be a premature celebration. She ain't beaten. She's about to try something different.

I scoop up me Rumpus Musket and Flashfire the great ugly beast in her gaping mouth. There be a satisfying gout of blood as me shot smashes through one of her teeth and sends bone shrapnel tearing through the soft flesh beyond.

Shot Damage = 200
The Bloodwyrm
Level 25
HP: 3130/5000

Then I Quickdraw Stormshot and add further injury to insult.

Shot Damage = 150
The Bloodwyrm
Level 25
HP: 2980/5000

Whatever the Bloodwyrm be preparing itself for, it takes long enough to give Maggie's 'beauties' time to do a tad more hacking and stabbing.

Stabbing Damage x39 strikes = 390
The Bloodwyrm
Level 25
HP: 2590/5000

But that be the last bit of helpful violence them zombies manage to perform. The bloody great sea snake sprouts spines like a sea urchin. Long, blood-red lances puncture Maggie's minions in so many places that they simply die, the lot of them, all over again.

I hear Maggie's pitiful wail, but I ain't got no time for sympathy as I activate me Anticipation skill. Something tells me this Bloodwyrm ain't satisfied with being merely prickly. It's about to show us that it's bloody well furious. And what Anticipation shows me be a blurring cloud of impending doom.

"Hit the sand! She's going to-"

Me final word was meant to be "blow", but it be drowned by a deafening thump as the wyrm's blood pressure sends every one of them javelin-sized spines hurtling through the air.

Anyone with a Quickness score of 10 or better manages to throw themselves onto the sand before the quills can hit them. Maggie ain't that quick, having focused on witchy attributes like Wit, Sand and Perception, but Inkman's quick enough for the two of them, bringing her down in a rough tackle.

Five of me burliest pirates ain't quick enough, having spent all their level-up points on Brawn and Stamina. Even their beefy HP ain't enough to accommodate half a dozen impaling javelins.

Landing Party: 16
Self-inflicted Damage due to blood loss = 500
The Bloodwyrm
Level 25
HP: 2090/5000

Her spiked barrage might have cost us dearly, all our zombies and five of me crew, but it's cost her a painful price too. Goes to show how desperate she be. Well, not quite so desperate as it turns out. The spikes ain't just sliced through me vanguard. They've also sliced through the ropes binding the wench.

With an almighty thrash, the Bloodwyrm turns herself about and plunges into the lagoon.

"Dammit!" I holler and kick a shower of sand into the air.

"Do not worry yourself, captain," offers a surprisingly calm

Sandwich. He be in the process of dusting sand and blood off his once-fine coat. "She will return shortly."

"How the hell do you know that?"

"She is the guardian of the Elder Sign. She will either slay us and recover her charge, or die in the attempt."

"And how the hell do you know *that*?" This time it ain't me doing the questioning. It be Shaka.

The Zulu's kneeling by one of our fallen mateys. The big Kenyan we call Rhino, mostly on account of him being horribly short-sighted. Could tear the head clean off a royal navy marine with them big hands though. There be blood dripping down Shaka's face. It ain't his. He must've been right behind Rhino when the bigger man got skewered by three of them flying spikes.

He has a point, but we don't got the time to explore it right now. I scowl Shaka into silence and then look to me gun crews. Both be a hand short now.

"Tarsi, Rumguts, help them gunners load the falconets with grapeshot. The rest of you, load your pistols. Give this lovely lady a bit of pepper with her lunch!"

I follow me own advice, reloading me Rumpus Musket and Stormshot as I run some numbers in me head. I've got ten crew not currently busy with the falconets, and assuming they can all hit the Bloodwyrm in its big ugly moosh, that be 500 Damage right there. With Rumpus, Stormshot and me two plain pistols, I can do at least another 450 Damage. Then the falconets will do 300 Damage apiece with grapeshot against her toughened hide, so that be 500 plus 450 plus 600 equals 1550 out of the 1990 remaining in her HP pool. A Critical Hit or two would certainly help, but I never count on those.

Thing be, now that she's free and easy, the Bloodwyrm will slither right up on this beach and try to chomp us to bits. Being out of shots, we'll have no choice but to have at her with our sabers. I don't fancy our chances against that leathery skin of hers, but we ain't got no other options right now.

"Here she comes!" shrieks Maggie, pointing at the V of the Bloodwyrm's approach just under the surface of the water.

It be with a glimmer of hope that I notice there be plenty of red in the monster's wake. And just as she's about to launch herself up onto the beach, the otherwords confirm me suspicions.

Damage due to blood loss = 300
The Bloodwyrm
Level 25
HP: 1690/5000

It's going to be close but we might just manage.

The Bloodwyrm launches herself out of the water and we honor her grand entrance with a thirteen gun salute. Bless me pirates. Every one of them holds their nerve and discharges their weapon right into the thing's mouth. Of course, having a reasonably high morale score helps there too.

The grapeshot shreds both sides of her head and me Stormshot feeds her some forked crackling right down her throat.

Ten Pistols Damage = 500
Falconet Grapeshot Damage = 600
Stormshot Damage = 150
Total Damage = 1250
The Bloodwyrm
Level 25
HP: 440/5000

The old snake ain't Level 25 for nothing. She proves it by pulling another trick out of her slimy backside. Quick as the lightning from me Stormshot, she lunges at the closest pirate, a

Scottish lass we call Pipes on account of her singing voice being like the drone on a set of bagpipes. Her dying noises sound like bagpipes too. Punctured ones.

Landing Party: 15

The Bloodwyrm disgorges Pipes and I groan as I see the update on her stats.

Healing drawn from a Level 4 Marine = 150
The Bloodwyrm
Level 25
HP: 590/5000

I feel a howl of rage rise in me throat, but I know it won't do the rest of me crew any good. They need their captain, their Deadeye, frosty as an Icelandic morning. I shoulder Rumpus Musket and feel a little satisfaction to know that me Anticipate skill be still active. I see a ghost image of the Bloodwyrm line up another pirate who be lying prone on the sand below her. White Russian. No, her sister would never forgive me if I let this happen.

I breathe out, feel me head empty of everything but the one big, black, soulless eye I be targeting. Then when ghost wyrm becomes Bloodwyrm, I pull the trigger.

Critical Hit!
Rumpus Musket Damage = 400
The Bloodwyrm
Level 25
HP: 190/5000

With her eye now ruptured and bleeding, the Bloodwyrm misjudges the distance of her strike. Her maw hits the sand below

White Russian's feet. The lass be hauled away by her sister as I Quickdraw me two remaining pistols and unload them in the wyrm's ravaged and bleeding head, landing a critical with me left-hand shot. Her hide be too torn up to protect her any longer.

Shot Damage = 150
The Bloodwyrm
Level 25
HP: 40/5000

The rest of me crew now charges at the Bloodwyrm, glass sabers flashing in the light of our Gleams. This time I let out that howl of fury I been holding in as I sprint down the beach to join them. Our next casualty be Kentucky, an ex-farm boy from Mississippi. Perhaps it's a blessing that I won't have to hear *that* convoluted origin story one more time. It took me too much rum to weather it the first time. Never one to invest in his Wit score, Kentucky runs right into the Bloodwyrm's mouth. Thank Bathala his 100 HP of blood prolongs the Bloodwyrm's demise only slightly.

Healing drawn from injured Level 3 Marine = 100
The Bloodwyrm
Level 25
HP: 140/5000

Landing Party: 14

It be Hyena what strikes the final blow. Before me startled eyes he spins away from Bloodwyrm's lunge, a move I seen him mocking Sandwich for during their Fencing lessons, then drives his saber right through the monster's one remaining eye. The beast thrashes blindly and knocks Hyena flying. I hear the barmy bugger cackling with hilarity right up until the point where he lands on top of one of them spines. It be stuck fast in a bank of sand and Hyena goes sliding onto the thing like a cube of lamb onto a kebab stick.

Landing Party: 13

But he least he gets the last laugh.

The Bloodwyrm
Level 25
HP: -85/5000

He would've liked that.

25

DREAMS OF THE DEAD

You have slain the Bloodwyrm and secured the Elder Sign!
The Bloodwyrm Lagoon XP pool is as follows:
One Level 25 Bloodwyrm = 2500 XP
Penalties for losing eight party members = -800 XP
Securing the Elder Sign = 5000 XP
Total to be divided between surviving party members = 6700 XP
As Leader of the party, you receive a double share of XP
Your personal XP reward total = 1030 XP
Progress to Pirate Captain Level 8 = 38140/40000

THERE BE a few smiles and nods from me surviving pirates as they level up; Inkman, Maggie and Sandwich among them.

Despite the heavy losses suffered during this venture, success has lifted your Landing Party's morale to 80%

With the exception of Sandwich, we be pirates. A long life be a pleasant surprise, not an expectation. Most of us are just happy to see another day. All the sweeter if we have a fat purse of coin to help us enjoy that day.

It takes us the entire afternoon to haul our loot to the ship and gather our dead. We build one big pyre from some of the spare timber we keep in the Albatross' hold, for both our crew and Bluegums' lot. As we set them poor buggers ablaze, I give them a butchered Catholic funeral prayer that be common among us pirates, to help send them on their final voyage.

I know that they not all be of a religious leaning in that pile, but it be the act of faith rather than its nature in moments like this. As me mother has always said on matters of spirituality, "a prayer is a prayer, no matter the words spoken".

"In sure and certain hope of the resurrection to eternal life,
Through our Lords and Ladies on high,
We commend to the Almighty these adventurous souls,
And we commit their bodies to the flames:
Fire to fire,
Ashes to ashes,
Sand to sand.
The Divine bless them and keep them,
The Divine make Their Faces to shine upon them,
And be gracious to them,
The Lord and Ladies lift Their countenance upon our departed,
And give them peace.
Amen."

"Amen," echoes me assembled crew in a dozen different languages and faiths.

We turn our backs on the flames and board the Albatross. Those of us who have survived the Maw of a Thousand Deaths are asleep before our heads even hit our bunks.

The next morning be a grey one. Inclement clouds loom overhead, threatening us with storm and fury before the day be done. Under normal circumstances, I'd have left us moored, sat out this tempest, but I simply can't bear the thought of another day on this shore. I know I be a fool for feeling this way. Hyena, Tabouli, Loretta, Pipes, Kentucky and all the rest; they be pirates. They knew the risks. Yet still the hounds of guilt nip at me heels.

Or maybe it be that golden sign in me cabin. Damn thing dominated me dreams last night. At one point I found meself hanging from it, a noose around me neck, and from every other branch, there be me crew, dangling like ripe plums. I woke in a sweat and it took me a couple of snifters of rum to get me back to sleep.

Come morning, the eyeless thing seemed to be watching me every step, reading me every thought from the corner of the room. I banished it to the darkest corner of the hold, but I can still feel it down there, a cold and clammy presence in the bowels of me ship.

Now I be up on the quarterdeck, me coat buttoned up against the cold wind, sipping strong, hot coffee while Jonesy guides us out of the bay. There ain't much talk this morning as me crew goes about their business. There be shadows under most eyes and the general mood be as overcast as the sky. Not the atmosphere you'd expect, considering the amount of booty we hauled aboard yesterday.

Your crew morale has dropped from 80% to 70% overnight.

"How'd you sleep last night, Jonesy?"

Me Navigator shrugs, trying to make light of her dreams. "I've had worse nights."

"And plenty better, I'd wager."

"Aye."

"Care to share?"

Jonesy manages a faint smile. "Looks to me you've had more than your fair share already, captain."

"Aye, probably. But these shoulders be broader than they look."

"I don't doubt it, captain." She sighs. "That thing we've brought aboard, what's it called again?"

"The Elder Sign."

"I dreamed we was all chained to it, sinking with the damned thing down into Davey Jones' Locker. But it weren't old Davey waiting down there for us. It were Squidbeard, like on them Atlantean crowns we've got so many of."

"Aye, the sooner we can swap the Elder Sign for the Star of Atlantis, the happier we'll all be." I ain't one to trouble the crew with me concerns, but Jonesy be different. She and Inkman be the ones I confide in from time to time. "Though we've done all right, I be having me regrets about coming to these islands."

"Atlantis not what you expected?"

"Not sure anyone knows what to expect from Atlantis. All I can reckon be that we've traded some fine skulls for some right horrible happenings."

Jonesy's normally full lips are a thin line of grim agreement. She led the second landing party to help us collect our loot and gather our corpses. She saw the cultists and the Bloodwyrm with her own lovely eyes.

"Sorry, captain, but I ain't got no cheery words for you. Was having a chat with Maggie last night. She reckons there be worse ahead."

"How much worse?"

"Enough to give a mistress of Baron Samedi the heebie-jeebies."

"Bloody hell. Now that be saying something."

Jonesy lowers her voice. "She ain't the only one saying things neither."

I follow her gaze down to Shaka on the deck below. The Zulu be sharpening sabers and cutlasses with a few of his mates; Goldilocks, Breezy and Redneck. Camel's with them too, his injured leg propped up on a barrel. His shin has grown back, and most of his ankle too. Just his foot to go now, and judging by the strained look of his bandages, that appendage be blooming into existence soon enough.

They be having a right good chinwag it seems. I watch them while pretending not to, until me coffee cup's run dry, and in that time I see half a dozen crew members stop in for some passing words with Shaka and his lot.

Your crew morale has dropped from 70% to 60%
There is discontent on board.

"What you been hearing?" I finally ask Jonesy.

"Sandwich comes up a lot. Shaka feels we should be chucking the toff to the sharks, then be heading for the Caribbean like the Narwhal. He reckons Atlantis be bad juju and that we ain't got no business here no more."

"He weren't complaining when he helped bring that chest of crowns on board."

"No, but he supposes we should cut our losses."

"And Sandwich's throat while be at it?"

"Aye."

I don't mind a difference in opinions. Pirates ain't renowned for being agreeable. But if I don't do something about Shaka, sooner or later, I be having a mutiny on me hands.

The wind picks up as Jonesy steers us out into the choppy open water. The gale be against us and I hear North order the trimming of the sails. Looks like it'll take all day to get back to Freeport. And it turns out that the wind ain't our only problem.

It be late morning, the day no lighter than before when the sky opens up and weeps like a teenage maiden over her lost lover. And through the deluge, Rumguts be shouting at me.

"A sail, captain!"

"What flag, Rumguts?!"

"Can't quite make it out, captain!" She peers into the gloom for a moment, then reels back as if she's just seen a ghost. "Bloody hell!"

"You ain't been drinking on your watch again, have you, Rumguts? I told you I be-"

"Nay, captain. I swear on Saint Patrick himself. I be as sober as a judge!"

I be seeing some right drunken judges in me time, but this ain't no time for nit-picking. "Then tell me what flag, you swab!"

"It be Squidface! Bright emerald on tattered black!"

There be several cries of alarm from the deck below, mostly from the Spaniards of the former Santa Lucia. One of them be heading for the railing like he's planning to throw himself overboard. I dissuade him by unslinging me musket and taking a bead on his bandana-clad head.

"No one be leaving me ship without me express permission, señor!"

He freezes in place and raises his hands. He be one of the survivors from me landing party. He saw what happened to Tabouli so ain't under no illusion that I be pulling the trigger if I have to.

"Diego, be it?" I ask around the muzzle of me firearm. "That the ship what waylaid the Santa Lucia?"

"Aye, capitana. The ghost ship, manned by men what got no right to be roaming beyond their graves."

"You be sure?"

He nods so emphatically that I be worried he'll snap his neck.

"Well, if that ain't all we bloody need," I mutter to meself as I lower me musket. I gesture for Diego to go back to his post and then turn to Jonesy. "Give us a good line on her. She might be bigger and uglier than us, and full of crazy deadmen, but we ain't making that dream of yours come true Jonesy. Not today." Into me hollering tube I yell, "Powderfinger! Ready the cannons! Let's make these Atlanteans wish they died a thousand years ago when they was supposed to!"

I allow meself a sharp smile as me crew braces themselves for the battle to come. We might be leaping from the frying pan into the fire, but we ain't cooked yet.

26

DO OR UNDIE

As we get closer, I see that the Atlantean ship be some kind of galley. While I be watching, it uses its oars to turn itself for the best angle on the wind and then launches at us with ragged sails billowing. I take the Peeper from me belt and has a gander at the gizzards of our opponent.

The Dreamer
Hull Defense: 200/200 (300/300)
+100 Defense from Stygian Planking
Sail Defense: 70/70 (100/100)
+30 Defense and +50% Fire Resistance from Dankthread Sails

Agility: 80 (100)
+10 Agility from Dankthread Sails
+10 Agility from Breath of the Sleeping One
Agility: 80 when sails trimmed care-of Skeletal Oarsmen

Speed: 120 (140)

+10 Speed from Dankthread Sails

+10 Speed from Breath of the Sleeping One

Speed: 80 when sails trimmed care-of Skeletal Oarsmen

Guns: 24

20 Antediluvian Artillery Cannons

Base Damage per Gun: 20

4 Cyclopean Swivel Cannons

Base Damage per Gun: 15

Crew: 200

I see that there crew now, standing stiff as boards on the Dreamer's deck, watching us impassively with milk-white eyes. They be a withered lot, like the wrapped-up Pharoah I once saw in Cairo. Each bears a cutlass of carved obsidian, and after hearing what happened to the Santa Lucia, I be in no doubt these ghouls have the strength and speed for butchery in their emaciated frames.

I stash me Peeper back into me belt and gulp down a thick lump of grisly fear. The Dreamer outguns us on every count, especially when it comes to them actual guns. One good broadside and we be off down to Davey's sodden nightmare. She be the same speed as us too, with those oars of hers to help her through the lulls. There be no way we can outrun her, unless…

"Chain shot, Powderfinger!" I shout into me hollering tube. "Aim for the sails and make every bloody shot count. You be the Master of Guns in this fracas." I quietly be wishing I hadn't traded in me 1st Class Gunner skill, but there ain't time for regrets right now.

I lean over the rail of me quarterdeck. "Mad Maggie! Get your witchy backside up here! You too, Sandwich!"

To the thump of hurried boots on the quarterdeck steps, I give me last order to Jonesy. "We cut across her bow, Cedella. Broadside her sails. It be our only chance."

Jonesy nods her understanding, her full lips pressed into a thin line of determination. I clap her on the shoulder and turn to me so-called brains of this outfit.

"Maggie, Sandwich, you best give me some advantage against these dead bastards or, frankly, *we* be the next dead bastards in line."

The witch purses her lips as she racks her crazy head for suitable spells. Sandwich cups his stubbled chin with his hand and taps his long, thin index fingers against his cheekbone. It be quite an endearing gesture, and I feel the tug of a smile upon me lips, despite the rather dire circumstances.

It be Sandwich what comes up with something first. His baby blues light up with excitement, then he's off bounding down the stairs.

"Sandwich?! What the bloody-"

"Be right back, captain!" be his answer, and he punctuates it by slamming open the trapdoor into the hold.

I look to Maggie, wondering if her madness be contagious, and am met with a wicked grin. "I hope that means you've got something for me, Ms MacDonald. Because I honestly don't know what's more unnerving. That boatload of deadmen or your sinister smirk."

"How close can you get us to that galley, captain?" she asks me, her voice fair trembling with anticipation.

"Pretty damned close. We be having a go at her sails with chain shot as we sweep across her bow."

"Good. I need to be seeing their milky whites."

"Would this help?" I ask her, gesturing at Squintlock's Peeper.

"Nay, needs to be with me naked eyes."

"Alrighty, hope all that peering into arcane tomes ain't ruined them jellies of yours."

"Don't be worrying about that, captain. I see more than most."

The implications there send a shiver down me spine. Can't say I'd ever want to see the world through Maggie's eyes. "Alright then. But let's make sure you don't get blasted by their falconets before you get a chance to work your magic." I look down at the main deck and point at Black and White Russian. "Ladies! Recruit a working party and build a wall of flour bags, starboard bow, to stop our witch here from getting peppered."

The Russians scamper off to do me bidding while Maggie makes her way up to the bow, already muttering some hoarse incantations under her breath. She crosses paths with Sandwich who be lugging the Elder Sign upstairs from the hold.

"What the hell are you doing with that thing?" I yell as I gesture for Inkman and Shaka to help him.

He doesn't answer just yet, too busy groaning and huffing as he drags the heavy thing across me deck. Inkman and Shaka take over, carrying the sign easily, proving that Sandwich needs to be working on his Brawn score. Not too much, mind. I prefer me men svelte rather than burly.

"Please take the sign up to the quarterdeck," he instructs them, "then raise it on a barrel or crate, and lash it down with ropes." Inkman looks amused, but Shaka simply scowls then looks to me for confirmation. I nod me assent and Shaka's scowl grows a few crinkles deeper. He don't like doing the toff's bidding, not one little bit. But he gets onto the job nonetheless, and soon he and Inkman have the sign sitting in pride of place.

"Very pretty," I say to Sandwich who has now joined us all on the quarterdeck. "Now care to explain why you be decorating me ship when you should be racking that educated grey of yours for solutions to our currently dubious situation?"

He points at the Dreamer. The damned ship be getting

dangerously close now. Jonesy's doing a beautiful job gliding the Albatross smoothly into our intercept course. Ain't long now before Powderfinger will be cutting loose at them sails. I raise me hand to stall Sandwich's answer and lean over to me hollering tube.

"Word of advice, Powderfinger! Wait until Jonesy turns us sharp-like when the starboard side be raising a little. Got it?"

Three knocks resound up me brass tube from the gundeck. We have a code, the gunners and me. One knock for nay. Two knocks for aye. And three knocks for "shut your gob and mind your ship, captain". That makes me feel a little better. Powderfinger ain't one for overconfidence.

I turn back to Sandwich. "Alright, m'lord. Out with it."

"The Dreamer is one of several warships that sailed with the Emperor's Dragon."

I gulp down another lump of fear so I can squeeze the next words out. "Don't be telling me it has one of them Stars what can help it jump about the place!"

Sandwich jiggles his hands up and down in a 'calm down' gesture. "I assure you, captain, that if the Dreamer possessed such a gem, it would be alongside us right this moment."

I heave a sigh of relief and gesture for him to go on.

"It is my hope," continues Sandwich, "that the captain of the Dreamer will recognize the Elder Sign and thereby be deterred from sinking us. It was a most precious artifact to the Atlanteans, and it will come as a shock to see it presented thus, far from the Maw of a Thousand Deaths."

"Meaning, they'll try to board us instead?"

"That would be my hope, yes."

I give him an approving wink, much to Shaka's obvious chagrin.

"You believe this limey silk-stocking?" he growls.

Inkman's hand moves slowly and deliberately to his taiaha. Shaka notices and bows his head.

"Sorry, captain. Meant no disrespect."

"None taken," I assure him. "And yes, I do believe this limey silk-stocking. His Atlantean knowledge has stood us in good stead so far." I shoot a sharp look at Sandwich, mostly for Shaka's sake. "Don't be giving me no cause to regret me confidence, you hear?"

"Absolutely not," promises Sandwich. "The captain of the Dreamer would never risk losing the Elder Sign to the depths."

"In that case," I conclude, "they'll be wanting to get close and pepper us with grapeshot, thin our ranks before the board and slaughter bit."

I glance out to sea. We're but moments away from our meet and greet with the Dreamer. Out of the corner of me eye, I can see a solid wall of flour bags and me witch crouching behind them, muttering and making some mighty strange hand gestures. Looks like we're all set. I take up me Rumpus Musket and move to the starboard gunwale. Then I raise me firearm in the air as I holler at me crew, adding a bit of Rallying Cry for good measure.

"Ladies and lads, I ain't going to lie to you. We be getting one shot at this, one fair moment to give that bloody tub of corpses all we got. We miss this porthole and we be worse than dead. We be joining the crew of that there bloody Dreamer." That gets more growls than gasps. A good sign. "I've seen no finer crew in all me days. The fine skulls of the fleet and fierce Albatross! By all the gods we believe in, good old fashioned luck if we don't, muster your muskets, gird your loins, and brace yourselves for the fight and flight of your miserable, rum-soaked lives!"

The cheer that follows be raucous with fear, but it be enough to shove their morale score from 60 percent up to 75 percent. That should be enough to stave off the panic, at least for now.

I nod me approval and take up me firing position against the gunwale. Sandwich hunkers down beside the sign, ready to protect it should we be boarded, while Inkman and Shaka join the rest of me crew as they prepare to repel boarders.

I take a deep breath and let it out nice and slow, calming me trembling hands. This be one of them do or 'undie' moments, and as I see the first ghoulish faces hove into view, I know the latter just ain't an attractive option.

GUNS AND GHOULS

THE DREAMER'S bow-mounted falconets swivel in our direction. I line up the farthest one and put a shot into the gunner's tattered face. The impact sends him reeling backwards, but to me disgust, he don't go down.

Shot Damage inflicted = 200
Ghoulish Gunner - Level 5
HP: 100/300

That confirms me suspicions right there. If the Dreamer's crew manages to board us, we'll be mincemeat served in a wooden tub. Even Inkman would be hard-pressed to lead a defense against these dead sea dogs. Me ladies and lads may have plenty of Sand between them, but that won't make their blood run any slower.

I judge the distance and glumly conclude that both the Dreamer's bow gunners be out of range of me Stormshot pistol. So I set to reloading me Rumpus Musket as I holler a request down to the main deck.

"Quartermaster! Bring me some loaded muskets, if you please!"

Unfortunately, it ain't Inkman what answers. It be the ghoulish gunners, their falconets speaking as one. Their aim be deadly true. The Albatross shudders as twin cannonballs plough into her timbers, just below the waterline.

Damage received from two Cyclopean Swivel Cannons = 30
The Albatross
Hull Defense: 120/150

There be a smattering of musket blasts as Inkman rallies me crew to return fire. I see the injured ghoul gunner go down and stay down this time.

The Dreamer
Crew: 199

Then our starboard-side falconet barks and blows a hole through the gunwale beneath the Dreamer's other swivel gun. The cannonball carries on too, smashing through the gunner's legs, snapping them like matchsticks. I look to see who be manning our falconet, and it turns out to be Rumguts. She be redder in the face than usual, having downed a bit more Dutch courage than most leading up to this here fracas. But as ever, those bleary eyes of hers be seeing true. And it seems she's been a bit quiet on the subject of her newfound gunner skills too.

Mary "Rumguts" O'Malley
Sailor Level 6
Gunner: 2nd Class

She must've leveled up while we was in the Maw of a Thousand Deaths and decided to try her hand at percussion. I make a mental note to congratulate her on that sober decision and line up the

Dreamer's now teetering swivel gun. Thanks to Rumguts' blast, the little cannon be holding onto that gunwale by splinters alone, so I place me next musket shot right where the cracks be showing worst.

The result be a most satisfying snap as the wood gives way. A pair of ghouls see what's happening and grab hold of their precious cannon, but it's already past its tipping point. All they succeed in doing be dragging themselves over the edge to sink with their gun into the sea below.

The Dreamer

Crew: 197

3 Cyclopean Swivel Cannons

Base Damage per Gun: 15

You have defeated two Level 5 Ghoulish Mariners and disabled one of the Dreamer's swivel guns with the help of Mary "Rumguts" O'Malley.

Your XP reward = 1250

Progress to Pirate Captain Level 8 = 39390/40000

I hear the thumping of boots behind me and turn to find a pair of loaded muskets on offer from Tarsi and Barber. "With compliments from the quartermaster, captain," says the latter.

I smile me thanks and grab me a fresh firearm just as another ghoul 'mans' the Dreamer's remaining bow falconet. This time I give the ugly bugger the old 'one-two'. Me first shot shatters his jaw. Me second shot blasts a hole out the back of his brittle skull.

Shot Damage inflicted = 300

Ghoulish Gunner - Level 5

HP: 0/300

You have killed a Level 5 Ghoulish Gunner.

Your XP reward = 500

Progress to Pirate Captain Level 8 = 39890/40000

As Tarsi, Barber and me set to reloading me muskets, Jonesy brings us around real sharp-like, putting us into the perfect line for a broadside. Powderfinger wastes no time in letting the Dreamer know what we're about. The six starboard cannons thunder in quick succession. The air between us and the ghoul ship whistles as it's sliced through by six sets of spinning chain shots. Four of those six shots hit their mark, shredding sailcloth and splintering one mast so badly it topples onto the Dreamer's deck, crushing several of its crew in the process.

The Dreamer
Crew: 192
Sail Defense: 32/100
Sail Speed: 48/150
Oar Speed: 80/80

The Dreamer's bow falconet answers back with a lone thump and I feel another shudder go through me poor Albatross.

The Albatross
Hull Defense: 105/150

Rumguts lets them ghouls know what she thinks about that with her falconet, shredding the Dreamer's gunner with grapeshot.

Thanks to Powderfinger and his gun crew, we're now almost five times faster than the Dreamer, but if we drop below 66 percent in Hull Defense, we'll suffer a lag in Speed due to taking on too much water. Of course, our sailing advantage be based on the assumption that the wind be with us. I shouldn't be assuming things like that.

I shiver as I feel the wind flip like a coin in a gambler's palm, and I ain't ever felt a breeze shift that fast. I look to the Dreamer and see the culprit standing on the prow, its ragged black robes flapping in this confounding squall of its creation.

The Dreamer's Gale Lich has changed the direction of its Breath of the Sleeping One spell to inflict an 80 point Speed penalty on both the Dreamer and the Albatross for 13 minutes.

The Albatross
Speed: 110 (70)
+10 from Sails of the Salamander
+10 from Navigator: 1st Class at the helm
+10 from Hero: 3rd Class on deck
+10 from Sailmaster: 1st Class on the rigging
-80 from Breath of the Sleeping One spell

"Trim the sails!" yells North from down on the deck. Tarsi abandons her musket-reloading duties to scramble up them ropes like a monkey with her tail on fire.

It be too late to shoot the Gale Lich down. The Damage already be done. And besides, I need to save me shots for the next ghoul what be stupid enough to try and fire that remaining falconet. But I have to admit, I be bemused by the Lich's decision to slow us both down. Ain't like it's going to help them catch us. At least, that's what I think until I see the Dreamer trim its sails and run out its oars. I watch with dawning horror as them paddles dip into the dark sea and start to make up all them points the ghoul ship has lost to the wind. They be catching up with us quicksmart unless we do something about it.

I check our angle against the Dreamer. We be off broadside angle now, so won't be able to use our cannons to slow the ghoul ship down. It be time our witch earned her share of the booty we have on board.

"Maggie!" I holler down at her. She be sitting with her back to the flour sacks, muttering and making some fairly obscene gesticulations at no one in particular. At least, no one *I* or any of me shipmates can see. Not that I know much about these things, but by the look on her face, I reckon she's trying to talk some*one* or some*thing* into helping us out. "Maggie!" This time she glances up at me. "Whatever you're going to do, do it now!"

Me request be punctuated by a distant boom, followed by a whoosh and spine-shivering crack as chain shot snaps off one of me yardarms. Splintered wood and tatters of sail rain down on the deck, narrowly missing a few of me crew members what have to scamper fast to get out of the way.

The Albatross
Sail Defense: 55/70
Speed: 55/70

Looking to the Dreamer I see that the captain has decided to cripple us first before rowing us down. He be turning his galley, and it be only thanks to the ponderous nature of the ship that we've not lost *every* scrap of sail to a full chain-shot broadside. Right now, the Dreamer's only turned far enough to bring its bow-most culverin to bear. We've about three seconds before we get hit again.

"Jonesy?"

"I see what he's up to, captain. I be keeping us ahead of his firing arc, though that's a helluva wind to tack into."

"Just do your-"

Me last few words to me pilot be lost to a god-awful howl from the main deck. It be Maggie.

A LITTLE DEATH

SEEMS Maggie has finally finished her chinwag with the spirits. Now she be waggling her fingers at the ghoulish galley while screeching like a banshee with a bowel blockage. Inkman looks at me from where he be standing nearby and raises his hands in quiet bewilderment. I shrug and force a hopeful smile onto me face. It be nice to see her doing *something*. I just hope it be something useful.

To find out, I take out Squintlock's Peeper and focus me lens on the Dreamer just in time to see a puff of smoke emerge from the ship's flank.

"Heads down!" I yell.

Me crew ducks for cover as another chain shot ploughs into our rigging. Shards of wood and shreds of sail fall to the deck, and that's not all this time. A small figure tumbles end over end to land with a sickening crunch on the boards. Tarsi.

Crew: 56
The Albatross
Sail Defense: 40/70
Speed: 40/70

I grit me teeth as anger flares in me guts. Time for us to return a little grief with our own cannons. Aye, if we broadside the ghoulish galley now, we be leaving ourselves sorely vulnerable in the aftermath. But frankly, the tide of certain death but tugging at us so this ain't no time to be getting squeamish over consequences.

"Broadside her masts, Powderfinger!" I scream into me hollering tube.

Me guns answer a close-shaved second later and I watch the resulting mayhem with grim satisfaction.

The Dreamer
Crew: 192
Sail Defense: 0/100
Sail Speed: 0/150
Trim Oar Speed: 80/80

I be pleased that the buggers be hurting, but I know it won't do any good with them oars still chopping away at the sea, propelling them ghouls forward at twice the clip we be managing. But just as I be making that glum observation, I notice something a little strange. One of them blades lifts out of the water, turns its angle, and starts rowing backwards. Another does it, followed by two more. Then before me wondering eyes, every one of them galley oars be rowing in reverse. At first, the change only slows the Dreamer's progress, being hard-pressed to counter the big ship's momentum. But then, sure enough, them oars bring the Dreamer to a full stop. Moments later, it be reversing at a growing pace.

I peer down at Maggie and follow the motion of her hands. She be playing the part of a rower, and them skeletons on the other ship be following her example. And as the distance between us and the Dreamer grows, I feel their foul ghoul wind weakening, easing off to no more than a breeze.

I look for me sailmaster on the main deck. She be crawling out from under some wrecked rigging, looking a little worse for wear.

"Ms North?"

"Aye, captain?"

"Looks like you've taken a battering. Do you need Croc?"

The sturdy lass straightens and places her hands on her hips, clearly put out at the very suggestion. "No, ma'am. But I would surely welcome some orders."

I smile, admiring the woman's Sand. "We be having a healthy breath of wind shortly, on account of us coming out of range of that damned spell of theirs. Unfurl what's left of our sails and get us the bloody hell out of here!"

"Aye, captain! With pleasure!"

She sets to barking at me sailors and it ain't long before I be hearing the welcoming snap of sailcloth and the comforting groan of the Albatross' timbers as she picks up speed.

The Albatross
Sail Defense: 40/70
Speed: 55/150
The Dreamer
Crew: 192
Sail Defense: 0/100
Sail Speed: 0/150
Trim Oar Speed: -40/80

Behind us, there be an almighty thundering as the Dreamer unleashes its broadside. But all them chain shots splash harmlessly into the sea off our stern. The wind be with us now, pressing us along as fast as me battered Albatross can manage.

The Albatross
Sail Defense: 40/70
Speed: 86/150

Ain't long before that accursed crate of cadavers be sinking behind the horizon.

The crew of the Albatross has fought the Dreamer and lived to tell the tale, something that very few ships can claim.
This is a Legendary Achievement of the High Seas!
Your XP reward = 50,000 XP
As Captain of the Albatross, you receive a double share
Your personal XP reward = 1790 XP
Progress to Pirate Captain Level 8 = 41680/40000
You be a barnacled and bedeviled buccaneer on a course to booty abundant!
A Level 8 Pirate Captain!
You receive eight points to apply to your core attributes.
You receive two free skill upgrades.

I turn to Jonesy and present her with such a big grin that I feel it from the soles of me feet to the top of me scalp. "To Freeport, on the double, Ms Jones."

The fair wind be setting the navigator's dreadlocks a-dancing. "Aye, captain!" she answers, the relief of our narrow escape glistening in her large, caramel eyes.

I be feeling that relief too, along with the aching desire for a cup of rum and a lie-down. I gesture for Sandwich to follow me to me cabin.

He raises a fine eyebrow in response. "Yes, captain, you wish to speak to me?"

"Aye, lad." I wink at Jonesy who smirks back at me, knowing full well what I be about. "You're going to give me a full debrief."

He looks suitably bemused. "I am afraid I will not be of much-"

"Anything you can give me will be most welcome at this juncture, m'lord, I can assure you of that."

Jonesy laughs as a flushed and grinning Sandwich follows me down the steps to me cabin. Out of the corner of me eye, I see Inkman and Barber wrapping Tarsi in a length of ripped sailcloth. We be pirates. We all die some time, and seldom will it be peaceful. Tarsi knew that. I know that. Which be why we corsairs live as large as we can for as long as we can. We take what we can while we still got warmth in our fingers and lust in our hearts.

"Inkman?" I call out.

He looks up from his needlework and his eyes flick between me and Sandwich. He don't miss a trick, that one. "Aye, captain?"

"About that ruby what Tarsi earned. Next time we hear of a merchantman headed for Indonesia, let's have them deliver it to her family."

"Duly noted, Deadeye."

Then he turns rather pointedly back to his work. It be clear enough he don't approve of me getting closer to Sandwich. I can tell by the tense set of his shoulders. But he'll just have to deal with the fact that he don't have any say in the matter.

After our close call with a whole shipful of death, this here Level 8 Pirate Captain be deserving a bit of warmth and lust while she still can. Not that I be planning on dying today. Well, maybe just a *little* death, as the French put it.

And Sandwich turns out to be quite the aficionado of stage and page. He's clearly studied the antics of Don Juan and been inspired by the adventurers of Giacomo Girolamo Casanova. But he hasn't stopped at the Europeans, no. In his readings he's ventured east to India, taken in the pungent pleasures of the Kamasutra, and even gone as far as the erotic Japanese inscriptions of shunga. Yes, he and I travel a *long* distance in a short time. Well, not *too* short.

When his boarding party has well and truly plundered me hold, I be floating like a freshly careened frigate with sails billowing on a stiff breeze.

We share a glass of red wine afterwards, still naked and wrapped in the sweaty linens of me bunk. His blue eyes glisten like a tropical lagoon at sunrise, and I swear I'll have to knock that grin off his face with a belaying pin.

I swig down the rest of me wine, a fine pinot I picked up in Australia, and point me glass at him.

"Don't be fixing me with them mooneyes and getting all lovey-dovey, Sandwich."

He blinks and his smooth skin takes on a rather fetching blush. "Whatever do you mean, Captain Deadeye?"

He be covering. I know it. "Me first love be me ship. Me second love be booty, of the gold and silver kind. Me third love be me crew. I ain't a big lady, as you can see, so me heart be already bursting at the seams. Don't be thinking that, just because we make a pretty wild beast with two backs, you be riding this same beast to some toffy English altar."

His fine-lipped mouth drops open, but it be utterly vacant of words. Just white teeth and that rather limber tongue of his. I take pity on the poor bugger and fill his glass with the remaining pinot, saving just a few splashes for meself. By the strain in the corner of his eyes, and the furrowing of his brow, I can tell he be feeling a little 'used'.

"Now don't get me wrong," I assure him. "You're a handsome chap, no two ways about it. Not to mention that you've got plenty of brains up top and...ah...vigor down below. I'm sure you have the English roses shedding their thorns over you back home. But here's the thing." I lean close, letting me sheet fall away. "Hey now. Be looking me in the eyes when we be speaking." His baby blues snap to attention. "Better. So here be the thing. I figured you for a bit of alright as soon as I laid me peepers on you. But I seen what marriage can do to people. Me mum came through it alright. Hell, more than alright. She owns her own fishing fleet now. One of the richest women in the Philippines. Me father though…"

I swill me wine to wash away the welling of tears in me throat. Don't know why I be opening up to this here lordling, but I am, so I might as well sail through the choppy weather while the wind be with me.

"He hit the dice tables the day I was born. By the time I were five, just old enough to remember, he gets hauled up in one of me mother's fishing nets with thirty-odd stab wounds in his paunch."

"I am truly sorry," murmurs Sandwich. And to his credit, he actually sounds it.

"Don't be. Best news she had since meeting the smooth-talking Don Juan bastard."

"Oh, so when I recited that passage about Don Juan from…"

"You weren't to know."

"Still…"

I wave away his concern. "You ain't heard the best bit."

He winces. "All right then. What is the 'best' bit."

"That me mum says I be his spitting image, only prettier. A chip off the old block."

"You gamble?"

"Not with money anymore. That be too valuable."

"With what then?"

"Me life."

It be out before I realize it. And now that I see it in the lantern light of this Atlantean evening, I know it for what it be. A comfortable truth. Something that's been following me about since the day I saw me father's beshrouded body slide off the edge of me mother's flagship.

"Me father was a fine sea captain. 1st Class in this, Special Ability in that. But when he weren't leveling up he be loafing and lechering and losing it all. He cared for nothing and nobody. Not me, and definitely not himself. Aye. A girl can learn a lot from a father like that."

Rather than try to offer his condolences or sympathies, Sandwich washes them down with the last of his wine. Then he's out with a few home truths of his own.

"Then perhaps you and I have more in common than one would think."

"How'd do you reckon that?"

"Among the aristocracy, children are a necessity, not a luxury. If managed correctly by each generation, wealth and power accumulate."

"Just like a ship and its crew should grow in strength and loot, no matter how many captains stand on the quarterdeck."

"Yes." He looks at me, his eyes dulled by sadness. "An accurate analogy, especially when you consider that a ship only functions with one captain on board."

"Aye. Chaotic as we corsairs may seem to the landlubbers, pirates thrive on order."

"So does the aristocracy, and it will happily expunge itself of elements that it deems surplus to requirements and potentially destabilizing."

"That what your mother and father figure? Their own flesh and blood be 'surplus to requirements'?"

He shrugs, a strangely boyish gesture from this man what's proved himself calm and capable in the face of danger.

"My parents are aristocrats first, people second."

"So you was told to bugger off and not to come back?"

He manages a weak smile. "It was not as explicit as that, but then polite society never is."

"At least they gave you a ship."

"Which a rather beautiful pirate then took from me."

I hide me smile behind me glass. I rather like being called 'beautiful', and his posh accent makes the word sound even lovelier.

"Now you have an even better ship to aid you in your quest and a much better crew."

His smile broadens and the twinkle returns to his baby blues. "Indeed. Though I may no longer be fully in charge of my destiny, my overall prospects have certainly improved."

He says that last phrase with a coy smirk that ain't subtle in its suggestiveness. Seems he's recovered already and be hoping I be polishing his prospects even more. Though it be tempting, I know I need to get some sleep. It's been a rough and tumble day.

I swill the rest of me wine and nod towards the clothing what he's discarded right across me nice, tidy cabin. "You'll be cleaning up after yourself on your way out, won't you, m'lord."

His smile falls away, and he looks like an admonished dog as he scurries off the bunk and hurries to don his clothing. I get a good view of those firm, white cheeks of his before they disappear into his breeches. They felt lush indeed beneath these calloused hands.

As he be reaching for the door, I peep over me emotional wall and offer him a wink, just because I be a kindhearted soul.

"If we live to see the sunset on the morrow, Sandwich, you fancy sharing another bottle of wine? I was sure to pick up a full case before we sailed out of Perth."

"Of course, Grace. I would like that very much."

Then he gently closes me door behind him. I sigh, actually quite relieved to be alone again, and sink back into me bunk. I be witness to many a horror today and I be needing some quiet time to consider me Character. I've lost forty-three crew and almost had me Albatross overtaken by a galley full of ghasts. That ain't good, not by *any* interpretation of the word. We was in some hairy situations, of that there be no doubt. But this quest for the Star of Atlantis will only get harder. That just be the way of the world. So if I don't want to see me ship sinking and me crew floating belly-up in the sea, I, Captain Deadeye, will have to get harder too.

NO HARBOR IN THE STORM

I STIFLE a yawn and ask the otherwords to show me the Level Up missive again.

You be a barnacled and bedeviled buccaneer on a course to booty abundant!
A Level 8 Pirate Captain!
You receive eight points to apply to your core attributes.
You receive two free skill upgrades.

Then I think back over the tribulations of the day and try to pick out moments that might've gone better had I been a bit more proficient in something or other.

Let's start with the fact that I didn't spot the tiles trap before we was standing on the bloody thing. Yes, I had the Perception score to be able to notice the whole red blue thing, but that ain't the point. Had me Perception been higher, I might've worked out what tiles we should be stepping on *before* we was perched and fearing the plunge.

Please note that a total Perception score of 30 will grant a 20% increased chance of Critical Hit for a Gunslinger and/or Sharpshooter.

I still find it unsettling when them otherwords read me thoughts like that. Feels like Bathala be peering right into me skull. Some might find that comforting, knowing that their beloved deity be taking an interest in their mental discourse. Me, I prefer to keep me notions private.

But in this case, I thank Bathala for the sage advice and drop five of me fresh points into Perception, bringing it from a base score of fifteen up to twenty.

Perception: 20 (30)

+2 Sharpshooter: 3rd Class

20% increased chance of a Critical Hit with a musket

+2 Gunslinger: 3rd Class

20% increased chance of a Critical Hit with a pistol

+2 Squintlock's Peeper

+2 Stormshot

+1 Musketeer: 1st Class

+1 Pistoleer: 1st Class

I stretch, turn over onto me side and take a deep breath as I consider another of today's mishaps what might've been avoided. I can still smell the musk of me lovely encounter with Sandwich, and it fills me chest with comforting warmth, cushioning me from the sharp edges of a rather unpleasant memory. That of me lifeblood being sucked out by a lamprey cultist. *Far* too close for comfort that was. To give meself a bit more leeway in future, I pop a couple of points into Brawn and a point into Stamina to give me Health Points a decent boost.

Brawn: 12 (15)

+1 Athlete: 1st Class

+1 Fencer: 1st Class

+1 Coat of the Salt

Stamina: 14 (18)

+1 Free Diver: 1st Class

+1 Athlete: 1st Class

+1 Coat of the Salt

+1 Seahawk Saber

Health Points: 270/270

HP = Brawn x Stamina

With me attributes thus bolstered, I look to me skills. As a rule, I should only be looking at me 1st Class skills, the ones what have capped out. If I'd been a Swashbuckler 3rd Class, the next step up from Fencer 1st Class, I'd have fared better against that lamprey cultist what nearly did me in. But while that might save me own skin, it ain't generally what's best for me crew. I save more lives with me guns than I ever will with a sword. And I'm surrounded by women and men with swashing blades. No, I need to be focusing on skills what can benefit us all, not just me.

Which means that both Athlete and Free Diver are out too. The latter was mighty handy when recovering the Elder Sign, but now that I think of it, we could've used the falconets to fire grapples across to that island.

No, the more I think on it, the more I know what the choice must be. When I cast me hindsight over our battle with the Dreamer, I realize now just how vital Jonesy was to our survival. Had she not been there to execute that broadside on the Dreamer's sails, had she not kept our speed up despite the Gale Ghoul's foul wind, the undead would've caught us. Maggie's spell might've delayed that capture for a bit, but it were Jonesy's sailing what kept us ahead of the deadmen long enough for the witch's incantation to seal the deal.

It sends a shiver down me spine to think that one of the Dreamer's falconets could've taken Jonesy out just like that. They was accurate enough to hole us on the waterline. Means they could've been accurate enough to turn our helmswoman into red mist. The fact that they chose a different target comes down to no more than the toss of a coin.

With Jonesy dead, *I* would've been the next best Navigator on the ship. And 2nd Class simply wouldn't have cut it. I can't be taking chances with me Albatross and all the lives she relies on, so I slot both me free upgrades into Navigator, sailing me through 1st Class and right into Shellback 3rd Class.

Navigator: 1st Class
Base Skill
Maintains all of the skills of a Navigator: 2nd Class while adding +1 to Wit and Sand, and increasing the ship at hand's Speed and Agility by 10
At 1st Class, Navigator unlocks the Special Skill or Read the Brine, the ability intuit tides, currents and disturbances in the sea.

Shellback: 3rd Class
Advanced Skill
Maintains all the skills of a Navigator: 1st Class while adding +2 to Wit and Sand, and increasing the ship at hand's Speed and Agility by 20
At 3rd Class, Shellback unlocks the Special Skill of Sailsnap, the ability to angle a ship so that it captures in the most subtle air currents and produces a 20% increase in speed that lasts for 10 minutes.

Now the Albatross has *two* helmswomen what can steer it out of troubled waters. That thought be a blessed relief to me, and when I close me eyes, it be to the creak of rigging and the flutter of sailcloth as I drift off into a merry slumber.

Well, that be the idea. Instead, I find meself on me quarterdeck, white-knuckled hands wrapped around the wheel in a death grip. I be drenched and water be sloshing across the timber as I desperately turn the Albatross this way and that to capture a wind that be dancing away from me like some mischievous child with too much sugar on its fevered brain.

But the water be strangely warm like we be in the heart of the tropics, but that be well out of sorts with the chill wind what bites at me even through me Coat of the Salt.

I look down and gag at the sight. There be blood lapping over the tops of me boots. The deck be awash, and in that sanguine wave faces be bobbing like apples in a Halloween bucket. Faces I know. Bonkers and Essex, pierced and torn by grapeshot. Odin, his one good eye now a punctured mess. Longshanks with blood running down her chin. Tabouli with part of his skull blown out. Hyena with his rictus grin. Tarsi, half her delicate face caved in. And many more. Every pirate what has sailed with me to their doom.

Tears stream from me eyes as I force me chin upwards, wrenching me own face away from its dead reflection. And that's when I see Him, bursting from the churning sea, looming over the Albatross, water streaming down from his writhing visage.

The Dreamer.

The Elder.

Squidbeard.

The wretched voyage afar,
Seeking to fill their empty hulls,
With promises made in eons past,
Empty whispers from drowned throats,

I feel his words slither about me ears, wriggling and thrashing to get inside. I let go of the wheel and squeeze me hands to the sides of me head, to no avail. Them words have boarded me, curled up inside me skull, coiling about me mind.

When they carry within them,
The sunken riches,
Doused in sanguine tides,

I wrap me hands around the wheel once more. I bring us about so sharp that we almost capsize, so all that blood, all them dead faces, cascade into the foaming ocean. I put me stern to the towering titan, and the howling gale drives us up and over a wave the size of a mountain. Higher and higher we climb, reaching a giddying peak. We teeter there for a moment, the Albatross and I, atop a yawning cliff of water, and then down we plunge, right into His cupped hands.

We grasp at life,
With gristle and sinew salted with despair,
And watch it drain through our fingers,

Me Albatross splinters into a million tiny shards. And so do I, flying apart, hither and thither, carried upon the breath of His voice.

No anchor in the drift,
No harbor in the storm,
Until the dead calm sea,
At journey's end.

With a scream, I come together. With a sob, I wake.
The creaking timbers be mercifully solid under me ribs, and the

stars be a blessed smattering of grapeshot holes in the black sail of the night.

I'm back. I know that much. The rest be a receding tide of blood and darkest omen.

3 0

EMPTY WHISPERS

IT BE a gloomy dawn that greets me on the quarterdeck. The clouds are bulbous and brooding, and the sea be gunmetal grey. It be a quiet relief when we round the ruin-speckled peninsula that wraps itself like a protective, tattooed arm around Freeport. The town's lights be burning bright and I recognize a familiar ship in the harbor. The Narwhal.

Inkman gestures at it with his coffee cup. "Thought Shogun was headed for warmer waters?"

I thought so too, and eye the bulky brigantine warily. "And he ain't one to change his mind on a whim. Most likely, he's chanced upon a more lucrative opportunity." I take a sip of me brew and savor its sweet and nutty flavor. It be a good salve against the grim temperament of the day.

I look up at them thunderous clouds and wonder if we've angered Atlantis by sacking its temple and stealing its Elder Sign. I feel the dregs of me nightmare at the back of me throat, like congealed chowder, and take another sip of me coffee to wash it away. Weather be weather, I remind meself. Ain't got no soul, no emotion. It just be winds and water.

Jonesy brings us into the docks, nice and smooth. I gather half me crew, twenty-eight including meself, to escort our loot to the old Italian for a fair exchange. When we get there, who should we find but Shogun, sat down with Medici, talking business over a glass of chianti.

The Italian's eyes remain shrewd and calm as the Russian sisters dump our treasure chest in front of him and open the lid. By contrast, Shogun's jaw drops and he almost knocks over his chianti in his haste to take a gander at our loot.

"Oni's Ass, Deadeye! Where in all hell did you find this little trove?"

"Same place I found Bluegums, though he ain't shining quite so pretty."

There be genuine sadness written across Shogun's face at that sour news. "Bluegums will be missed. He was one of the good ones."

I nod me agreement. "Was thinking of holding a wake for him tonight up at the Simpering Siren, if you lot would care to join us?"

"We'd be honored, but don't be thinking you have to pay the tab alone. The Narwhal will cover its share."

I tilt me head in Medici's direction. "Business picked up a bit since we sailed out, eh?"

Shogun looks to the old man for permission to speak freely of their dealings. The Italian's rheumy eyes disappear under a tide of wrinkles as he smiles his assent.

"Aye," agrees Shogun. "Seniore Medici wishes us to haul his crowns and such to Venice. Needs someone to keep those Moroccan marauders off his back as we pass through Gibraltar."

"And I bet the Venetians have tasty Letters of Marque on offer for any willing to pick a squabble with the Ottomans?"

Shogun offers me a gapped-tooth grin. "You're a sharp one, Deadeye. Tis why I already be mentioning the Albatross as our possible escort. Maybe you lot should come with us, eh?"

After what we just been through, it's a mighty tempting offer. I've lost thirty-five women and men to these Atlantean monstrosities, and am sure to lose many more before this Star of Atlantis quest be done. Even if we *do* find and recover the Star? What then? Aye, we'll be able to jump all over the show, raid where we please. But we'll also be the arch envy of every damned navy on the globe. We'll be hunted from pole to pole. A hard quarry to catch, able to hide in places no warship could ever reach, but it'd be a knife-edge life with no room for mistakes.

Then again, perhaps that be old Squidbeard talking. Perhaps I be so busy listening to the whispers of the shadows that I haven't thought to open me eyes to the light. Inside that there chest we hauled out of the Maw of a Thousand Deaths be more loot than we'd likely accrue in a dozen raids, the toll of which could have been twice me current casualties or more. Though Atlantis be home to horrors, there clearly be riches aplenty with which to drown them midnight terrors.

I give Shogun a friendly slap on the shoulder as I look past him to Medici. "A kind and generous offer, seniore," I assure him, "but we of the Albatross ain't quite done with Atlantis." I give the treasure a tap with me boot. So full it be with silver that it barely offers a thud in response. "And could you be persuaded to delay your departure by a few days? At least until we've brought you a couple more of these?"

His parchment-dry fingertips rasp through his grey stubble as he ponders me chances. I can almost hear the click of abacus and tap of quill against inkwell as he makes his mental calculations.

"Six days," he offers me. "I give you two for one, plus twenty percent, as before. Then we sail for Venice. The invitation still stands if breath you still have, Captain Deadeye."

"Breathing be one of me favorite pastimes, Seniore Medici. I ain't planning to give it up any time soon."

Shogun rolls his eyes, thinking I be a fool for pushing me luck, but he makes no move to challenge me decision. Understandable really. The larger Medici's haul, the larger the Narwhal's fee for protecting it.

On the matter of our existing loot, Medici be true to his word, swapping our one large chest for four smaller chests packed with doubloons.

The Albatross
Treasury = 111508 doubloons

As we head down to the docks to do some shopping for the Albatross, I can't shake the feeling that I should've taken Shogun and Medici up on their offer. Some good honest mercenary work followed by a healthy dose of privateering. The sensible course for a sensible corsair.

I motion with a glare of warning for Sandwich to fall into step beside me and wipe the goofy grin off his face. I enjoyed our bunk time together. No doubt about it. But this ain't no time to be mixing business with pleasure.

"Now that I've turned down a perfectly good contract with Medici, you best be telling me what we be sailing into next."

Sandwich's golden grin melts down into a grim, leaden line. For the first time, I notice the dark shadows under his slightly bloodshot eyes. "I spent much of last night scouring my tomes for references to the Dreamer, in the hopes of unearthing the hazards and horrors that await us on our course to the Star of Atlantis."

"Well, I ain't sailing me ship into unknown waters without *some* inkling of me destination, so you best be coughing that up right now."

He casts a couple of sidelong glances at our companions before leaning in closer. "With promises made in eons past. Empty whispers from drowned throats."

Now there's a phrase to shiver me bloody timbers! "Where did you hear that?!"

Me demand's a little on the loud side. Several of me crew look over and Inkman shoots me a look of concern.

"Everything alright, captain?"

I try to be nonchalant as I wave me crewmates on. "Fine, fine. You lot go ahead and scout out some better sails and hull-cladding for our Albatross. Don't sign no pieces of paper though, unless one of you be hiding a Merchant 1st Class skill somewhere up your collective asses."

A smattering of laughter goes through the assembled pirates and a smile crosses Inkman's face, though I notice it ain't touching his eyes. "Aye captain. I'll have the purveyors set aside our selections for your inspection."

"Right you are, quartermaster."

I wait until me crew's moved off and then round on Sandwich. "That there 'empty whispers' malarky. Where'd you learn it?"

He blinks at me for a long, dumb moment, clearly taken aback. "Have you heard it before?"

"Aye, and more besides."

"How?"

"A dream, last night. A nightmare starring old Squidbeard himself."

Sandwich's pale face blanches even further. He takes a deep breath and lets it out all shuddery like. Though there be a brisk and biting breeze blowing in off the Atlantic, a fine patina of sweat breaks out on the young man's forehead.

"What's wrong, Sandwich? What do them words mean?"

Sandwich's eyes be wide and wild as he looks into mine. His voice be a half-choked rasp, like that of a dying man.

"He has spoken to you, Grace. He knows you are coming for him."

QUEEN OF THE PHILIPPINES

BEFORE I KNOW IT, I feel the smooth handle of Stormshot pressing into me palm. Sandwich's eyes flick down to me holstered pistol and back to me face.

"Steady there, captain. Do not shoot the messenger."

I ease me hand away from me pistol, silently cursing me own skittishness. Don't know what's bloody getting into me. I ain't usually this jumpy.

"Alright, but you need to be uttering some perfectly logical explanation before me trigger finger gets any itchier."

I've no intention of shooting the bugger. In fact, if he plays his cards right, he might get to shoot *me* again once or twice before this quest is over. But it never pays to let your captives get too comfy. And Sandwich, bunk time and shared adventures aside, is still me prisoner. There'll be no more shared confessions and *definitely* no using of me first name.

He raises his hands in a vain attempt at placation and takes a deep breath in a vainer attempt to calm his nerves. Perhaps it just be his jitters I be picking up on. Fear be contagious, as any good captain knows.

"Empty whispers and drowned throats. That is a reference to the Murmurs. A network of coastal caves that festoon the eastern edge of a particularly sacred island."

"What island?"

"The Isle of Mourning. A necropolis."

"City of the Dead?" Them ghouls on the Dreamer spring to mind with alarming clarity.

"In a manner of speaking, yes, and the Murmurs were reserved for the monarchs of Atlantis. Hence it was the final mooring of the Emperor's Dragon. On the brink of Atlantis' submergence, those that could, fled. A few chose to remain with their emperor, to stand vigil over their drowning civilization."

"Fishmen and eelheads, eh?"

"Quite so, although I believe they were as you and I before the submergence."

"A thousand years under the sea will have that effect on people."

"Quite so." He clears the cloying dregs of anxiety from his throat. His color has improved too. "As the final sail disappeared below the horizon, as the sea lapped at the city's foundations, the last emperor sailed to the Murmurs to take his place among his ancestors, taking with him the choicest jewels in the Atlantean Crown."

"When they carry within them, The sunken riches, Doused in sanguine tides." The words be out of me mouth before I know they be on me mind.

"We grasp at life, With gristle and sinew salted with despair," he responds, "And watch it drain through our fingers."

The pieces be starting to fall into place. "Ain't nothing grasps at life quite so much as a ghoul does."

A smile twitches at the edge of Sandwich's lips. There be pride in his eyes, like he be a schoolmaster and me his favorite student. "My thoughts *exactly*, Gra... I mean, captain."

"Well, me brain be conjuring up a few thoughts what you might *not* want to be having."

"Like what?"

"How many ships used to sail with the Emperor's Dragon?"

"Four, including the Dreamer. The Champion, the Weeper and the Sentinel."

"And the Dragon was a warship?"

"The pride of the Atlantean fleet, yes."

I shake me head. Those ain't good odds, no matter how you try to square them. "After a few upgrades, we might just be able to take the Dreamer. *Just.* We don't stand a chance in hell if we encounter all five of them bastards."

"Agreed, captain, but I don't think it will come to that."

"Why not?"

"As Atlantis sank beneath the waves, the Champion, the Weeper and the Sentinel escorted their fleeing comrades to safety."

"Are you sure about that?"

"I have cross-referenced several accounts, yes. They left and did not return. Only the Dreamer remained, to guard the Dragon while the emperor performed his final rites within the Murmurs."

"Aright, then what about this last bit. No anchor in the drift, No harbor in the storm, Until the deadcalm sea, At journey's end."

His brow beetles as he searches his orderly mind and comes up empty-handed. "Forgive me. Alas, I have not heard that part before."

"Nor have you yet mentioned what part Squidbeard plays in all this. And what the hell do you mean He knows we're coming?"

Sandwich's eyes flick to me shooting hand again, and when they come back up, they can't quite meet me gaze. "My understanding is that Squidbeard communicates predominantly through dreams."

"Meaning, you've dreamed about him too?"

He looks suitably abashed. "Yes, back in England."

Now it all be starting to make sense. "And that be why you came all the way out to Atlantis, eh?"

He bites his lip and nods, looking all the world like a schoolboy what has been caught sharing a tobacco pipe in the handball courts.

"Then you best be telling me Squidbeard's real name, because it sure as hell ain't Neptune as you said back at the lighthouse."

"I...I do not know his real name. I do not think anyone does. At least, the Atlanteans certainly did not mention it. They simply referred to him as He Who Slumbers In The Drowning Dark."

"And let me guess," I growl, doing me very best to contain me rising temper, "He What's Snoozing Below Decks has me bloody Star of Atlantis. That about right?"

The lordling audibly gulps before answering. "It would seem likely, yes."

I raise me right hand and pinch me thumb and forefinger so there's about half an inch between them. "You know I'm *this* close to shooting you in the head and sailing off with Shogun?"

His Adam's Apple bobs up and down as he swallows his fear so his words can come out. "Would the words 'mind-bogglingly rich' stay your trigger finger, captain?"

I clamp me thumb and forefinger together and feel me lips curl back into a wild grin. "Barely, Sandwich. Just barely." I put me hands on me hips and fix him with me best 'don't mess me about' glare. "I've a greedy imagination, Sandwich. It ain't easily boggled, so you best be giving me some numbers."

Sandwich glances up to his left as he thinks, a good sign that he be searching for facts rather than making up fictions. "The accounts differ, but they all agree on one thing."

"What be that?"

"Although the Atlantean fleet took the lion's share of the treasury with it, the emperor retained a significant amount in the eventuality that the city's fate could be avoided."

"How significant? More than what we plundered from the Maw of a Thousand Deaths?"

His face lights up a little, like it be feeling a glimmer of hope. "A thousand times more, at the very least."

Now it be me palms itching rather than me trigger finger as I tally the accounts in me head. If Sandwich be correct, that be fifty million Atlantean crowns. Divided among a full complement of one hundred crew, with double shares going to the captain and the quartermaster, and the sailmaster, chief gunner, helmswoman and doctor getting one and a half shares, that means I stand to walk away with over nine hundred thousand crowns. That be two million doubloons going by me current exchange rate. I could set meself up as governor of me own Caribbean island with that amount of cash. Hell, I could buy the Philippines off the Spaniards, or at the very least fund a revolution what could see me homeland free of colonial rule once and for all.

Me, Queen of the Philippines. Now *that* would make me mother proud.

"Alright, Sandwich," I say, "but you best be open with me as the wide, blue skies. If Squidbeard be expecting us to visit him, I be needing to know *everything* you got stored in that noggin of yours." I give him a friendly whack across the head to hammer home me point. "You hearing me?"

"Yes, captain. Loud and clear."

"Good. Now let's be finishing this shopping trip of ours with a view to being well equipped for the rigors ahead. Got to spend it to make it, they say."

I stride off in the direction me crew has taken with a subdued Sandwich in tow, feigning more confidence than I feel. Aye, spending it to make it be all very well, but it only works with money, not blood.

A BIT OF SHOPPING

SANDWICH and I catch up with Inkman and Abigail North down at Hu's Haberdashery. Inkman's sent the rest of the crew off with Rumguts and Silverback, and one of our chests of doubloons, to secure water, food, and various sundry supplies like rope and timber. He's kept the Russian sisters, Barber, Powderfinger and Shaka with him to carry and guard the remaining two chests. I note that he's also rejigged the contents of the chests so that these two contain about forty thousand doubloons each. A wise move, keeping the lion's share under the watchful gaze of responsible eyes. Rumguts and Silverback have their heads screwed on right, but still, pirates ain't renowned for their impulse control.

Hu of Hong Kong might not know what haberdashery means, but he sure does know his sailcloth. So does Ms North. In fact, it be a little distracting how lovingly she strokes them sails as she talks, like a lady of leisure petting her prize pussy cat. I try to focus on her words, best I can.

"Sails of the Cyclone," explains North. "Threaded with tungsten into a hemp and cotton blend that'll withstand everything from a gale-force wind to a long-range hit by chain shot. Nothing short of a point-blank blast is going to shred these beautiful bolts. Not to mention that they've been blessed by an Adept Shaolin Elementalist."

The otherwords confirm her appraisal.

Sails of the Cyclone

+50 Sail Defense, +50% Resistance to All Elements

+30 Speed

Special Ability: Howling Wind

Sails of the Cyclone can consume surplus wind, storing it up for the moment when your ship requires an instant burst of speed.

The storage process takes a typical day at sea to complete.

Strong winds will accelerate the process.

Howling Wind = +50 Speed for up to 5 minutes

"To defeat the storm you must be the storm." - Shaolin Wang

I ask Mister Hu what his price be and wince at the answer. Twenty thousand doubloons. Then I think back to how close we came to being taken by the Dreamer and me reluctance evaporates like mist in the morning sun. Them Cyclones will give us a +30 Speed advantage over the Dreamer and the chance to get well clear of them should their lich try sucking the wind out of our sails again. I put me Merchant skill into practice and manage to get us a twenty percent discount plus a modest trade-in on our well-used Sails of the Salamander. All up, it's a saving of five thousand doubloons. I hand Hu his fifteen thousand and ask North to organize the delivery of her new sails to the Albatross. She wouldn't have had it any other way, I can tell.

"Ain't going to be parted from her precious cloth, eh North?"

She folds her arms and there be a right determined set to her broad features. "Something happens to me, captain, you're going to have to wrap me in these here sails before you throw me overboard.

Otherwise," she adds with a wink, "I'll be coming back to haunt your bedchamber."

Me laugh be doubly hearty at the sight of Sandwich's obvious discomfort. "Does this mean, Ms North, that you are relinquishing your loyalties to the English crown in favor of a bit of buccaneering?"

She don't even spare a glance for her former captain. "Me dear mother weren't the best at paying her taxes, so I found meself drafted into the royal navy at the tender age of seventeen. So as far as I be concerned, me mother and me king can go kiss each other's asses."

I slap her on the shoulder. "Then welcome to the pirate's life, Sailmaster North. May your woes be brief and your booty bountiful."

"Aye, thank you, captain!"

Inkman leads the way to our next shopping stop, the small shipyard that's sprung up next door to the Freeport docks. There be a Dutch fluyt in dry dock, being careened of its barnacles and teredo navalis, the shipworms that bore into a ship's timbers and can sink the damned vessel out from under your feet if you don't manage the buggers.

We track down Chaperon, the burly French shipwright, and see what sort of cladding he has on offer. He shows us his stock of Dunkle Plating, fresh from the cargo of the very fluyt that he's now careening. The plating be named after the extinct Dunkleoteus, the most heavily-armored fish to have hunted the seas. Having neither the Alchemist nor Metallurgist skill, I barely follow the Frenchman's excited rant, but I do pick up the words 'lightest', 'hardest' and 'will not rust'. Then there's the fact that they been imbued with 'inanimate recuperative properties' by the rather infamous Dutch alchemist, Doctor Rudolf Glauber. And of course, I be having Inkman here to assure the quality of the stuff.

Tamaki "Inkman" McKenzie
Marine Level 7
Metallurgist 2nd Class

He gives me that Polynesian nod of his, a quick lift of the eyebrows timed with an upward jerk of his chin. He approves, and the otherwords come in to reinforce his case.

Dunkle Plating
+100 Hull Defense, +50% Resistance to Fire
+40 Agility

Special Ability: Glauber's Purge
Glauber's Purge
+25% Hull Strength Recovery
Removal of Hull-related Debuffs
If the ship's hull comes to suffer from ailments such as acid corrosion, parasitic infestation, or any form of decay, magical or otherwise, Glauber's Purge can be incited to rid the ship of said malaise.
This ability can only be activated by a Metallurgist of 3rd Class or better and requires the use of a twenty pound bag of Glauber's Salts.
"A good laxative empties the bowels of silt and the soul of sin."- Dr Rudolf Glauber

The price of twenty-four thousand doubloons brings tears to me eyes, but once again I think of the Dreamer.

Guns: 24
20 Antediluvian Artillery Cannons
Base Damage per Gun: 20
4 Cyclopean Swivel Cannons
Base Damage per Gun: 15

If worst comes to worst, we can face down a full broadside and *maybe* live to tell the tale. Who knows? It might make all the difference. The difference between beating them dead bastards or joining them.

I work me mercantile wiles and get us a twenty percent discount and an eight hundred doubloon trade-in on our copper plating. That'll need to come off to make way for the Dunkle Plating. A total price of eighteen thousand, four hundred doubloons.

That leaves us with forty-six thousand, six hundred doubloons with which to go cannon shopping. I leave Inkman to work out the Dunkle installation details with the shipwright and lead me little group up to Carruthers Cannoneers. As I'd hoped, the Thunder Gods are still on display.

Thunder God Culverins
Base Damage per Gun: 30
Allows the Chief Gunner to shoot one Class higher than normal.
Reload and firing times reduced by 50%
"None fully appreciated Thor's might until the invention of the cannon." - Admiral Bjorn Sigurdson

I haggle with the lean, sunburned Carruthers for a bit and get me customary twenty percent off, but that still means each cannon be worth eight thousand doubloons. Me sloop of war be already at capacity for gunports, six a side, so the artilleryman gives me a generous five hundred doubloon buyback per Barking Mastiff, a healthy three thousand doubloons total. And he throws in a restock of shot and powder to boot. The total price comes to forty-five thousand doubloons, leaving me with only sixteen thousand doubloons. I be budgeting fifteen thousand for Rumguts and Silverback's shopping spree, so we should have enough to give Bluegums a hearty wake tonight *and* have about a thousand in the kitty for emergencies.

Of course, one of these days there'll have to be a reckoning with the crew. Aye, the Albatross be covering their daily needs and the odd bit of revelry, but ten thousand won't go far for those wishing to split and retire. That be the aim of every pirate once the sun goes down on their seafaring career. A tidy sum upon which to live out the rest of their days without lifting a single finger in work or risk. Let's just be hoping them 'mind-bogglingly rich' words are more than mere aristocratic romance on Sandwich's part. Our gains from the Maw of a Thousand Deaths be a good sign for the future, but you just never know.

I ease me anxieties by doing a bit of projective naval gazing, comparing me prospective Albatross numbers with those of the Dreamer.

The Albatross
Hull Defense: 120/120 (250/250)
+30 Hull Defense from Iron Scantlings
+100 Hull Defense and +50% Resistance to Fire from Dunkle Plating
Sail Defense: 50/50 (100/100)
+50 Sail Defense and +25% Resistance to All Elements from Sails of the Cyclone

The Dreamer
Hull Defense: 200/200 (300/300)
+100 Defense from Stygian Planking
Sail Defense: 70/70 (100/100)
+30 Defense and +50% Fire Resistance from Dankthread Sails

The corpse crate might still be a tougher nut than us to crack, but she's a great bloody galley after all. It be like comparing a coconut to a walnut.

The Albatross

Agility: 100 (180)

+40 from Dunkle Plating

+10 from Navigator: 1st Class at the helm

+10 from Sailmaster: 1st Class at the rigging

+20 from Shellback: 3rd Class on deck

+10 Agility from Hero: 3rd Class on deck

Speed: 110 (190)

+30 from Sails of the Cyclone

+10 from Navigator: 1st Class at the helm

+10 from Sailmaster: 1st Class at the rigging

+20 from Shellback: 3rd Class on deck

+10 from Hero: 3rd Class on deck

The Dreamer

Agility: 80 (100)

+10 from Dankthread Sails

+10 from Breath of the Sleeping One

Agility: 80 when sails trimmed care-of Skeletal Oarsmen

Speed: 120 (140)

+10 from Dankthread Sails

+10 from Breath of the Sleeping One

Speed: 80 when sails trimmed care-of Skeletal Oarsmen

We can sail rings around that floating cemetery, meaning we can pepper her good and proper without *ever* having to weather one of them brutal broadsides of hers.

The Albatross

Guns: 14

6 Thunder God Culverins

Base Damage per Gun: 30

6 Barking Mastiff Culverins

Base Damage per Gun: 12

+5 Damage per Gun from Gunner: 1st Class on the gun deck

2 Barking Mastiff Falconets

Base Damage per Gun: 8

The Dreamer

Guns: 24

20 Antediluvian Artillery Cannons

Base Damage per Gun: 20

4 Cyclopean Swivel Cannons

Base Damage per Gun: 15

Our broadside total be 156 Damage to their 200 Damage. Aye, they still outgun us, but then they always will, having four more gun ports per side than we have. But the important thing be that, if we can stay nimble, keep yapping at that great old dane without giving her the chance to bark back, we might just wear her down.

Aye we be ready for the Dreamer now. We be ready to give her a long-overdue burial at sea.

33

GRAIN OF SALT

THE SETTING SUN be bleeding across the cloud-choked sky by the time we all get back to the Albatross. Firelight be popping up all over Freeport now and the echoes of revelry be reaching our hungry ears. We've many a pirate to mourn tonight, the likes of Hyena and Bluegums being at the forefront of me mind. The former was a bloody good shipmate and the latter was a mentor to me, a gruff yet patient teacher of the Buccaneer's Way.

Me and Bluegums was the terrors of the South Pacific for a time there, until those damned Frenchies caught up with us. Now I be wishing for Bluegums' sake that he *had* gone down in a blaze of gunpowder while going pound for pound with that French frigate. Would've been a legendary end for a legendary pirate. Instead, I hear me own crew whispering about Bluegums' fate. Sucked dry of blood in some demon's sphincter of a cavern. He and his crew fell to the darkness while we blasted our way to victory. There's a few among me lot what be of more religious leanings than me. Barber, for instance. She be a Roman Catholic, and now she's making little signs of the cross with her fingers every time Bluegums' name be mentioned. Like the poor bastard was cursed somehow.

It pains me that people be thinking of Captain Bluegums in that way. It would've gotten right under his skin, no mistake. But I have to admit to meself that it's not only Bluegums' posterity that I be worrying about. I be worrying about me own posterior. If a veteran of the sea can meet his grisly end here in Atlantis, so can a bolshie upstart like me. Some of me crew say I was just smarter than Bluegums, and I appreciate the praise. But I don't reckon they was right. I reckon I was plain old lucky that Bluegums went first. That me old mentor paved the way with his bones and wrote of the dangers ahead in his blood.

We all be walking up to the Simpering Siren now, passing through the hustle and bustle of an evening in Freeport. It be all fifty-six of us this time since the Albatross be safe and sound in dry dock, having her Dunkle Plating installed.

It amazes me how quickly this town has sprung up, especially since it be located smack dab in the middle of a dead metropolis full of foul beasties. But the shipwright assured me that the now three thousand or so 'citizens' of Freeport be well prepared to run off any nasties what poke their ugly heads over them makeshift walls. Military folk aplenty have flocked to this lawless place, mostly deserters from the various wars, civil and otherwise, being waged on every continent. And then there be the boatloads of refugees arriving every day, escaping the follies of kings and their big, bloody egos.

While Atlantis might seem like a barren hellhole on the surface, it ain't taken long for the Freeporters to scrape off the silted surfaces and plunder the resources hiding beneath. Turns out Atlantis sank fast enough to produce a whole plethora of air pockets. Them pockets have kept large parts of the undercity preserved, the contents fairly pristine. Refugee farmers have put Atlantean tools to good use, carting fertile soil up from the ruins, making gardens and planting them with the seeds they've brought with them. It rains often enough here for there to be an abundance of fresh water, and kelp makes for excellent fertilizer, I'm told. So as we wind our way through the town, I notice luscious crops of tomatoes, beets, sweet potato and all manner of other vegetables. No chance of going down with scurvy in these parts.

The air too be rich with delicacy. The aromas of steamed and fried fish waft over us from hundreds of cooking fires. There be wood aplenty for those fires too. The peaks of Atlantis have poked up out of the sea for millennia, causing some right gnarly tides and storms in this stretch of water. Many a ship was waylaid during that time, and all that timber be up those slopes, dried and ready for the hearth.

I've half a mind to stick around Freeport for a bit after securing the Star. We could use it as our base while we raid the trade routes of Europe, Africa and the Americas. But strangely, the thought don't offer me much cheer. There be dread in me gut, curled like some slimy worm behind me sternum. I be hoping a few ales at the Simpering Siren will wash the thing out, but I ain't holding out much hope.

So I fall back from the group, lagging me pace until I be a few feet behind. I be subtle about it, not wanting me crewmates to see the brave captain all glum and broody. But Inkman notices, bugger him. He always does. He drops back to join me, matching me pace though his legs be almost twice as long.

"Something troubling you, captain?" He keeps his voice low, a soft growl that goes a little way to warming me clammy ruminations.

No point in lying to Inkman. Those dark eyes of his have a way of piercing through even me lightest fibs. "Bit worried we've bitten off more than we can chew on this one."

His brow wrinkles, just a tiny bit. "How so?"

"Sandwich reckons we might be brushing fins with some old sea god. He Who Slumbers In The Drowning Dark. Fondly referred to as Squidbeard."

Inkman snorts. "You believe him?"

I bridle a bit at that, me response coming out pretty sharp. "You got a problem with me believing him?"

Inkman shrugs. "Books ain't just memories from someone else's eyes and ears. Books contain their stories too. A story be a story. Don't matter how much you believe in one. It still ain't truth."

"I thought you lot believed in gods."

"Never met a god I didn't believe in."

I throw me hands up in frustration. "So you're saying I shouldn't believe him? You don't think Squidbeard's waiting for us at the end of this damn Star of Atlantis quest?"

"Nay, I think he might be right there. Stands to reason after what we seen so far. Fishmen, lamprey people, liches, ghouls and zombies. An old tentacle-chinned sea god would fit right in. After all, that be why we recruited Maggie, aye or nay? Magic versus magic."

"Aye. Don't know if she'll be enough though."

"If Squidbeard's flesh and blood, whether it be warm and running or cold and congealed, we'll blow him all the way to Hine-nui-te-pō's underworld."

"Hine-nui-te-pō? Who be that?"

"Māori goddess of death."

"Reckon she'd like to join our crew?"

"While we've got a witch that steals the dead and turns them into puppets? Not likely."

"Ah well. Worth asking." I bite me lower lip as I imagine us broadsiding some looming hulk of a fish deity. "So what's your point about Sandwich? Sounds like you and him are on the same page."

"Far from it, captain. I believe me own eyes and ears. I saw that Squidbeard mosaic in the lighthouse, and I noticed how similar the style was to them carvings in the Maw of a Thousand Deaths. Ain't no mistaking they were made by the same hands."

"Didn't know you had such an eye for art."

He grins and taps his chin. "Me people be trained to look for the world's patterns from a tender age."

"You reckon these Atlanteans worshipped Squidbeard?"

"Nay. I reckon they feared him. The mosaic, the carvings, they all had that fear crafted into their lines. They weren't pieces of admiration. They was reminders."

The worm of fear in me solar plexus gives a wriggle. "Reminders of what?"

"Only the Atlanteans know that, and they don't seem inclined to talk to us."

"Nay, they ain't been hospitable."

"You ever wonder why?"

A flush of embarrassment creeps up me neck and onto me cheeks. I be glad for the waning sunlight. "Not until now. I figure they be protecting what's theirs."

"Maybe. What if they're not protecting? What if they're *guarding*?"

"Like Squidbeard be some sort of prisoner?" That thought feels like dipping me hands in cold brine. "According to Sandwich, Squidbeard's the reason Atlantis sank."

"And the reason it be risen again?"

"Aye, could be."

"Did those fishmen and lampreys *look* like they'd be too worried about living underwater?"

"Nay. So you reckon it was them what sank the city, not Squidbeard?"

"I don't reckon nothing that me eyes and ears ain't gathered. I'm only saying that we need to sail into this with Wits sharpened and Sand at the ready. Ain't no book going to tell me where to jab me taiaha."

"Alright then. A grain of salt with me Sandwich, eh?"

"A whole bloody shaker, Grace."

I clap the smart bastard on the back and step with him into the circle of light what be spilling out of the Simpering Siren. He flashes me a grin and strides inside. I wait a moment, pausing to let me friend's words sink in before joining him in the bright din of revelry. Plenty of time for thinking on the morrow. Now be the time for drinking.

34

ONCE IN A DARK ALLEY

"WELCOME ABOARD THE GOOD SHIP, Albatross, mateys!"

The assembly of sailors and rogues gives a resounding cheer in response and me otherwords confirm their recruitment.

The Albatross
Crew: 85

Not a full complement for me ship, but me Hero 3rd Class skill be helping me attract more quality rather than quantity. Most of them be Level 5 or 6, and a dozen or so be 1st Class Fencers and Musketeers, deserters from the war between England and Spain. Strangely enough, they be a mixture of both nations, drawn together by the promise of freedom from idiot monarchs.

Having promised me fresh recruits a drink on the Albatross, I pass the innkeeper a pouchful of doubloons. In return, he palms me a tightly folded bit of parchment. I raise me eyebrow at this surprise delivery but he already be off pouring the drinks and pointedly ignoring me.

After checking quickly to make sure no one be watching me, I unfold the paper and read it. The roughly-scrawled words send a jab of anxiety through me guts.

WE HAV YOR PRITTY TOFF
GO TO THE LAVS AND KEP WALKING
COM ALONE AND BE KWIK ABOWT IT

It ain't signed but a glance around tells me who be writing this note. Shaka and his motley mates be missing. So be Sandwich. I grit me teeth and tuck the note into me inside jacket pocket. For a moment I consider collaring Inkman, maybe ask him and some of me most loyal to sweep out across the town, see if they can sneak up on these traitorous blighters. But even though I be having several pints of the Siren's finest sloshing about in me guts, I ain't drunk enough to be playing dice with Sandwich's life. For one, he be the only one what knows where the Murmurs be. Secondly, and rather embarrassingly, I'd feel a might guilty if he got his throat slit on me watch. Against me better judgement, I seem to have grown a little fond of that lofty limey.

I duck out of the stifling barroom, taking the side door what leads out to the long drops, and hide meself in the shadows for a bit while I check that all me pistols be loaded. I left me Rumpus Musket on the Albatross, but I'd have felt naked without *some* form of firearm on me person so made sure to wear me brace of handguns. Besides, Stormshot be the closest thing I have to 'stepping out' jewelry. Damned sight more useful than a broach.

Before I carry on me way to face these malcontents, I check in on me vitals, knowing already that they be a tad impaired thanks to the ale I been swilling.

Perception: 20 (27)

+2 Sharpshooter: 3rd Class

20% increased chance of a Critical Hit with a musket

+2 Gunslinger: 3rd Class

20% increased chance of a Critical Hit with a pistol

+2 Squintlock's Peeper

+2 Stormshot

+1 Musketeer: 1st Class

+1 Pistoleer: 1st Class

-3 for Moderate Inebriation

Quickness: 13 (17)

+2 Sharpshooter: 3rd Class

+2 Gunslinger: 3rd Class

+1 Fencer: 1st Class

+1 Musketeer: 1st Class

+1 Pistoleer: 1st Class

-3 for Moderate Inebriation

Could be worse. I should still be a shade sharper and faster than Shaka and his lot, especially if they be knocking back a bit of Dutch courage leading up to this bit of backstabbing.

I gird me loins and strike off into the gloom, holding me breath as I pass the stinking long drops. Shaka's chosen his spot well, as there only be a single alleyway what leads uphill between a huddle of shacks. There ain't any fires burning in them. The inhabitants are inside the Simpering Siren. This makes the alleyway pretty dark so I take out me Gleam and hold it in me right hand as I make me way up the dirt pathway.

A voice stops me in me tracks just as I pass the last of the shacks.

"Far enough, captain, and keep them hands of yours at your sides. You be having four muskets trained on you, so don't be trying nothing stupid."

I do as I be told, though I be quietly firing up me Hasty Hands and Quickdraw skills while I be at it. Sure, I might be able to talk some sense into Shaka, but I ain't going to resist the urge to put a lead ball through his skull if I get the chance.

"Show me Sandwich first, Shaka. I ain't making no deals until I know he be alive."

"Aw, hear that, mateys? Deadeye Cortez, hard-as-flint pirate captain, be all worried and weepy over her toffy toyboy."

His taunt makes the shadows snicker in four different places. I fight the smile that threatens to break me staunch demeanor. Them numbskulls have just given away their sniping positions.

"Ain't like that, Shaka," I answer him evenly.

"That right, Grace? I can call you 'Grace', can't I? Without your ship and your crew, that's all you be after all. A little girl from the Philippines called Grace Cortez."

"You can call me whatever name you want from the grave, Shaka."

He growls and his voice takes on a fierce edge as he steps into the light of me Gleam. He be holding Sandwich in front of him. The lordling has taken a beating already. His left eye be puffed up and there be blood running down his chin. But he still be breathing. Thank Bathala for that.

"No, Grace. No one but this blighter be dying tonight. This here toff's killed enough of us already."

"Last time I checked, Shaka, it were fishmen, giant lampreys and the odd ghoul what be killing us. I know Sandwich there be a bit on the pasty side, but even you be smart enough to see that he ain't no ghoul."

Shaka's lips curl back from his large white teeth in a feral snarl. "You be blind, Deadeye. His highness here be killing us as sure as bad eggs. He be the one leading you by the nose with his Star of Atlantis story. He be the one whispering across your pillow at night, filling you with fancy while you *should* be leading us to cold, hard treasure."

I shake me head in disbelief. "What do you call all them crowns what we hauled out of the Maw, Shaka?"

"I call that a good start. A good omen what we should be listening too."

"And what do you reckon it be saying?"

"It be plain for anyone to hear. These ruins be full of riches what we should be finding and taking for ourselves. Like that Elder Sign. Bloody thing be made of solid gold. Worth a small fortune. But the toff here be telling you it be some sort of key. He be telling you to sail with it into some hellhole where the devil himself be waiting for us. He be pointing the way like he be the captain and you be his mast monkey, scampering about at his beck and call, helping sail us right down the throat of a *bloody great sea god!*"

Me heart sinks as I realize what's pushed Shaka over the edge. Whether while in his cups or under duress, Sandwich has gone and spilled his guts about He Who Slumbers In The Drowning Dark.

"So what be your plan then, Shaka? What be your great theory about how we all get rich and live happily ever after?"

"It be right simple." A knife glints in me Gleamlight, right next to Sandwich's throat.

The lordling's eyes look at me pleadingly, but he has the good sense to keep his mouth shut. Any word now would likely be his last.

"I slit this here toff's throat and we both agree that he got himself boozed up and wandered into a part of Freeport what his noble self had no business in frequenting. Then we forget all about this sea god and his bloody Star, sink a few celebratory ales together, and get back to the honest trades of pirating and plundering. No more fancy stories. No more grappling with sea monsters what have slithered out of myth just to take a chunk out of us, and no more nabbing keys for doors what should never be opened. Instead, we do what makes sense. We pick the low-hanging fruit from this here bountiful vine and then we bugger off to the Caribbean for a long and happy retirement, just like we all planned."

Shaka's right on that front. It be what we *all* planned on our way here. Fill our hull with Atlantean wealth and find ourselves some nice spots in the tropics in which to fish, drink and fornicate away our remaining years. But then came Sandwich, his Atlantis Star thing and his 'mind-boggling riches'. I mention that latter notion to Shaka but his only response be to spit in disgust, his gobbet of phlegm landing squarely on the toe of one of Sandwich's boots.

"Don't believe it, Shaka?"

"Sure I believe it. Don't mean I think it be worth the risk though. One and a million be all the same when you're dead!"

Shaka be making some sense, which be why I ain't shot him yet. But something in me just don't want to hear it. Before we reached Atlantis, the thought of a quiet, Caribbean life seemed quite tasty. Smooth and sweet like a nice Pinot Gris. Now it seems as flat and dull as lukewarm barrel water. It don't stir me like the thought of flashing about the world like some seafaring willow 'o the wisp. It don't thrill me like the tale of that daring pirate lass what swiped her fortune out from under the tentacled beard of a great and ancient deity. It don't live up to the legend of Captain Deadeye.

It be in this moment, in this darkened alleyway, that I realize why I need the lordling to live, and for these five traitorous bastards to die. I don't want their rationality to be turning the heads of me crew in sensible directions.

I think I knew it the first time I laid eyes on Sandwich, the first time them otherwords offered up the Star of Atlantis quest. I ain't in this pirate life for the money. I was born into money. I could've stayed home and grown fat and content on the proceeds of a fishing empire. And that notion be exactly what drove me, screaming, out of me mother's house, down to the docks, and onto the first smuggler's barque leaving the Philippines.

I almost feel grateful to Shaka for shedding more light on me situation. So much filled with gratitude that I resolve to shed a bit of light on his situation too. Having filled me Gleam up with a few health points, I toss it in the air so that its glow highlights all four of Shaka's musketeers at once.

And without further adieu, I go for me guns.

35

VOYAGE FOR COWARDS

SHAKA BE CONCENTRATING SO hard on me, he forgets to tuck in the elbow of his blade arm. It be sticking out into the night air, just begging to be shattered by a pistol ball. I oblige him, Quickdraw one of me plain pistols, and snap off a shot. There be a satisfying crunch and a spray of blood as the shot finds its mark. Shaka hisses in pain as his knife drops from his now useless arm.

Sandwich makes the most of Shaka's incapacitation by slamming his elbow in the Zulu's face. Shaka goes down, but I don't have no time to see what follows. I be too busy diving for the cover of a water barrel.

Muskets roar and two shots go 'thunk thunk' into the oak at me back. The sound of trickling water follows as the barrel's contents escape out through the subsequent holes. Above me, I hear two of the traitors shifting their aim, bringing their muskets to bear. The bad news for them be that they be planting themselves too close together. Barely five feet between them.

Before the first one, Goldilocks, can pull her trigger, I draw Stormshot and plonk a lead ball into her chest.

Your pistol Damage = 300

Greta "Goldilocks" Schwindler
Level 5 Marine
HP: -80/220

You have killed a Level 5 Marine under difficult conditions!
Your XP reward = 750 XP
Progress to Pirate Captain Level 9 = 42430/60000

Lightning crackles through the dead Austrian's body and arcs across to her partner in crime, Breezy. The wrinkled Fijian shrieks with pain and his shot goes wide, shattering a nearby pot of pickled herrings. With the smell of briny fish wafting over me, I draw me third pistol, take careful aim, and shoot the man through the throat while the sparks still be crackling through his steaming hair.

Your lightning Damage = 50

Critical Hit!
Your pistol Damage = 300

Juita "Breezy" Koroi
Level 5 Marine
HP: -140/210

You have killed a Level 5 Marine under difficult conditions!
Your XP reward = 750 XP
Progress to Pirate Captain Level 9 = 43180/60000

I reload while calling out to the two remaining shooters. Me Gleam's hit the ground now, but a quick glance offers up me targets' shadows. Whether they planned it that way, or have moved after seeing what Stormshot did to Goldilocks and Breezy, this pair has made sure they be well away from each other.

Perhaps it be the grog in me veins, but I feel charitable enough to offer them a chance to surrender.

"Oi, you two. I don't know what bilge Shaka be telling you, but we don't need to be doing this. Drop them muskets into the street and stand up with your hands raised. Do that and I promise you both be walking out of here and up the gangplank of any ship what'll take you. I won't be seeking no retribution, you have me word on it!"

"Sorry, captain, but we ain't neither that scared nor that stupid."

The speaker has the light male tone of a young man and the warm lilt of an Egyptian.

"Damn me ears! That you, Camel?"

"Aye."

A swell of anger sweeps any notions of sympathy from me bleeding heart. I think over the times I've seen Shaka huddled with his chums on deck, and reckon I know who the fifth turncoat be.

"That MacCarthy with you?"

"Aye, Deadeye," replies the former cotton farmer from Alabama. "But you be welcome to take a good hard look if you want to make sure."

I let out a rough guffaw. "You must think I be dumber than you look, Redneck!"

Shaka and Redneck have always been an odd pairing. The latter being a Dixie boy with a fairly dim view when it comes to 'folks of color', a phrase he'd use on me and Camel as much as Shaka, truth be told. But it seems that mutiny trumps all racial boundaries.

"Sharp enough to put a shot through that pretty face of yours, Deadeye," be Redneck's answer.

It be kind of him to keep talking, to help me pinpoint his position in the dark. I lunge out from me barrel, Stormshot in hand, but I don't unleash me lightning just yet. Instead I pause just long enough for Camel and Redneck to take their aim. But when their muskets thunder and their shots cut through the air, I ain't no longer where I was. Daring Dash has taken me into the middle of the street.

From there it be a simple matter of plugging Redneck in the flank. From the wheeze he lets out, sounds like he got a punctured lung for his troubles. He don't suffer long though. Stormshot's lightning finishes him off mercifully quick.

Your pistol Damage = 300

Robert "Redneck" McCarthy
Level 5 Musketeer
HP: -70/230

You have killed a Level 5 Musketeer under difficult conditions!
Your XP reward = 750 XP
Progress to Pirate Captain Level 9 = 43930/60000

Camel be frantically reloading so I draw me two plain pistols and shoot him in both legs. The result be a tumbling mess of boy what hits the ground with a thump and a couple of cracks.

Pistol and fall Damage = 150

Ramses "Camel" Mesbah
Level 4 Marine
HP: 30/180

I leave Camel groaning in the dirt while I take cover behind a low stone wall and have a thorough gander up and down the street. Nothing stirs except the wounded Egyptian and Sandwich who now be sitting astride Shaka and pounding the sailor's face with his bloodied fists.

"Sandwich!" The mention of his name does nothing to stop him, so I try a more maternal approach.

"James Montagu Sandwich, that be enough!"

He stops and looks in me direction, his eyes wild, his face awash with sweat.

"Mother?"

"Nay, it be your captain, you daft bugger. Quit beating on that mutineer! I want a word with him."

Sandwich staggers to his feet but there be no movement from Shaka. Neither groan nor gurgle. The otherwords confirm me suspicions.

Sibusiso "Shaka" Ibubesi
Level 6 Marine
HP: -5/270

You and James Montagu have killed a Level 6 Marine under difficult conditions!
Your XP reward per person = 450 XP
Progress to Pirate Captain Level 9 = 44380/60000

"Bloody hell, Sandwich! Didn't think you had it in you to beat some poor bastard to death."

The look he gives me raises goose pimples on the back of me neck. The baby blue be gone from his eyes. It be like his pupils have dilated so much that they've eclipsed his irises. And the words that come out of his mouth be a roiling mess of brine and slime. Not like words at all. More like the moist slithering of unfurling tentacles.

I blink and Sandwich be standing before me, his bright blue eyes full of concern, his soft lips moving gently.

"Are you alright, Grace?"

I serve him up a deep scowl, masking the fluttering of me heart. "Stow that 'Grace' malarky, Sandwich. I be Captain Deadeye to you."

"Indeed. Sorry." He clears his throat and stands up straight. "Thank you, captain. It certainly appears that I owe you my life."

"Nay, Sandwich. You merely owe me a mind-boggling amount of wealth."

I turn away from him so he don't notice me unease, and draw me saber as I stride over to Camel. I press the tip to his throat, putting a stop to his pitiful moans.

"You really need to be more careful of them legs of yours, lad. One of them be brand new, remember?"

He coughs and whispers something.

"Didn't quite catch that, Camel. Need me to open up your windpipe, make it easier for them words to get out?"

He gulps and this time his voice comes out like the whine of a frightened dog. "I be sorry, captain. Truly."

"You tell me what you be sorry about, lad."

"Shaka, he told me that the Englishman had twisted your mind, said that you was about to sail us all to our deaths."

"And you reckon Shaka was speaking with his right mind? Don't think he might've still been a tad upset that this same Englishman put a rapier through his cute German bunkmate?"

"Aye, captain, he was angry about that. But it weren't why we agreed to his plan."

"Why then? I be giving you no reason to mutiny, lad. I been as fair as any captain you're likely to meet."

He gulps and his next words be weaker than before. Seems like I might've clipped an artery with one of me shots.

Bleeding Damage = 10

Ramses "Camel" Mesbah
Level 4 Marine
HP: 20/180

"Even the fairest wind can blow us off course," Camel tells me, and the boy's audacity sets me blood to boiling. I be the captain, not him. I be the one to know me course, not this Cairo street rat what can't even grow a proper beard yet.

"Me course be true, lad," I hiss as I press down a little harder with me Seahawk Saber, "but this ain't a voyage for cowards."

His dark eyes go wide as me swordpoint pierces his jugular and carves a slice into his smooth neck. His remaining health points spurt out into the dirt. I wipe me blade clean on his shirt and sheath it.

You have killed a Level 4 Marine under difficult conditions!
Your XP reward = 600 XP
Progress to Pirate Captain Level 9 = 44980/60000

"Well said, captain."

I don't bother to look at Sandwich. Instead, I set out for the welcoming lights of the Simpering Siren. The fires be burning bright in me belly, and I need more than a few ales to put them out.

36

MARRIED TO THE SEA

I WAKE the next morning with an Argentinian coffee steaming under me nose. I grunt me thanks to Inkman as I sit up and accept the mug with trembling hands.

"Remember much about last night?" he asks me.

The bunk creaks in protest as Inkman sits down on the end of it. He be sipping a brew too, though he takes his with a dollop of honey. Me, I prefer me coffee like I prefer me life. Full-bodied and a tad bitter.

"Aside from murdering five of me own crew, no, not a great deal."

"Shaka and his lot had it coming. If you'd not shot them, I'd have hung them for you. Mutineers deserve no less."

"Aye, it were just, but it don't make it any easier to stomach."

"I take that as a good sign," he offers with a smirk.

"How do you figure that?"

"Means you've still got a soul in there somewhere."

I nod and smile, making an appearance of agreement. But I be thinking about Sandwich, his eyes as black as night and his words slithering from his mouth like them baby lampreys of the Maw. I might still be having a soul, but seems like it be up for sale and I ain't sure who be buying.

"How soon until we sail for the Murmurs, Tamaki?"

"The crew be about as sluggish as you this morning, but we'll be ready by the time you stagger up onto the quarterdeck."

"I'll take me time then, shall I?"

"Aye, that would be appreciated, Grace."

It takes me a good hour to muster me faculties enough to give the order to set sail. It be a gloomy day overlooked by a dark and brooding sky. The gun-metal grey sea be choppy as hell. It don't sit so well with me queasy belly and I can see that most of me crew be feeling it too.

Not Sandwich though. He be looking as perky as a fresh-plucked rose as he bounds up them quarterdeck steps, two at a time, and plants himself at me side. He has a bandage wrapped around his left forearm that I don't remember him having before. He didn't sustain no injury to his arm during our scrap with Shaka, so I suppose he must've done himself a mischief while in his cups last night.

"You're looking disturbingly chipper," I venture. "Was you spilling your drinks on the sly last night?"

Once we got back to the Simpering Siren, we matched each other drink for drink, and I remember him spilling his guts out the door and then curling up under a table like a beleaguered cur. Didn't look like an act, but then, I ain't so sure I know what's what with this lordling no more.

He shrugs and offers me a charming half-smile what I be inclined to match. His presence be a comfort, strangely enough. I feel me hangover ebbing away, vanquished by a rising tide of energy and purpose. I should be paying more attention to me instincts, like me mother and experience have taught me, but something about this lordling gets me pondering such malarky as 'higher purpose' and all that guff. In this moment, I feel like I be on exactly the right course with the fair wind of destiny at me back. It be a strange feeling, but not unpleasant.

And though the light of day be rightly cold, Sandwich be looking warm and human. That moment last night with him all fish-faced and speaking in tongues must've been the stress of battle talking. Perhaps a throwback to our battles up to this point. Hell, if I spend too much longer in Atlantis, most *everyone* be starting to look like a fishman to me. Time to get this damn Star, make it rich, and sail as far from these accursed islands as possible. That fleeting notion of staying at Freeport be a distant and derelict wreck this morning. I got better things to be doing with me life. Perhaps I could sail to the Carribean, buy a sugar plantation, free all the slaves and hire them as me workers. For a silly, girlish moment, as I feel the warm sun of fantasy on me back, I wonder if Sandwich might join me there. After all, I'd be living like a lady, so I might as well have a lord to go with the scene.

"I suppose it is the excitement of adventure that puts the spring in my step today, captain."

"Then tell me what manner of excitement we can expect as we approach them Murmurs."

He points at the rugged outline of the island up ahead. It be a few hours sail from the Maw of a Thousand Deaths, so it be no wonder that we crossed paths with the Dreamer. Most likely, we sailed right into her course of patrol, maybe a loop she does around the Murmurs once a day.

"We will not have any bother from the Dreamer, if that is your concern."

"Why not?"

"I woke early this morning and poured over my books until I found an elegant solution. A relatively simple incantation and a small amount of sacrificial blood."

He holds up his injured forearm for me to see, and for the first time, I notice the wet glint of blood on the Elder Sign behind us. We stashed it below decks before heading off to the Siren last night. Now it be back in pride of place at the stern.

"And what be the outcome of this muttering and bleeding of yours?"

"The Dreamer will keep its distance. As far as ghouls are concerned, we are sanctioned emissaries of the Atlantean Emperor. The Albatross is now surrounded by an aura of imperial devotion."

I look about me ship, trying to spot if anything be different. Nothing seems amiss. "For corpse's peepers only, eh?"

"Indeed, captain. Although Ms MacDonald can likely see it."

Aye, now that Sandwich mentions it, there be Maggie down on the main deck, standing at the gunwale, staring into space. What I took at first glance to be simple Maggie strangeness, I now see for what it be. She be inspecting Sandwich's handiwork, and by that faint and frankly unnatural smile on her face, looks like she be impressed.

"We should start calling you the Sand Witch or somesuch."

Sandwich laughs. "My arcane skills are narrow. Outside of Atlantis, I am as mundane as the next man."

"Feel rather at home here, do you?" There be a clammy feeling in me guts as I say that. Something akin to disappointment, but with the stink of rot about it.

"Strangely, yes. But I am sure that will change once we have the Star of Atlantis. This place is simply a means to an end."

"And what be that end?"

"Freedom. Absolute freedom."

That clammy feeling evaporates under the warmth of his sunny grin and thoughts of an open and glittering sea. I be fooling meself with fancies of plantations and happily-ever-afters. I be a pirate lass, married to the sea and no other. Aye, once I have the Star in me grubby mitts, I be seeing the world and taking from it whatever I damned well like. A pirate captain don't retire. A pirate captain sails until she can't sail no more.

"On that notion, Sandwich," I reply, "we be in absolute agreement."

37

FIGHTING WORDS

Turns out that the Murmurs be shrouded in fog so thick that I could add peas and call it a soup. Jonesy navigates us through it with her usual aplomb, picking our course by the currents and the gulls. In fact, she be doing such a bang-up job that I sidle over to her with a query in me mind.

"Jonesy?"

"Aye, captain?"

"Be you a Shellback now?"

"Aye. Takes one to know one, does it, captain?"

Me laugh be sponged away by the cloying fog. "Weren't thinking of replacing you, Jonesy. Just wanted to make sure we was alright, you know, if…" I let me statement trail and she picks up the slack.

"If I catch a stray cannonball?"

"Aye, that be the gist of it. And when did you level up from Navigator, if you don't mind me asking?"

"During our tussle with the Dreamer."

I peer into the mist, but there ain't no penetrating it. If the Dreamer be out there, she be as blind as us. Hopefully.

"Reckon the dead can see through this fog?"

"Not according to Maggie, nay."

I glance back at the Elder Sign, wondering if this sodden milieu be Sandwich's doing somehow. Considering how au fait with the fey he be, I wouldn't put it past him.

"Reckon we should be easing off the speed now? Can't be far to landfall?"

"You teaching me how to suck eggs now, captain?"

I raise me eyebrow, noting the edge to Jonesy's tone. "Nay. And it ain't like you to be tetchy, Jonesy. Something wrong?"

Jonesy offers me a smile, but it be a thin one. "Sorry, captain. I be a little nervous about our destination. You ain't exactly been verbose about our purpose here, and begging your pardon, but it ain't like *you* to be so circumspect with your crew. We ain't hankering to question your decisions if that be what worries you. Shaka and his lot weren't speaking for the rest of us when they had a go at you and Sandwich."

She has me there, and the otherwords confirm it.

Your crew morale is 70% but behavioral indicators suggest a downward trend.

I cast me eyes about me ship and see what them otherwords be on about. Me crew be moving slower than usual, their heads bowed for the most part. There be a few nervous ticks too, jiggling of legs, habitual picking of noses, that sorta carry on. There be no sense of purpose, not like I be feeling right now. Seems I'd best rectify that in short order.

"You get us into safe harbor, Jonesy, and as soon as we've dropped anchor, I'll offer up the most illuminating sermon you've ever heard. How about that?"

This time Jonesy's smile be fuller, more genuine. "Much appreciated, captain."

I be true to me word too. The Murmurs loom over us, a series of cavernous mouths that have been molded and carved by skilled hands to form archways. Once again, the decorative taste leans towards the wriggly and slimy. Plenty of spirals, swirls and hints of writhing masses. The darkness within them caverns fair heaves with menace and a soft wind sets the whole place moaning and whimpering like a widower at her husband's funeral.

Your crew moral has dropped to 65% due to the unsettling aspect of the Murmurs.

To the hum of rope against the deck, and the plunk of our anchors plunging into the sea, I gather me crew together with a whistle. Once I have all seventy-nine pairs of eyes looking me way, I clear me throat and activate me Stirring Words skill.

"Mateys, I imagine many of you be wondering why we be sailing into the most dreary of waters, where that ghoulish warship be roaming and the rocks themselves be groaning."

A growl of agreement utters from every throat. A unanimous 'aye' of collective trepidation.

"And I ain't been so forthcoming with me intentions. I know that, and I be hoping you'll accept me apologies."

That gets me more nods than folded arms. A good enough sign.

"I thank you for your patience and loyalty, especially those what have only newly joined us and ain't yet sure of how things be on the Albatross. Well, here it be, the truth, rough and ugly just like you lot."

A chuckle sweeps through their ranks, and it be like the first embers flaring in a near-dead fire.

"We be on the brink of completing the Star of Atlantis quest, me ladies and lads. Our prize lies within these ruins, brought here by the emperor of Atlantis himself only moments before this once fair nation sank beneath the waves. And that's not all he brought with him on his Dragon. Not by a long shot."

I pause for a moment, playing out their anticipation. Me Hero skill tells me that leadership be as much about the story as it be about the decisions.

"Within the straining belly of his flagship, he brought with him the full wealth of Atlantis. More riches than most of you can likely imagine. At least, more than most of you can count, that's for sure."

I punctuate that jest with a wink and it gets the desired result. A bout of hearty laughter what reflects the growing sense of excitement among them.

Your crew morale has increased to 75%

"I be making no bones about it, mateys. We be in for the lark of our lives in this here place." I point into the closest of the caverns, at the lurking darkness within. "We be sailing into the bedchamber of He Who Slumbers In the Drowning Dark. An old and cranky sea god, and no mistake about it."

Though that gets a few shivers and gasps, morale be holding steady at 75%. So far so good. It likely be the promise of uncountable riches what be keeping them buoyant, like a wreck survivor clinging to a barrel.

"But look around you ladies and lads. Look at this fine ship what you be having the honor of occupying. A hull what can withstand the fiercest of poundings, and cannons what can deliver the wrath of Thor's hammer. A helmswoman who can steer us through the Devil's fangs and sails what can carry us off faster than a ten doubloon happy ending at Nice's finest massage parlour."

The latter quip gets a right bark of hilarity from me assembled sailors and be likely the sole cause of the 5 percent boost to their morale. Simple minds, simple pleasures.

Your crew morale has increased to 80%

"You've all been in Atlantis long enough to be casting your peepers on Squidbeard's betentacled visage. Aye, he be a fearsome opponent. Ain't no doubt about that. But you know what, mateys?"

I lean over the railing of the quarterdeck, drawing me crew in with a conspiratorial smile like I be about to share with them the juiciest secret they ever laid ears on.

"Fearsome be in the eye of the beholder, and he ain't never beheld the likes of us before. We ain't no scale-bellied fish lovers. We ain't no lily-livered Atlanteans, fleeing like rats from their sinking ship. We be pirates! We sail under the skull and bones, and ain't no woman nor man, alive nor dead, going to stop us taking what we please!"

Aye, they like being told how fierce and powerful they be. It shows in the 5 percent increase in their morale. 85 percent be a good number, but I ain't finished just yet. I draw me pair of plain pistols, already primed and ready to fire.

"Join me, ladies and lads. Wake this salted old calamari from his snoozing, let him know we be coming for him! Make him quake in his sodden boots for fear of our violent visitation! For we be snatching that shiny gem from under his stinking tentacles, and a king's ransom of booty from his barnacled sea chest. And once we be done and the Star be mounted there upon our helm, we shall go where we please and let the riches of the whole damned world be ours for the taking!"

I fire me Stormshot in the air, and me echo be the thunderous report of seventy-nine assorted pistols. The concussion bounds through the caverns like a great, barking hound, its blood up and its quarry in sight.

On cue, Rumguts cracks a keg of grog and starts pouring out some Dutch courage for me suitably enlivened mateys.

Your crew's morale is now 95% and holding steady.

A grin sets me cheeks to aching as I holster me pistols and survey the now buoyant hubbub on deck. One of the new sailors has broken out his violin and be playing a jaunty shanty. He be called Fiddler from this point on, piratical imaginations being what they are. A dozen or so sailors respond to his tune in short order, dancing up a jig that trembles the boards beneath their boots.

Aye, we be ready for old Squidbeard. And now that me crew believes it, I can almost believe it meself.

THE INEFFABLE

WE SAIL into the yawning darkness, like krill swimming down the gullet of a whale. Inkman be panning his spotlight contraption across the cavern, illuminating the way while the linemen measure the depth beneath us from their perches at port and starboard. They be calling out their measurements at regular turns, guiding us away from the shallows so we don't beach ourselves.

The spotlight itself be a nifty invention of Inkman's devising. It be a barrel full of pre-charged Gleams, mounted on a swivel what he's whipped up and installed at the bow of the Albatross. He be sweeping the way ahead of us, watching for rocks and Bathala-knows what else we might encounter in the Murmurs.

I try not to imagine a mass of tentacles rising all of a sudden to wrap themselves around me ship, dragging us all down to be food for whatever marine monsters be swimming beneath us.

We be sailing for quite some time now, but by me own measure, we should've hit a dead-end or popped out the other side of the island some time ago. The Murmurs didn't look all that big from the outside. Roughly nine miles across at me best guess, and here we been travelling at a steady five knots per hour for almost four hours.

There be a light yet steady breeze what blows through these caves, giving them the constant murmur of their namesake.

Though it be giving me the creepy crawlies right up and down me back, I know for certain that the Murmurs be somehow larger on the inside. Much larger, it seems, for another two hours sail on by before we pass out of the metaphorical whale's intestines and into an impossibly large cavern.

Inkman's spotlight be swallowed up by the darkness like a lone needle plunged into a bolt of black velvet. As he pans upwards, trying to find the cavern's roof, I catch a glimmer of something on the closest wall. Silvery threads be hanging beneath a rocky ledge. That gets me to wondering.

"Inkman?" I call out.

Me words echo back at me, but me voice no longer sounds like mine. There be a damp, gurgling quality to it, like it be uttered from some Atlantean's throat, freshly moistened with brine and blood.

"Aye, captain?" answers Inkman.

His echoes have that same marine quality like they be breathed out by gills instead of lungs.

"Cap that light of yours. I want to try something."

Inkman does as he's bade, plunging us into pitch black. I can't see me hand in front of me face, it be so dark, but then a single light springs into life above us. A lone star in a sable sky. Another be following suit nearby, then a few more. Then the light spreads across the cavern roof, illuminating fissures and stalactites, glittering veins of ore and clusters of crystal.

Me crewmates have the good sense to stay their tongues, though I know they be wanting to whoop with wonder. Glowworms be sensitive to sound, dimming themselves if they think they be under threat from a larger predator. And here be millions of them, covering the entirety of this mighty enclave, lighting our way and illuminating both promises and threats of what be to come.

Looming ahead there be the largest gateway I ever seen in me life, a great archway carved with them same sinuous and slithering forms we witnessed both outside and in the Maw of a Thousand Deaths. The gates themselves look to be carved from obsidian. They be almost invisible in the wan light of the glowworms above, save for the faintest sheen on their polished surface. The weak light be enough to set off a host of writhing horrors not discernible to the eye, but chillingly perceptible to the soul.

And as we draw closer to that edifice of eerie fancies, a nightmarish malaise wraps around meself and me crew like tentacles around our trembling flesh.

The Ineffable Arch assaults the sanity of any who dare approach it. Those lacking the will to resist shall be drowned in the depths of delusion.
The Ineffable Arch Challenge is considered complete when all victims are rendered unable to inflict violence upon themselves or others.
The Ineffable Arch Challenge = 40
The Elder Sign is in your possession.
This antediluvian artifact provides a 30% Sand bonus to each sentient creature on your ship.

Me Sand score be 23, and with the 30 percent bonus from the Elder Sign, that gives me a total of 30 Sand. That's a 75 percent chance of coming through this with me sanity intact. Problem be, I be possessing one of the highest Sand scores on the ship. If Lady Luck ain't inclined to flash us a bit of cleavage, we might find ourselves in a sloop full of lunatics.

The dice of Fate rattle through me mind, cartwheeling and cavorting off the inside of me skull. It be a maddening feeling all by itself. Here's hoping it be the only crazy thought I be having today.

Your mind is a bonfire of enlightenment, blazing bright and clear against the murk of lurking hysteria.

The Ineffable Arch Challenge has rolled 13 to your 72 Nothing to fear but fear itself, Captain Deadeye.

I feel the Ineffable Arch relinquish its clammy grip on me noggin. I heave a sigh of relief, but me moment of serenity be shattered by an inhuman howl.

Going on instinct, I Quickdraw one of me mundane pistols and aim at the howler. It be one of the new recruits, a big Inuit bruiser what I be hearing some call Nanuk. His peepers be wild and full of hunger like his polar bear namesake. The madness has him, hook, line and sinker. He lets out a bellow of rage and charges up the quarterdeck steps at me, his fingers curled like claws, his stained teeth bared.

Not wanting to hurt him too badly, I holster me pistol and sidestep Nanuk with the help of me Fencer 1st Class skill, just as he be about to wrap his paws around me throat. For good measure, I drag me left boot so that he trips on it and goes sprawling on the deck. Then before he can get up, I jump onto his back and press me knee down onto the nape of his neck while also twisting one of his arms up behind his shoulder blades. It takes all of me Brawn to stop him from thrashing free.

You have incapacitated a Level 1 Lunatic.

Your XP reward = 50 XP

Progress to Pirate Captain Level 9 = 45030/60000

A Level 1 Lunatic? Nanuk be a Level 6 Marine. That be why I recruited the bugger! Yet somehow this Ineffable Archway malarky has stripped him of everything bar his most base urges. I just be hoping this bothersome bear be getting back his faculties once the challenge be over.

Banishing that dark thought from me mind, I hold onto Nanuk and do me best to take in the mayhem about me. From bow to stern, mad-eyed pirates be tangling with their shipmates. In a few cases already, the fracas has been final.

Crew: 77/80

Me only consolation be that I see a good number of clear, non-maniacal eyes among me crew still. And to their credit, me sane sailors, those with the Sand to withstand the curse, be doing their best *not* to kill their shipmates. Right convivial of them, considering the circumstances.

For instance, I see Rumguts drop Barber from behind with a cannonball to the back of the head. The Irishwoman's face be redder and wilder than I've ever seen it, even during one of Rumguts' most stormy benders. On either side of her, two of me new recruits, Ratface and Borscht, be bearing down on me sailmaster, Ms North.

I draw Stormshot and take careful aim at Rumguts' raised cannonball, the one what she be about to crush Barber's skull with. Me shot strikes the top of the iron ball and the lightning does the rest, arcing down onto Rumguts, Ratface and Borscht, stopping them in their tracks long enough for North to drop them all with the plank she be wielding.

You and Abigail North have incapacitated three Level 1 Lunatics.
Your XP reward per person = 75 XP
Progress to Pirate Captain Level 9 = 45105/60000

I sense movement behind me and Quickdraw me a pistol, stopping meself just short of blowing Jonesy's head off. She looks up from her work only for a moment to offer a wink of reassurance before finishing her binding job on Nanuk's legs. I sigh with relief, holster me pistol, and help her bind the Alaskan's burly arms.

With our immediate threat thus hogtied, and the quarterdeck mercifully clear of crazies, I set me mind to the task of returning sanity to me delusional crew members. I be having to think fast too. There be five more sailors down with mortal wounds, and a rough headcount of clear-eyes versus mad-eyes tells me that I might lose a third of me crew if I don't break this curse.

Crew: 72/80

I need to be finding a way to distract these nutters so me sane sailors can wrap them up in ropes. I feel me Wits twitch, putting four and four together to make eight. There be only one thing that be drawing a pirate's attention before all else. That be if these lunatics still have even the faintest inkling of their piratical nature.

I take a doubloon out of me pocket, kneel down by Nanuk, and wave the coin in front of his snarling face. It takes him a moment or two, but then the glint of the gold catches his eyes and he goes still as a dog eyeing a juicy treat.

Aye then. The ineffable ain't infallible. There be hope for us yet.

I wink at Jonesy. "Help me fight me way into me cabin. Fists and feet only."

Me navigator grins at me like I've just told her it be Christmas Morning. "Aye, captain."

And with that, we two ladies wade into the fray.

SMITHEREENS

JONESY DON'T GENERALLY DIVULGE this in polite company. She be a Brawler 1st Class. Having escaped a sugar plantation near Havana, Jonesy stowed away on a ship and headed home to Port Royal. There she made a living pounding people's faces for cash.

Thing with Jonesy be that her stunning smile be her first punch, able to give pause to most men and not a few women neither. Then while they be gazing at her beauteous visage, good old Jonesy pops them one in the kisser.

Naturally, that don't work so well on lunatics, so there be a ferocious scowl on her face instead as she clears me a path to me cabin. I wince at a few of them elbows and knees she applies to parts most tender. When me crew wakes up from this bad dream, there'll be many a nasty bruise for Doc the Croc to attend to.

Speaking of that Aussie devil, he already be making some headway with containing our maniacs. With syringes in both hands, he be filling his fellows full of dope, jabbing a thigh here and a buttock there. Have to admire the bugger. Even in the thick of bedlam, he be as cool as a cucumber. Though in some books, that emotionless demeanor would be classed as its own special kind of pathology.

Jonesy removes a different Australian from our path, a dog-breathed chap called Dingo, sending him to the floor with a sharp jab to his throat. Then we burst into me cabin and lay our hands on our salvation. The ship's treasure chest. I unlock it with the key I keep tucked under me shirt and fling the lid open.

There be roughly fifteen thousand doubloons here, more than enough to grab them mad privateers by the eyeballs, so me and Jonesy haul the booty out onto the deck. I give Jonesy the nod and she kicks the chest over, spilling them shiny gold coins all over the boards.

The effect be immediate. The closest lunatics lunge for the loot, scooping coins up in their hands, eyes twitching here, there and everywhere as their beleaguered minds try to take it all in.

I scoop up a bunch of doubloons meself and hurl them into the air. The clatter they make on the deck grabs the attention of the farther flung lunatics, and soon every one of them be at the treasure like rats at a freshly murdered corpse.

Jonesy wastes no time. She grabs up some nearby rope, knocks the closest crazy flat and proceeds to hogtie the woman. This time the lunatic don't even seem to notice, so fixated she be on the pile of coins she's scraped together from the scramble. Doc the Croc follows suit in his own way, filling his syringes from a flask clipped to his belt and sticking them lunatics with swift and clinical precision.

Near the bow, I see Inkman grab up a coil of rope and collar a couple of clear-eyed sailors to help him. They soon have a bundle of bedlamites lashed to the mainmast.

It occurs to me that I ain't seen Sandwich nowhere. I cast me eyes about the deck, looking for that lily-white face of his, and that be when I spot the open hatch. Quicksmart I be over there and down into the hull.

It don't smell pretty down there, but what can one expect when you have almost eighty unwashed pirates slumming it below decks. And it be dark as a closed coffin.

I take out me Gleam to light me way. There ain't no mad lordling leaping out at me from the shadows, but I do see spots glistening wet on the floor. I kneel down to take a better look, already suspecting what it might be. Blood. I ain't liking the direction of them sanguine splatters neither. He be headed for the bow and there be only one thing of interest to a homicidal maniac down there.

The powder store.

I weave me way through the crates and barrels of our supplies, grabbing up a coil of rope as I go. The Albatross ain't a big ship, so I be at the bow soon after, and the sight I behold there near turns me bowels to water.

There be Sandwich, grinning like a ghoul, his face streaked with blood from a cut on his forehead. Must've taken a knock from a fellow lunatic before reaching the hatch above.

He be crouching over a fuse what he's laid out on the floor. The fuse runs but a few feet, right into an uncorked barrel of gunpowder, one barrel of a whole bloody stack what makes up our entire powder store. If this lot goes up, me ship and me crew will be so many splinters of wood and bone.

"James?"

He looks up at me, turning slightly so I can see the flint and tinder in his hands. His eyes be wide and bloodshot, but unlike them mad buggers up on deck, there be an inkling of cunning too.

"Put the lighter down, James. There's a good lad."

In his current state of mind, he ain't a good lad at all, so of course he don't do as he be told. Instead his grin widens, threatening to break his pretty face in half, as he puts flint to tinder and strikes a spark.

Me Daring Dash puts me between Sandwich and the powder

store just as the fuse flares into life. It be a quick-burning one so it takes all of me 20 Quickness and me Fencer 1st Class skill to draw me Seahawk and sever that damned line before its fizzing payload can reach the kegs.

I stamp down hard on the flame, grinding it to ash beneath me boot. Disaster averted. But with me distracted by the fuse, I ain't quick enough to sidestep Sandwich's shoulder charge. Next thing I know, I be flat on me back with Sandwich's boot plonked right between me breasts.

He grins down at me before leaning forward and strikes up another spark right beside me ear. Off goes the fuse again.

With a howl that be a mere semitone shy of terror, I twist out from under Sandwich's foot, toppling the toff in the process. Then I leap toward the powder store, arms outstretched. It be like the world's turned to slow-flowing treacle as I watch that fluttering flame crawl away from me.

I slap me palm down onto the fuse and the sparks sear me tender flesh. I grit me teeth against the pain and clap me right hand over the left, applying pressure, grinding them flames out against me skin. But just as I be struggling up onto me hands and knees, I be shoved back down by Sandwich's body weight. The bugger's jumped on me, and by the sound of the clacking in his hands, he be at it with that damned flint and tinder again.

This time he has me cold, kneeling right onto me shoulders so that I can't bloody move a muscle. Out the corner of me eye, I see sparks flare in the dark.

"Don't do this, James," I wheeze. "Think of the prize, man. Think of the quest. You've come all this way just to blow yourself to smithereens?"

"Smithereens," he murmurs, seeming to enjoy the word. It be a frightening sound, devoid of the tiniest scrap of rationality. "Smither-"

A thunk cuts his word short and I feel Sandwich's weight be

lifted away. I roll onto me back with a sigh and note that Sandwich be out cold, another light trickle of blood running down his forehead from the whack Inkman dealt with the flat of his taiaha.

Then I look up into Inkman's smiling face. "Bloody hell, Tamaki. What took you so long?"

"Island time," be his answer.

I laugh and take the hand he be offering me.

40

ALL THAT GLITTERS

W ITH THE MADDENED portion of me crew now bound, gagged, and gathered amidships, I take stock of our brush with insanity while Doc the Croc tends to the injured. Truth be told, it could've been a lot worse. And if we hadn't got that 30 percent Sand bonus from the Elder Sign, it would've been.

Crew: 72/80

Your crew's morale has dropped to 65%

Aye, nothing like having a crazy shipmate at your throat to dampen your spirits. And the gloomy ambience of this cavern ain't helping neither.

Then there be the fact that eight of us be dead, murdered by our fellow pirates. Seven of our eight fatalities be new recruits what I haven't had the chance to get to know. That always saddens me a bit. If a pirate be following me to their death, I at least like to know beforehand what their names be. And normally there'd be that opportunity. We'd be out patrolling the shipping line for days, sometimes weeks, before we might happen upon a juicy prize. Plenty of time to shoot dice and chew the fat over a glass or six of rum. But here in Atlantis it be feeling like a sailor no sooner steps on me tub than they be gutted, gashed or gunned down by some abomination or other. It be weighing on me conscience something vicious, but something tells me there ain't much to be done about it until the Star of Atlantis be mounted on the helm, and our hold be full of imperial treasure.

I offer me usual prayer as Inkman, Silverback and the Russian sisters finish wrapping the dead and throwing them overboard. Barber be the one I offer special attention to. That crack Rumguts gave her on the head proved a little too hard. She kept breathing right through until we'd hogtied that last lunatic, and then she gave up the ghost on us. I wrap her meself, then add a Sign of the Cross and a "Requiescat in pace" in honor of her Catholicism. She's been with me crew since the very beginning, Barber has, cutting hair and throats since I took the Albatross as me own.

I pick her up, carrying her to the gunwale, and gently drop her over the edge. Weighted down as she be by a cannonball, Barber sinks into the dark water and be gone in a mere moment.

With a sigh, I paint over me sadness with a thick coat of stoicism and return me attention to me living crew. I look to Rumguts first. She be wriggling at her bonds and gnawing at her gag, but as I watch her, her struggles become less certain and that mad glint in her eye fades away. The transition takes a few minutes, but soon there be confusion rather than chaos in her look, and she be uttering something into her gag that I can't understand.

I remove the offending cloth in time to hear, "By the leprechaun's golden curlies, what the bloody hell just happened?!" I see the sanity return to others nearby, and soon there be a muffled chorus of moans and protests.

Your ship and crew have survived the vexatious curse of the Ineffable Arch.
This is a Legendary Achievement of the High Seas!
Your XP reward = 60,000 XP
Less 100 XP per crew casualty = 800 XP
As Captain of the Albatross, you receive a double share. Your personal XP reward = 1640 XP
Progress to Pirate Captain Level 9 = 46745/60000

"You don't remember anything?" I ask as I untie Rumguts' bonds.

I quietly be hoping that the answer be 'no', for I ain't sure Rumguts will cope with the knowledge that she murdered Barber. She was one of Rumguts' favorite drinking mates, although Barber generally knew when enough was enough, curbing the Irish soak away from drowning in booze on more than one occasion. Aye, if Rumguts don't remember, and there ain't no witnesses aside from meself, then I see no reason to drive me purveyor of calming brews over the edge. I need her too much.

There be a long pause as Rumguts sorts through her scattered memories. To me relief she comes up empty.

"Don't remember nothing since laying eyes on that ugly bloody archway."

"What about the rest of you what we tied up?" I ask me crewmates. "Big blank spot where your memories should be?"

There be unanimous consent, so I cast a warning glare about those what resisted the archway's corrupting notions.

"What be forgotten best stay that way!" I announce, hoping me Hero 3rd Class skill be enough to hammer the point home. "There were trouble, a bad dream that eight of us didn't wake up from. But it ain't the fault of no one here." I point at the archway. "Blame lies with that accursed lump of stone and malice. Nowhere else. Are we agreed on this?"

Seventy-one 'ayes' come back to me. The jury be of one mind and the plea of insanity be accepted.

I help Rumguts to her feet and order her to break out the rum rations to wash away the dregs of this here stressful encounter. And while me crew be lining up for their refreshment, I sit down beside Sandwich. Doc the Croc has wrapped a bandage around his head, but the lordling be looking clear-eyed and sharp. No sign of a concussion. Thank Bathala for that. This be one egghead I don't need scrambled right now.

"You remember anything?" I ask him.

He tenses with obvious guilt and leans a little closer to whisper in me ear. "I tried to blow up the ship."

"Seems you recall more than most," I whisper back. "Makes sense as you were more compos mentis than most. The rest went feral, resorting to tooth and claw. You behaved like you was possessed by a demon or something. Not that I believe in demons, but you know what I be saying, right?"

"I am afraid I do." He shrugs and there be a pleading cast to his eyes. "Perhaps it is because I have communed with He Who Slumbers?"

"You reckon his lot made that arch?"

Sandwich shakes his head. "In a manner of speaking. It was built by the Atlanteans, I think. Most likely to protect what lies beyond from the likes of us."

"Aye, maybe. What be your Sand score?"

"Fourteen."

"Making it eighteen with the Elder Sign bonus. Eighteen divided by the challenge score of forty equals fourty-six percent, give or take. Almost a coin toss."

"Yes," he agrees glumly. "One that came down Tails."

"Well, don't beat yourself up about it, Sandwich." I wink at him and tap him on the head. He winces, it still being rather tender. "Inkman be your best bet for that."

"If he had not come along when he did…"

I tap him on the head again. "Stop right there. I be giving the crew a clean slate. I offer you the same and I advise you to take it."

He manages a smile. Well, more like the ghost of a smile, but it be something. "Thank you, captain."

"You be welcome." I gesture at the Ineffable Arch. "Now tell me how to open that thing."

"Of course." He points to where the gates plunge into the waterline. "If I have understood my readings correctly, we simply sail on through with the Elder Sign aboard."

"What? No 'open sesame' or nothing like that?"

"Not that I am aware of."

"And on the other side? What should we expect?"

"The Emperor's Sanctum, if the accounts are correct."

"What about guardians and wards? The Dreamer, perhaps? The Dragon even? Or maybe something akin to that damned Bloodwyrm?"

"Your guess is as good as mine, captain."

"In that case," I say, slapping me hand down on his thigh as I stand up, "I be expecting the worst with a view to being pleasantly surprised."

And pleasantly surprised I be when them looming gates rumble aside to allow us safe passage. Even more so at there being no ghoulish broadside awaiting us, nor a great betentacled beastie ready to scoop us into its slavering maw.

We sail on through the perturbing portal with nary a concern, into the dark and tranquil waters beyond. Once again, the glowworms are kind enough to bathe us in their gentle illuminations, giving us a clear view of a truly beauteous vista. The temple stands alone on a rugged island in the center of an underground lagoon. The cavern that surrounds it be similar to the Bloodwyrm's lair, only much *much* larger. As for the holy structure itself, it be rich on the eye and it'll be even richer on the coffers once we get amongst it.

Whoever said "all that glitters ain't gold" was right. Diamonds be glittery too.

41

EMPEROR OF ATLANTIS

"TAKE US IN, JONESY," I say, "but keep us well clear of that thing."

I be pointing at the pier what be sticking out into the water from the foot of the temple. There be a mighty ship docked there already, the Emperor's Dragon I be assuming. I look to Sandwich for confirmation and he acknowledges me suspicions.

I use Squintlock's Peeper to scan the decks for ghouls and such but they look to be empty. The vessel be in such shoddy repair, so caked in cobwebs and dust, that it don't seem to have been out to sea in a full thousand years.

I order Powderfinger to be at the ready nonetheless, to blast that old tub if it be showing any signs of life. Or undeath, as the case may be.

"No sign of the Dreamer neither," I observe.

"We have been lucky on that front," Sandwich agrees. "Perhaps they are out patrolling the waters around the Murmurs?"

"Aye, perhaps." But I ain't buying it.

Inkman can see me doubts. "I'd have thought we put their dead noses out of joint enough to be of *some* concern to their rotten brains. If I were them, seeing we have the Elder Sign, I'd have stuck closer to home, guarded this here temple with the expectation that we'd be coming here sooner or later."

"That be me thinking too," I concur. "It don't feel right."

"Then where could she be?" asks Sandwich, a tremor of anxiety in his voice.

By way of answer, I get the attention of Rumguts down on the main deck. "Get up that crow's nest, Mary, and watch for the Dreamer."

Then to Jonesy I say, "Let's anchor a little offshore so we can present our starboard broadside to the Ineffable Arch. If the Dreamer be sailing in here after us, we'll be ready with a friendly six-gun salute."

"Aye, captain," answers Jonesy as she adjusts our course to suit.

As we get into position, I instruct the crew to drop our fore and aft anchors at particular intervals, letting them run out as we drift so we have plenty of slack. Once we're set, this will allow us to reel in or let out the anchor lines at four different angles, enabling us to pivot on the spot. This way the Albatross becomes an artillery battery what we can turn on a doubloon. We can track the Dreamer's course as she enters the cavern and keep plugging her with shot as she tries to get close. I noticed the ghast ship had shorter, heavier cannons than our long-nosed culverins. Means we'll get plenty of opportunities to punish her before she be in range to unleash her broadside.

Once we be settled into place, I leave a skeleton crew of twenty-two on the Albatross, under Jonesy's command, and with Powderfinger and his best gunners on board, to give the Dreamer hell should she decide to poke her nose into our business.

The remaining fifty of us take to the longboats and paddle for shore. We be bringing the two falconets with us again, and plenty of grapeshot and powder. Harpoons and ropes too. No telling what we might face in this here temple.

"Nobody touches nothing unless I say so," I order me motley lot as we land.

I see the fires of greed blazing in their eyes as they look upon this great stone edifice what be encrusted in diamonds. Even the normally calm and collected Inkman has a glint in his dark orbs. "And have your firearms at the ready. Ain't no way this treasure be sitting by its lonesome, just begging for the company of us buccaneers."

I take me own advice, unsling me Rumpus Musket, and lead me raiding party up to the yawning archway what seems to serve as the main entrance. As we approach, I cast me eyes over the ornate edifice, both watching for snipers and speculating how we might be gathering up all them gems. Once the temple be secured, me better climbers, with ropes, grappling hooks and pickaxes, could probably pluck the surface clean in two or three hours. It be a shame to vandalize such a pretty building, but it ain't like it be an accessible spot for public perusal. And I ain't never been one to believe in expensive art anyway. Stinking cities aside, the world be beautiful enough without slathering the place in gilt.

We stop just shy of the entrance because me Wits be telling me to be careful. "Inkman, you take ten musketeers and head right. See if you can find a side entrance or can climb in through one of them lower windows. Silverback, you take another ten and do the same out left. The rest of you, follow me."

Me crew does as they be told, and as I lead the way into the temple, I quietly hope me tactics will result in some sort of crossfire on whatever be awaiting us inside.

Sandwich be walking beside me, and for a moment I consider seeking his advice on what to expect. But then I remember Inkman's warning about listening to his stories. Assumptions could get us all killed. Best I just keep me Wits about me and react in kind to what I see with me own eyes.

As we pass through the entrance chamber and into the main

vault of worship, that be exactly what I do. I note the ornate throne and the figure what be sitting on it. His robes and regalia be splendid indeed considering they be over a thousand years old. The body within be neatly preserved, though he be chalky white and his prominent veins stand out like a tracery of black ink across his skin. He could be mistaken for a human were he not completely hairless, and that he be having gills in his neck what be moving ever so slightly, soft and steady, like he be breathing in his sleep. They must be strange gills indeed to be sucking in air rather than water, but then I ain't no expert in Atlantean anatomy.

It be difficult to say where the throne ends and the man begins. The throne itself be forged in the image of a Kraken. Its bulbous body forms the seat while petrified tentacles curl and twist together to make the back, arms and legs. More tentacles rise from the chair and plunge through the emperor, for that's who he must be. A dozen or more have stabbed through his limbs and torso. A thin one has even entered through his ear and then poked out through his eye. He be a sight both wondrous and ghastly.

But he ain't what I be chiefly concerned with at this juncture. Surrounding him be a company of thirty-one soldiers, their uniforms as clean and neat as the day they was donned. They be armored, too, with breastplates and helmets, not dissimilar to Spanish Conquistadors in style. With the Spanish Empire and Atlantis not being contemporaries in any way, I'd wager that the similarity either be coincidental or that some portion of the Atlantean fleet made their way to the Mediterranean. Europe's rise to power influenced by fishmen? Now *that* would be a turnup for the history books.

Each Atlantean soldier be standing to attention and presenting a musket what be tipped with a nasty looking bayonet. Their gills be moving too, flaring and shrinking. By some dint of Atlantean magic, they be alive... after a fashion.

They ain't noticed us yet. We mustn't have crossed whatever

threshold that they be willing to defend. I be almost tempted to leave and make do with the riches on the outside of the structure until Sandwich sidles up to me and puts his lips close to me ear.

"Captain, look. At the emperor's feet."

Sitting there on its own little pedestal be the biggest damned diamond I ever seen, and it be glowing from within, projecting a wan and unholy light upon the emperor and his guards.

Congratulations!

You and your landing party have discovered the location of the Star of Atlantis!

This is a truly mythological achievement!

Your XP reward = 100,000 XP

As Captain of the Albatross, you receive a double share.

Your personal XP reward = 4000 XP

Progress to Pirate Captain Level 9 = 50745/60000

I look to the balconies and walkways above us and notice another dozen Atlantean soldiers in sniping positions, six on each side. I quietly call the Russian sisters over and order them to catch up with Inkman and Silverback and warn them of the snipers. They'll need to take that higher ground if we're to win this battle.

I arrange me two falconet gun crews, four pirates apiece, flanking the entranceway. They be close enough together to top each other up with powder and shot, and well placed to send someone back to the ship for more supplies if it comes to that.

The remaining twenty, including meself, spread out to the left and right. We make the most of the various statues and altars as cover, but I ensure that none of us step any further into the chamber. All the time I be keeping one eye on the emperor and his guards, watching for movement. Still nothing. I ain't sure what's going to trigger them, whether it be proximity or when one of us fires a shot, but I want to be ready when this fracas kicks off.

Now we just have to wait for Silverback and Inkman to make their move on the balconies above. We don't have to wait long.

265

42

SHOOTING GALLERY

BLACK RUSSIAN ARRIVES BACK FIRST. "Silverback waits on your signal, captain."

White Russian be only moments behind. "Inkman be eager to begin the fray, captain."

I take a deep breath, let it out slowly in a vain attempt to steady me nerves, and then flash the sisters a false cavalier grin. "Aye, let's be having them then!"

Seeing as I have all the time in the world, I rest me Rumpus Musket on the outstretched arm of a statue and consider me shot real careful like. I could put a bullet between the eyes of the emperor, but by the way he be pinioned to that chair by them tentacles, it don't seem like he be something we need to worry about. To me it looks like he sacrificed himself in some weird Atlantean ritual.

Me chief concern be for what did he give his life exactly? Some magic to protect him and his treasures? Aye, no one be giving up their life for nothing, at least not where I be from. But I ain't going to find out his payoff by ruminating on suppositions. And since this emperor's given his life already, there ain't much point in me trying to take something that ain't no longer there.

I switch me aim to one of the soldiers, a proud-looking chap whose uniform be more decorated than the rest. Likely as not, he be the commanding officer of this here guard. Might as well remove the brains of the outfit.

I take a bead on his face, let me breath out slowly, and smoothly squeeze me trigger. The boom of me musket echoes through the vaulted chamber, shattering the sinister serenity like a rock through a stained glass window.

Me little lead ball finds its mark, puncturing the officer's brow and exiting with a spray of grey and black out the back of his skull. He drops like a ragdoll to the floor.

Critical Hit!
Your shot Damage = 600
You have killed a Level 9 Atlantean Colonel.
HP: -100/500

But I ain't congratulating meself just yet. Where be the experience points? Me silent query be answered in short order by the emperor himself. His eyelids flutter open to reveal eyes of the brightest blue I ever seen. Gleaming sapphire irises surrounded by pupils of the deepest jet. And them eyes be looking right at me.

The tentacles within his chair come to life. They raise the emperor to his feet like strings pulling a puppet up from the stage floor for the edification of some eager kiddies. They stretch out his arms and splay his fingers. Sparks crackle into life around them dead digits. I feel the air in the room electrify. Me hairs on me forearms raise like they too are little emperors on tentacle strings.

From his fingertips leap bolts of lightning. But he ain't aiming at us. The lightning arcs down to the fallen colonel. They course through his corpse, making him flap and dance like a freshly landed fish. Then, as the emperor closes his hands, cutting off the storm, the colonel gets to his feet, dusts off his uniform, and turns to his troops.

He opens his mouth and gurgles something in that foul Atlantean language of theirs. His troops respond instantly, forming firing ranks around the emperor to protect him, and presenting a formidable front while they be at it, I must say.

I catch movement out of the corner of me eye, up on the balconies, and soon after I hear the crack and thump of pistols and muskets as Inkman and Silverback's parties fire on the snipers. Some of them Atlanteans fall before reaching cover, but the emperor simply opens up those life-giving hands of his and shocks them back into active duty.

The goal be clear to me now, and I curse meself for not going with me first instinct, to plug that morbid monarch when I had the chance.

"Fire on the throne!" I roar at me gun crews and am rewarded by two thunderous reports.

Me falconets send grapeshot ploughing into the emperor's guards, but the colonel has already thought of that. He's made his defensive formation thickest in the middle, four men deep. Our grapeshot carves through the first two rows easy enough, peppers the third a bit, but don't even touch the fourth, nor even scratch the emperor himself. And in return, the whole of the remaining force, sixteen musketeers, fires a focused volley at me left-hand gun crew, cutting them down to a man.

Landing Party: 46/50

Poor bastards didn't stand a chance, and they ain't coming back neither, not like the fourteen Altantean musketeers what are right now being given the stormy kiss of life by their beloved bloody ruler.

Emperor's Elite Guard: 42/42

With an utterance what sounds like some morbid cross between a tortured dolphin and a man drowning in his blood, the colonel forms up his men again. Those fourteen what didn't fire before, on account of them being cannon fodder, level their muskets at me remaining gun crew. Me pirates be valiantly, and rather stupidly, trying to reload their cannon.

"Abandon your gun!" I yell at them. "Duck for cover, you daft blighters!"

Ratface be in charge of this crew. He be a wiry Welshman who we picked up in Australia. An escaped convict from one of the penal colonies there. Got done for sheep rustling, if memory serves. I imagine you have to be quick on your feet to be a stock thief, able to outrun the buckshot from a farmer's blunderbuss. Me theory holds with Ratface. He be clearly investing points in Quickness, for he ducks behind a sturdy stone altar four paces sooner than anyone else. A shame the other three ain't so nimble. The Atlantean volley makes them dance like drunken sailors before laying them down to bleed out on the floor.

Landing Party: 43/50

Meself and me neighboring pirates return fire. We knock down a fair few musketeers but the bastards get back up again while we be reloading. And in the meantime, the soldiers still standing be taking potshots at us. We keep our heads down, but one of them manages to put a bullet in Fiddler off to me left. Damned shame. It were nice to have some music onboard.

Landing Party: 42/50

This can't go on, so I rack me noggin for a solution as I look up to the balconies for inspiration. Inkman and Silverback be trading shots with the Atlantean snipers, but it be a fool's errand. Me pirates have the drop on the buggers in terms of cover and firing positions, but they be just wasting lead and powder. Every time a sniper goes down, the emperor just props him up again with his crackling damned fingers.

The sisters be flanking me so I wave them over. "We can give you some cover so you can go tell our mateys up top to charge them buggers rather than treat them as bloody target practice. Ready?"

The sisters nod in unison, so I shout the order to me party. "Reload and fire on me count mateys!" Then I count down from ten, giving them plenty of time to charge their pistols and muskets. Once I hit one, we all pop up and let loose at the musketeers while the sisters bolt for the entranceway.

Once again, we shoot down many a musketeer, but the rest of them make the most of our few seconds of exposure. Five of me pirates go down. For two of them, death be instant, lead shots passing straight through their skulls. The other three get clipped in the shoulder or arm and be needing immediate attention from Doc the Croc.

Landing Party: 40/50

"Stay down, reload, and wait for me command!" I shout.

While we be waiting on blessed help from above, I look to Mad Maggie who be hunkering down with Sandwich on me right. She's been making good use of her pistols, but it be her magic we could do with right now.

"Maggie!" I shout at her, "Got anything in your spellbook what can help? Can you stop that imperial bastard from resurrecting his cronies?"

Maggie's eyes roll back into her skull as she thinks fast and hard. It looks like she be peering into her own mind, but turns out it be too murky in there for her right now. Her eyes roll back to me and she shakes her head.

"Nothing what I can use directly against him, captain!"

Well, at least her bad news be mitigated in that moment by some good news from above. Sounds like the sisters have got me message across, for all of a sudden I hear hollering and bellowing as Inkman and Silverback lead their pirates against the snipers on them balconies. The din be punctuated by the popping of musket shots as the snipers' fire at their charging foes. Accurate bastards they be too.

Landing Party: 36/50

Could've been worse though. Inkman and Silverback have had the sense to push forward when some of the snipers have been reloading. Had they got that wrong, we'd likely be looking at a full dozen casualties.

Soon the sky be raining soldiers as me pirates disarm the snipers and heave them off the balconies. The Atlanteans make a satisfying crunch when they hit the floor, but even broken bones seem fixable by their benevolent monarch. Crackle, crackle and up they hop.

The colonel calls them in and forms them up as a fleshy shield around the emperor. Some of them even clamber up onto the throne so they can shield him from me pirates what can now shoot down at him from above.

And that's when I notice something interesting about the colonel's formation. He be leaving the back of the throne unmanned, perhaps figuring that the sturdy piece of furniture be protection enough for his posterior. Being made of them thick tentacles, it be impossible to shoot through. But as I've seen already, shooting ain't proving so helpful.

We need to shake things up and I think I might have an idea of how to do that.

43

SHARING A KEG

"Maggie!" I bark through the cacophony of gunfire. "Get over here!"

The witch launches herself across the gap between her cover and mine. Wishing she'd at least picked a lull in the shooting, I grit me teeth, half expecting her to arrive at me side with a hole in her mad bloody head.

While a couple of shots do whizz by dangerously close, Maggie makes it unscathed and presents me with that wild grin of hers. "You be wanting me to raise some zombies, captain?"

I grimace at the thought. Turning mateys into meat puppets be a sure way to scuttle me crew's morale and bring on a mutiny. "Nay, Maggie."

Her disappointment be palpable. "Then what you have in mind?"

"That magical shield you had back in the Maw. Can you walk about while you've got it up?"

"Aye, captain. I can even run if I want to."

"What be the area of effect on that thing?"

"Five-meter diameter."

"And how much punishment can it take?"

"Thirteen hundred and thirteen health points."

"Why that number?" I wonder.

"Because thirteen be me lucky number."

I raise me eyebrow but know better than to question Maggie's logic. There ain't none.

Judging by how me pirates be getting knocked down by them things, the Atlantean muskets seem to be doing 100 Damage per hit. 300 on a critical, which them musketeers seem to be nailing disturbingly often.

To punctuate me mental point, I hear a cry from above and see one of Silverback's lot topple over the edge of the balcony.

Landing Party: 35/50

"Right then, Maggie. Get that shadowy aura of yours around us."

"Aye, captain."

As she mutters the appropriate Voodoo words, I look over at Sandwich who be firing his pistol at the Atlanteans for the umpteenth time. He ain't hit nothing vital the whole time we been trading shots with them buggers. Must be a Pistoleer 3rd Class at the very best. Time to put him to better use.

"Sandwich! Get your ass over here."

Spotting Ratface nearby, I wave him over too. The two gents join us just as Maggie's shadowy shield swims into place. Sandwich don't seem perturbed by it, but Ratface's skinny moosh goes a shade paler.

"Calm yourself, sailor," I assure him. "The shadow be protecting us. Your soul be safe, for today at least."

He relaxes a little and manages a crook-toothed smile. "What be the plan, captain?"

"Follow me and do as I tell you. Good enough?"

"Aye, works for me."

I cup me hands about me mouth and holler up at the balconies as loud as I can. "Shoot at the colonel, you blighters! Keep him dancing!"

Inkman gives me the thumbs up, but Silverback ain't so quick on the uptake.

"Which one be the colonel?" he yells back, almost getting his sluggish head blown off for his troubles. The shot in question ricochets off the balcony rail a scant few centimeters from his face.

"The fancy one, you lughead!"

Realization dawns and he too gives me the thumbs up. I sigh and wonder if I should recruit meself a school teacher for future voyages. Me crew got plenty of Sand, but Wits are in short supply.

I wait a few moments to see if me instructions have the desired effect, and sure enough, the colonel goes down with a trio of shots in his chest. Crackle, pop, he be back up again in time to take a couple of bullets to the gut. Aye, he'll be too busy dying and undying to notice what we be up to, and his musketeers seem only smart enough to follow orders. I ain't seen none of them take any sort of initiative yet.

"Stay close," I tell me three companions.

I run for the archway, making a beeline for one of the powder kegs what we brought with the falconets. Reacting to the movement, a couple of musketeers make us their mark and Maggie's shield ripples as it absorbs the impacts of their shots.

Mad Maggie's Shadow Shield has taken 200 Damage.
HP remaining = 1113

"Nab that keg, Ratface!"

The sailor does as he be told, and then we be off to the second powder keg on the other side of the archway. We take another shot for our efforts too.

Mad Maggie's Shadow Shield has taken 100 Damage.
HP remaining = 1013

Sandwich scoops that one up and we all duck for cover behind a statue of three naked Atlantean ladies doing some sort of cancan dance.

I lead off again, skirting the edge of the chamber, hurrying us from cover to cover, doing me best to time our dashes so we don't take too much punishment. Can't be avoiding it all though. They ain't the sharpest bayonets in the armory, these Atlantean musketeers. Brains have probably atrophied after a thousand years of guard duty. But they still be pretty good at reacting to movement.

Mad Maggie's Shadow Shield has taken 300 Damage.
HP remaining = 713

Me pirates be finding that out the hard way too. Above us, a couple of Inkman's lot try to break from cover to get cleaner shots at the colonel. Instead, they both get facefuls of lead.

Landing Party: 33/50

And so it goes on until we've circled behind the throne and managed ourselves a bit of respite from the barrage. Much needed too, for Maggie's shield be on its last metaphorical legs.

Mad Maggie's Shadow Shield has taken 500 Damage.
HP remaining = 213

We catch our breath while I fill me mateys in on the last stage of me dastardly design.

"Now's the tricky bit, lads and lady. We sneak up to the back of that throne, plonk one of them kegs down and create a powder trail with the other one, leading back over here."

Ratface grins as he takes a flint and tinder out of his jacket. "Then emperor fishface goes kaboom, right?"

"Right you are, Ratface. So let's be having him."

We creep up on the throne, real stealthy like, and almost make it to the back before one of them musketeers sees us out of the corner of his dead blue eyes. He turns, raises his musket and… boom.

Critical Hit!
Mad Maggie's Shadow Shield has taken 300 Damage.
HP remaining = -87

Our protective shield vanishes in a puff of smoke and Maggie be knocked to the floor by the aftermath. She screeches with pain as her hand goes to her side. There be blood on her palm when it comes away. Looks like she's taken the remaining 87 Damage points right in the breadbasket.

I take careful aim while the musketeer be reloading, and put me shot through one of his sapphire blues.

Critical Hit!
Your shot Damage = 600
Level 6 Atlantean Musketeer
HP: -300/300
You have killed a Level 6 Atlantean Musketeer.

"Hop to it, lads!" I hiss at Sandwich and Ratface as I draw me mundane pistols and cover Maggie.

To their credit, they be frosty under pressure, these two. Sandwich uncorks his keg and makes a pile of powder before placing the barrel next to it, snug against the back legs of the throne.

Ratface starts his powder trail at Sandwich's pile and then backs towards us, laying out his makeshift fuse as he goes.

"Behind me, Maggie," I order as the Atlantean musketeer I just killed gets back to his feet.

He be joined by a colleague what has noticed our retreat. At this close range, it ain't much trouble to send me twin shots through their skulls.

Critical Hits!
Your shot Damage total = 600
Two Level 6 Atlantean Musketeers
HP: -0/300
HP: -0/300
You have killed two Level 6 Atlantean Musketeers.

Aye, and if only they'd be staying dead!

Sandwich draws his pistol and clips a third musketeer what's noticed us. It ain't enough to drop the bugger, but at least it throws his shot off.

I distract our three assailants a little longer with a blast from Stormshot, but now it be me own time to reload, and in that time we have ourselves a fourth musketeer to contend with. A bloody D'artagnan to them Porthos, Aramis and Athos bastards.

Ain't nothing I can do as he lines up Ratface and plugs him right in the throat. Poor bugger goes down, thrashing and gurgling, and his keg tumbles to the floor.

Landing Party: 32/50

I be grateful for Sandwich's high Wits score, as he be reacting straight away, grabbing up that keg and carrying on where Ratface left off.

With me Hasty Hands skill on the go, I beat D'artagnan to the reload and fry him good with Stormshot. I nab Ratface's lighter from his twitching cadaver and hustle us along so we reach cover just as the other three musketeers raise their guns and let loose. Lead balls careen off the stone plinth we be cowering behind.

I take the near empty keg from Sandwich and roll it towards the throne before ducking back under cover. Then it be out with the flint and tinder.

"Reckon they be paying their passages to hell?" I ask me mateys.

"Many times over," answers Maggie. "Send them packing, captain."

"Don't mind if I do, Maggie."

I strike a spark. It catches and the resulting fizz of fire streaks across the floor and into the bunghole of Sandwich's powder keg mere moments later. The resulting thunder be a welcome herald to the rain of gore that pours down upon us.

44

SANDY SOVEREIGN

WE COVER our heads and huddle together, sheltering from the deluge of wood, metal and bits of imperial highness. I peek through me fingers in time to see another of me pirates tumble off the balcony, a nasty length of shrapnel embedded in his chest.

Landing Party: 31/50

It be a damned shame, and one I feel a wee bit responsible for, but me guilt be alleviated a little by the casualty report for the Atlantean musketeers.

Your explosives team has killed eight Level 6 Atlantean musketeers!
Your XP reward per team member = 1600 XP
Progress to Pirate Captain Level 9 = 52345/60000

Your explosives team has destroyed the Level 30 Undying Emperor of Atlantis!
Your XP reward per team member = 1000 XP
Progress to Pirate Captain Level 9 = 53345/60000

Emperor's Elite Guard: 34/42

Beside us, Maggie groans, and it ain't with joy. She be pressing her hands to the wound in her gut and the blood be bubbling out between her fingers. I need to get her to Doc the Croc, quicksmart.

"Sandwich!"

He don't respond. His big blue eyes be glued to the Star of Atlantis and his lips be trembling weirdly like he be about to cry.

"Oi!" I grip his forearm and squeeze hard to get his attention. "We've got to get Maggie to the doc. She be bleeding out on us."

He looks at me but there be little recognition in his eyes. "The Star." He points at the jewel what now be lying a few meters from the throne, nestled into the remains of a musketeer. "We have broken it!"

I ain't got time for this. More to the point, Maggie ain't got time for this. But the witch be too heavy for me to haul by meself, and right now Doc the Croc be pinned down by enemy fire. He ain't in no position to make a house call. Still, looks like the only way to get Sandwich moving be to allay his fears, so I take out Squintlock's Peeper and hone in on the Star.

Sure enough, the diamond be showing a nasty crack along its flank. Damn thing must've had a flaw in it, one which we've aggravated with our fireworks display. Still, it be in one piece and it ain't given up the unholy glowing it seems wont to do. Bodes well for the magic it holds inside.

And, of course, there be another reason why I ain't panicking about the Star of Atlantis.

"If it were damaged beyond use," I tell Sandwich, "them otherwords would've told us. We'd have failed the quest." I stow me Peeper with one hand while patting him on the cheek with the other. "So secure that whimpering, sailor, and help me get our witch some medical attention before the poor lass gives up her ghost to Baron Samedi."

He blinks the fog of distress from his eyes and then has the good grace to look embarrassed at his momentary conniption. "Sorr-"

I turn me pat into a slap. "Save that bilge too. Come on!"

For the barest moment, a shadow passes across his eyes. He rubs his cheek then helps me haul Maggie to her feet. To the blazing of muskets and pistols, we carry the witch from cover to cover. Though we've removed that damned emperor from the picture, me party still be hard-pressed to put down the remaining musketeers.

Emperor's Elite Guard: 31/42

Landing Party: 29/50

No longer needing to protect their monarch, the Atlanteans have spread out and taken cover, determined to keep us from fetching the Star. Aye, having taken the balconies, we now have the best firing positions, but them musketeers be proving brutally accurate. I need to get in there and help me ladies and lads before I be losing me whole damned landing party.

As we make the final dash to Croc's hiding place, Sandwich's right thigh takes a bullet and he goes down with a cry of pain. By Poseidon's barnacled posterior, it be taking all me Brawn and Sand to drag *both* of them the rest of the way, but by Bathala I do it.

Croc offers me a cold smile as I dump me patients at his feet. "Nurse Deadeye to the rescue, eh?"

"Aye, and you'll be nursing a cracked jaw if you don't save these two buggers."

He shrugs. Even in the heat of battle, Croc still be his implacable self. Makes me wonder what happened to him, what nasty business in his childhood made him lock up his emotions and throw away the key.

"I'll do me best, captain."

I nod me thanks and then do a Daring Dash out through the

archway. I hurtle around the outside of the temple, find the steps what Inkman and his lot used to ascend to the balcony, and take them two at a time until I be skidding to a halt at me quartermaster's side.

"What kept you?" he asks me with a tattooed smirk.

"Island time," I answer as I set to reloading me guns.

The pickings be much finer from up here, so I set about evening the odds. One Rumpus shot, a Stormshot, and a twin blast from me mundanes later, and we have three less musketeers to worry about.

You have gunned down three Level 6 Atlantean musketeers!
Your XP reward = 1800 XP
Progress to Pirate Captain Level 9 = 55145/60000

In that time we lose another of our lot. Big Nanuk proves to be too generous a target as he lumbers from one bit of cover to the next. Down he goes with half a dozen holes in his chest and ample belly. But me fellow pirates do in a few more musketeers in vengeance, with Silverback across the way proving himself to be a damned fine marksman, popping the head off an Atlantean the moment he be peeking over one of them altars.

Emperor's Elite Guard: 24/42

Landing Party: 28/50

"We've got their backs to the wall now, mateys!" I holler across the chamber, triggering Rallying Cry to give me words a little extra oomph.

I get a ragged cheer in response and next thing four more Atlanteans have met their maker.

Emperor's Elite Guard: 20/42

Alas, me Rallying Cry goes to the head of one poor lass, a Punjabi girl we call Banshee on account of her singing voice. She feels compelled to charge the enemy with her saber. To her credit, she manages to impale one musketeer and take the head off a second before she gets drilled right in her screaming mouth.

Emperor's Elite Guard: 18/42

Landing Party: 27/50

Fortunately, the rest of me raiders keep their heads where they belong, behind cover.

To drive a nail into the Atlantean coffin, I focus me fire on the colonel, softening him up with Stormshot and me two pistols before putting a Rumpus shot through his black heart.

You have killed a Level 9 Atlantean Colonel.
Your XP reward = 900 XP
Progress to Pirate Captain Level 9 = 56045/60000

With their leader gone, the stuffing goes out of the remaining musketeers, and me landing party don't have too much trouble mopping them up, especially when four of me pirates, led by Dingo, have the good sense to bring one of our falconets back into play. Grapeshot sure can clear a room in a hurry.

Congratulations!
You have secured the Emperor's Sanctum!
This is a Legendary Achievement of the High Seas!
Clearing the Sanctum = 100,000 XP
Securing the Star of Atlantis = 200,000 XP
Less 100 XP per party casualty = 2300 XP
Total to be divided between surviving party members = 297700 XP
As Captain of the Albatross, you receive a double share
Your personal XP reward = 22050 XP
Progress to Pirate Captain Level 9 = 78095/60000

You be a sandy sovereign of the seven seas on a true course to
international infamy!
A Level 9 Pirate Captain!
You receive nine points to apply to your core attributes.
You receive two free skill upgrades.

I join me crewmates in the resounding jubilation, dancing me a
jig with a bemused Inkman. Then I be scuttling down them steps,
charging into the chamber, and scooping up that Star in me sticky
mitts.

The power of the thing washes away me post-battle aches and
pains, bathing me in what I can only describe as a victory. Aye, it be
a fine feeling indeed.

45

OPEN FIRE

WE HAVE ourselves a somber ceremony and sink our dead before spending the rest of the day plundering the temple and hauling our booty onto the Albatross. All fifty-five of me skulls be grinning ear to ear as they work, extracting gold and chipping away at diamonds and other precious gems on the outer structure. Despite everything we've been through, all the pain we've suffered and the friends we've lost, our morale score pretty much says it all.

Morale = 100%

Aye, nothing like making a pirate ridiculously rich to make her as happy as a babe at a boob.

Meanwhile, meself and Sandwich go fossicking through the guts and gore of the Emperor's throne room. Sandwich finds the colonel's rapier, a magically forged Atlantean blade with a rather macabre yet fetching hilt guard. It be a silver octopus what be draping its tentacles as protection over the wielder's hand. For me part, I find an emerald broach what be pinned to a ragged slab of

285

imperial chest. I extricate the jewelry, wash it in the brine outside, and pin it at me throat.

Since I too be ridiculously rich, the time seems ripe to be smartening up this salty sailor lass. Of course, the broach ain't just a useless piece of fancy neither.

Emerald of Longevity
Health Points are increased by 20%

Captain Grace "Deadeye" Cortez
HP: 270 (324)

Since there be no way of telling night from the day inside this cavern, we just keep going until we run out of wind. We manage to recover everything of value from the temple exterior. That just leaves the decorations in the throne room itself, something we should be able to polish off in the course of a morning.

I order Rumguts to break out the grog and we soon be wiling away the evening in the drunken recollection of everyone's most daring and daft moments during the battle. When it comes time to retire for the night, I grab Sandwich by the hand and lead him into me cabin for a bit of after-quest stress relief.

The poor lad be so tuckered out once we be done, he passes out as soon as his head touches the pillow. And I be receiving an extra boost to me sexual after-glow.

Congratulations!
You have gained the skill of Lover: 3rd Class.

Interesting. Seems that when I be paying for it, I ain't getting no leveling done. But when the loving be free, it also be educational. Unless, of course, I actually paid for some strumpet lads to teach me a thing or two what I could practise with them. But that would be cutting into me 'me' time. Ah well, better to have 3rd Class love than no love at all, I say. Which gets me to thinking about me Character, even though sleep be gently dragging at me eyelids.

Turning me mind to other recent incidents, I recall how touch and go it were with the Ineffable Arch. I ain't never before encountered magic what can drive a girl batty, but it seems wise to be preparing for such eventualities in Atlantis, so I drop three of me nine attribute points into Sand.

And since I don't want to be lagging behind the likes of Sandwich in the brains department, I drop another three points into Wits, and round meself out with three points of Quickness. After all, while me shooting be mighty handy, it be me ability to think on me feet what's saved our hides more often than not.

Then there be the question of me two skill points. Me naked Sandwich shifts in his sleep beside me. I be sorely tempted to bestow upon meself the title of Lover 1st Class. But when I think harder about it, that be a skill I don't mind leveling up the natural way. Practice makes perfect, after all.

So I turn me thoughts to more captainly matters, especially the fact that I be losing so many of me pirates in these violent ventures of ours. Hoping it might give me a nice crew-based special skill, I slide a point into Hero.

Hero 2nd Class
Advanced Skill
Maintains all the abilities of a Hero 3rd Class while adding another +2 to Wit and +2 to Sand, increasing the ship-at-hand's Speed and Agility by another 30, and giving your crew a bonus of +2 to their Sand scores.

Please note that you cannot attain Hero 1st Class with a skill upgrade. Hero 1st Class can only be attained via an act of true heroism.

Act of true heroism, eh? A tall order for a pirate, but I satisfy meself with me tasty new skill.

At 2nd Class, Hero unlocks the Special Skill of Touched by Fate, the ability to shrug off Damage and look like a demi-god while doing it. The Hero is surrounded by a glowing aura which can absorb up to 2000 points of Damage.
The aura will dissolve after 3 seconds.

A shame that it be short-lived, but I quietly can't wait to impress me crew by stopping a cannonball with me glowing behind.

I mull over me other skills for a good while before I settle on turning Athlete 1st Class into Kinesthete 3rd Class.

Kinesthete: 3rd Class
Advanced Skill
Maintains all the abilities of an Athlete 1st Class while adding +2 to Brawn and +2 to Stamina, and noticeably improving the Kinesthete's coordination and athleticism.

At 3rd Class, Kinesthete unlocks the Special Skill of Leap of Faith, the ability to make a horizontal jump of 10 meters after a run-up of at least 12 strides, and to land safely with weapons drawn, if required.

Aye, that could come in mighty handy, I reckon. Specially when it comes to boarding enemy ships. I could be first over, secure the helm before me crew invades the main deck. In fact, if I managed to capture the enemy captain, I could force a surrender and save a lot of lives. I stow that strategy away for the future and take one last look at me Character.

Grace "Deadeye" Cortez

Level 9 Pirate Captain

Progress to Pirate Captain Level 10 = 78095/100000

Core Attributes:

Perception: 20 (30)

+2 Sharpshooter: 3rd Class

+2 Gunslinger: 3rd Class

+1 Pistoleer: 1st Class

+1 Musketeer: 1st Class

+2 Squintlock's Peeper

+2 Stormshot

Quickness: 16 (24)

+2 Sharpshooter: 3rd Class

+2 Gunslinger: 3rd Class

+1 Pistoleer: 1st Class

+1 Musketeer: 1st Class

+1 Fencer: 1st Class

+1 Rumpus Musket

Wit: 19 (27)

+4 Hero: 2nd Class

+1 Leader: 1st Class

+2 Shellback: 3rd Class

+1 Navigator: 1st Class

Sand: 18 (28)

+1 Free Diver: 1st Class

+4 Hero: 2nd Class

+1 Leader: 1st Class

+2 Shellback: 3rd Class

+1 Navigator: 1st Class

+1 Seahawk Saber

Brawn: 12 (17)

+2 Kinesthete: 3rd Class

+1 Athlete: 1st Class

+1 Fencer: 1st Class

+1 Coat of the Salt

Stamina: 14 (20)

+1 Free Diver: 1st Class

+2 Kinesthete: 3rd Class

+1 Athlete: 1st Class

+1 Coat of the Salt

+1 Seahawk Saber

Health Points: 340/340 (408/408)

HP = Brawn x Stamina

+20% Emerald of Longevity

Advanced Core Skills

2nd Class

Hero

3rd Class
Sharpshooter
Gunslinger
Shellback
Kinesthete

Base Core Skills
1st Class
Musketeer
Pistoleer
Leader
Free Diver
Athlete
Fencer
Navigator

2nd Class
Merchant
Chess Player
Angler

3rd Class
Lover

Special Skills
Flashfire (Required: Musketeer 1st Class)
Anticipation (Required: Sharpshooter 3rd Class)
Hasty Hands (Required: Pistoleer 1st Class)
Quickdraw (Required: Gunslinger 3rd Class)
Stirring Words (Required: Leader 1st Class)
Rallying Cry (Required: Hero 3rd Class)
Lungfish (Required: Free Diver 1st Class)
Daring Dash (Required: Athlete 1st Class)
Reaver Rage (Required: Fencer 1st Class)
Sailsnap (Required: Shellback 3rd Class)
Read the Brine (Required: Navigator 1st Class)
Touched by Fate (Required: Hero 2nd Class)
Leap of Faith (Required: Kinesthete 3rd Class)

Kit
Squintlock's Peeper (+2 Perception)
Rumpus Musket (+1 Quickness, -2 Reload)
Coat of the Salt (+1 Brawn, +1 Stamina)
Stormshot Pistol (+2 Perception)
Seahawk Saber (+1 Sand, +1Stamina)

I close me eyes, feeling warm and snug beside Sandwich even though we be in the middle of the Murmurs with Bathala-knows-what horror to greet us on the morrow. I feel meself drift off to sleep, and damned if it only seems like five minutes later that I be rudely awakened by hollering and thumping at me cabin door.

"Whaddissit?!" I manage to growl.

Me waking ears make out Rumguts' voice, though it takes a few sluggish moments for me brain to make sense of the words.

"A sail?" Then me brain be clear as day and me skin be prickled with a cold sweat. "A sail?!"

"Aye, captain! May I enter?"

I pull me sheets up to me neck, exposing Sandwich's naked and still-sleeping form beside me. "Nay, you may bloody not!" I scramble to get me clothes on. "Be it the Dreamer?"

"Nay, it be the Narwhal! She be passing under the archway and her gunports be open. And there be more besides."

"What bloody more besides?"

"There be a longboat missing, two sentries missing too. Judging by the blood pools, I wouldn't fancy their chances, not with Mad Maggie being nowhere to be found."

Crew: 54

Me intestines play skip rope with themselves at that sincerely dire news. It be meaning only one thing. Betrayal. The injured witch has back-stabbed two of me crew and turned them into zombies so she could row off back to the sodding Narwhal.

"Tell Powderfinger to ready the cannons!"

"He already has, captain! He be waiting on your orders."

"Then me orders be, open fire!"

46

PLUNDERING PIRATES

I EMERGE FROM ME CABIN, dressed and ready for battle, just as Powderfinger's broadside sets the Albatross abuzz with activity. All around me, pirates be loading muskets, scooping up sabers and cutlasses. A well-salted crew getting themselves ready to prepare borders.

That said, I see me surprise at the Narwhal's attack reflected on me crewmates' faces, plain as day, but we ain't got time for feelings like hurt and disappointment. We've some plundering pirates to be thwarting. Ain't nothing worse than having your plunder plundered.

"Musketeers to your posts and everyone else take cover," I bellow at them. "Make no mistake. Shogun and his scurvy scum have their lecherous peepers fixed on our booty!"

I climb the steps to me quarterdeck and unsling Squintlock's Peeper so I can take a gander at the Narwhal's gizzards.

The Narwhal
Hull Defense: 66/150 (216/300)
+50 Hull Defense from Tungsten Scantlings
+100 Hull Defense and +50% Resistance to Fire from Dunkle Plating

Powderfinger be getting his eye in already. 84 Damage, meaning two hits from the Thunder Gods and two hits from the Mastiffs. But it be little more than a slap to a sea lion so far.

Seems Shogun be a cunning bastard. He must've gone shopping straight after we did, picking up the rest of that plating from the Frenchman before setting out in pursuit of us. And considering the price of that armor, I've no doubt that Medici be financing this underhanded expedition. As I rove me Peeper across the Narwhal's deck, I see the old Italian prune up on Shogun's quarterdeck, flanked by Mad Maggie and the slimy samurai himself.

Sail Defense: 60/60 (85/85)
+25 for Refurbished Sails of the Salamander
+25% Fire Resistance

He's even bought and patched up me old sails. The bald bloody nerve of the scoundrel!

Guns: 24
20 Screaming Demon Sakers
Base Damage per Gun: 20
4 Screaming Demon Falconets
Base Damage per Gun: 10

Not as powerful as our Thunder Gods, but what Shogun be lacking in quality, he be making up for in quantity. A ten cannon broadside ain't nothing to sneeze at, and as I watch the Narwhal come about, I know we be about to hear them demons scream.

"Heads down, mateys!" I yell, getting me point across a fraction before the Narwhal roars its retort.

We all be showered in splinters as the Narwhal's cannonballs pound into us. Three of me crew go down screaming, their bodies impaled by jagged shards of timber.

Crew: 51/80

We be lucky that Shogun's got a 2nd Class Gunner or worse in charge of his gun crews. Four hits out of ten ain't exactly crack shooting. Especially when we be a sitting target.

The Albatross
Hull Defense: 170/250

Though Shogun be trying to come in erratic-like to make him hard to aim at, I be cutting through that malarky, study his bow wave and wake with me Read the Brine skill so I can predict his course changes. I tell me sailors on the anchor lines which leads to shorten and which to give some slack and feel the Albatross turn gently in the water to the whine of running ropes. From the gun deck, Powderfinger be noting me maneuvering and it ain't long before he acknowledges our dance with thunderous applause.

The Narwhal
Hull Defense: 114/300

Three hits from the Thunder Gods, two from the Mastiffs. That keen-eyed Russian be finding his rhythm now.

The bugger of it be, we don't have to wait long for an answer, neither. Shogun be trying to make up for lack of accuracy with speed of firing. It be a risky call, but might just work if he gets lucky.

Once again we cower behind our gunwales as splinters rain down on us. A bit of blood in that shower too. One of Shogun's shots passes straight across the main deck, catching Borscht along the way. Ain't much left of him to mourn.

Crew: 50/80

The Albatross
Hull Defense: 70/250

Five out of ten this time. Me beleaguered boat can't take another hit like that.

"Why ain't most of them off their nuts and at each other's throats right now?!" This be from Jonesy. She be sheltering by the wheelbase and, aside from a few scratches, she's managed to avoid the shrapnel so far. Good thing too. I be needing her piloting skills in a moment.

"Because the gates are open, I reckon. Now get your hands on that wheel, Jonesy, and be ready to hold a steady course for us."

"Aye, captain!"

Then I peek me face over the quarterdeck railing and direct me anchor crew to cut the lines with boarding axes. They hesitate for a moment, wondering what I be about, but one look at me determined face gets them chopping away at them ropes. Then I address the rest of me crew, giving them fair warning of what's to come.

"Hold on tight, ladies and lads!" I call out across me ship. "Brace yourselves for a gust!"

I hold on tight to the railing, look up at me newly purchased Sails of the Cyclone, note the shimmer of a full charge in the tungsten threads. But I ain't the Sailmaster.

"North!" I yell down to the main deck. "A stiff breeze, if you please!"

She catches me drift, cups her hands to her mouth and shouts "Howling Wind!" to her beloved cloth.

The sails billow as our stored wind be released in one mighty exhale. The Albatross lurches forward, accelerating from zero to fifty Speed in a mere second or two. The Narwhal fires its broadside but their aim be where we no longer be. Their cannonballs crash into the temple, smashing through its pretty lines.

As we cut across the Narwhal's bow, the boards beneath our

boots tremble with the report of six cannons, fired in perfect unison. I feel a surge of pride at the sound. I've chosen me Chief Gunner well.

I look to the Narwhal, and me pride turns into a deluge of elation as I see six neat holes appear just above our enemy's waterline, three each side of their bowsprit. Six out of six, and the result be celebrated with fireworks.

The Narwhal's powder stores explode as one, blowing the ship's pointy nose right off. The subsequent explosions go off amidships as the flames ignite the powder barrels along the gun deck. Shards of timber and pirate go flying into the air across two-thirds of Shogun's doomed boat. Only the aft castle be spared the combustion, but soon enough it be bathed in flames. And if I listen close enough, peeling back the roar of the fire, I reckon I hear a pleasant trio of screams as three treacherous bastards be cooked alive in their just deserts.

A cheer sweeps across me Albatross as the last flaming bit of the Narwhal sinks below the waves and the otherwords confirm our triumph.

The Albatross has destroyed the Narwhal, a pirate brigantine under the command of Shogun, a Level 7 Pirate Captain.

The XP reward = 75,000 XP

Less 500 XP per crew casualty = 3000 XP

Total to be divided between surviving crew members = 72,000 XP

As Captain of the Albatross, you receive a double share. Your personal XP reward = 2880 XP

Progress to Pirate Captain Level 10 = 80975/90000

I run down the quarterdeck steps, almost bowling a disheveled Sandwich over as he emerges from me cabin, and hug Powderfinger as he emerges from the trapdoor in the gundeck. The lanky Russian looks a little bemused to be receiving such affection from his captain and returns me an awkward pat on the back. I don't care a jot, giving him a final squeeze before letting go to turn me attention to matters of a rather less salutary nature.

A stooped and weeping Jonesy makes her way down the quarterdeck steps, her hand on the bannister, the only thing keeping her steady. I cross the boards to her and wrap her in a hug. She buries her face in me shoulder and tries to offer me a muffled apology.

"No, it be me that should be sorry, Jonesy. It were me own idea to recruit Maggie and me own fault for not seeing that Shogun and Maggie were playing us from the start."

"I should've-"

"Stow that, Jonesy. I be the captain. It be me job to sniff out treachery, and seems I've been remiss in me duties. First Shaka and now Maggie. I be starting to wonder what this Hero skill of mine be good for."

Jonesy lifts her head and steps back a pace to look me full in the face. Though there still be tears streaming down her cheeks, the brave lass forces a smile for me.

"Heroes lead by example, captain. You be trusting in us so we be trusting in each other. Ain't your fault that some folks don't believe in heroes."

"Warms me heart to hear you say that, Jonesy. Thank you."

"You be welcome, captain." She wipes her eyes with the back of her hand and her smile fades away. "Now will you be wanting me to beach the ship, captain?"

"And why would we be doing that?"

Me fair navigator blinks with surprise. "We're holed pretty bad. We can't sail more than three or four leagues before we sink. We need to drag the Albatross ashore to make repairs. We've got enough timber aboard to make her seaworthy, and a few weeks of food and water if we ration-"

"Hold your seahorses there!" I laugh. Then I take the Star of

Atlantis from the pouch on me belt and look to me expert in such things. "Sandwich! Limp your way over here. I've no idea how to use this bloody thing, so we be needing that Atlantean learning of yours."

And limp Sandwich does. There be a bandage around his thigh, care of Croc. We had to be a bit careful of that leg last night. It looks to be healing fast, but by the way he be wincing as he hobbles across the deck, the flesh ain't quite knitted yet. Or he be playing for me sympathies, hoping I be nursing him in me bunk no doubt. By Bathala's booty, I might even be tempted again if he gets us out of this here predicament.

I plonk the Star in his cupped hands. "Get us to Freeport, if you please. No more than a league out, eh?"

"Of course, right away," he answers, his voice barely a whisper, his eyes locked onto the glowing gem.

We follow him as he walks up the stairs to the quarterdeck and goes straight to the helm. He takes the gem and presses it to the center of the wheel. It flashes brightly for a moment, forcing Jonesy and me to shield our eyes, and once we've blinked away them light spots, we both exchange a startled glance. The Star of Atlantis be melted right into the wood.

Without looking at us, Sandwich places both hands on the wheel, and out of his pretty mouth comes just one word.

"R'lyeh."

In a flash, we be gone.

When we reappear, it be pretty damned clear that we ain't in Freeport.

47

THE DROWNING DARK

It be hard to say if we be *anywhere* one might consider 'earthly' or 'real' or even goddamned understandable!

The sky be the sea, just for starters. An inky depth where the weird and the unknowable breeds and multiplies, their sickly lights gleaming through the liquid pitch, offering mere glimpses of nightmares as they swim and hunt in that swallowing sea.

Around us be a sea more like the sky, so thick with low-lying fog that it feels like we be sailing among the clouds. From the mists jut looming structures of impossible architecture, splashes of grey and black obscenity across an already grim canvas.

And speaking of obscenities, there be the Dreamer, sitting alongside us, its gangplank lowering onto our gunwale, its crew motionless and staring with them long-dead eyes. I recognize the Gale Lich, and beside him be the Dreamer's captain, a tall and gaunt figure resplendent in a rotting uniform and tattered tri-quarter hat.

I hear a quiet curse to me right, and catch the movement of a musket being raised. A young Samoan lad we call Mako, fixing to take a potshot at the captain while he just be standing there gawping at us. Before I can stop him a shot rings out and Mako drops to the deck like a stone, his head blown half away. There be a smoking pistol in the captain's hand now and I didn't even see him draw it.

Crew: 49/80

Ain't sure at all if I can outdraw *that* fetid freak, even on a good day.

"Don't nobody else make a move," I order me crew with a voice much steadier than I be expecting.

By rights, I should be soiling meself right now, as a few of me mateys have already done by the smell of it. But I be feeling calm and steady as a rock. Means that I've either gone completely starkers or Hero 2nd Class be having some bolstering effect on me nerves. I be quietly hoping for the latter.

I see movement again, this time on me other side, and I be about to give the sailor a right barrelling when the sod hoves into view and stops me words in me throat. It be Sandwich and there in his hands be me Star. He's drawn it out of the wheel and now he be walking straight toward the Dreamer's gangplank.

"Where you going with that, Sandwich?"

He pauses and looks at me over his shoulder. Them baby blues are as dark as the waters above us and near as impenetrable as the mist clawing its way up the sides of our boat.

"To free a god."

Even his tone be different now, his lovely noble notes now distorted with brine and baleful monstrosity.

"He Who Slumbers in the Drowning Dark?"

"He who was imprisoned before the dawn of history," he answers. "He who has languished and suffered, chained by those who would deny his rightful place."

He holds up the Star in his corpse-white hands. His voice rises to a fever pitch and spittle froths in the corners of his mouth. "They stole his Star, kept it for themselves. Yet I shall return his blessed light, thrust open the door to his ancient prison, and from the Drowning Dark, Cthulhu shall rise!"

Them words be bitter and painful to swallow indeed, shoved down a throat what be suddenly tight with fury and sorrow. I be a 3rd Class Lover alright. A moon-eyed idiot what be falling for a pretty face so hard that I be sinking all the way to hell.

I glance at the ghast captain and the second pistol tucked into his belt. Sandwich follows me gaze and quirks an eyebrow.

"They will not kill you, Grace."

"That be bloody Captain Deadeye to you, turncoat," growls North.

"Easy there, Sailmaster," I placate her, though there be a whole tsunami of foul words I be wishing to drown this bastard in. But this ain't no time for self-satisfaction.

Sandwich sighs. "I am no traitor, Ms North. My loyalties have never swayed. Cthulhu commands and I obey. I sailed from England to answer his call." He turns to me and the bastard has the gall to smile. "You, captain, were simply a fortunate turn of events."

"Nay. Nothing fortunate about the cast of your dice, Sandwich. That pack of ghouls be slitting your throat as soon as you step aboard that tomb of a tub. They be sinking you to join that drowned god of yours, and then they be sailing on their merry way back to Atlantis."

He smiles, and I've seen warmer expressions on a shark. "No, captain. They will not. The captain there and I had a good heart to heart, you see." He unwinds the bandage around his forearm and shows me the still livid cut lurking beneath. Unlike all his other wounds, this one ain't healed even a smidge. "Remember my little ritual, the one that bathed the Albatross in imperial radiance?"

Understanding dawns and it be a blood-red sunrise. "You weren't protecting us. You were reaching out to these dead bastards for help."

"Quite so, captain. I see you have been investing some points in Wit of late."

Oh, I be sorely wanting to punch that smug smirk right off his face. "What's in it for them, then? They was meant to be guarding the emperor and the Star, to stop some mad bastard like you from freeing that great bugger of a monster down below."

"A thousand years of guard duty? That grows tiresome for even the most stoic of hearts." He looks to the Dreamer and there be genuine sympathy in his eyes. "They only wish to rest now. To enjoy the peace of death they have been denied for so long."

"Cthulhu's going to give them that?"

"Indeed."

"And what plans does he have for everyone else? A god like that, imprisoned for millenia, I imagine he has a few things he wants to get off his chest."

"Quite so, captain. This corrupt and violent world shall be washed away, and a new world of purity and peace shall emerge with the receding tide."

"He be offering you a lifeboat during all this?"

His grin be that of a proud child. "And his faithful shall inherit the earth."

And with that, he turns and crosses the gangplank. Then he pauses at the gunwale and glances at me over his shoulder.

"Do not worry, *Captain* Deadeye. You and your crew will not be expected to stand by as dumb witnesses to this wondrous event. Cthulhu has slept for a long time. I thought it might be nice to treat him. A little breakfast in bed? After all, he has a *very* big day ahead of him."

Then he nods to the ghast captain who in turn whispers a command that be too quiet to catch. But his crew seem to hear it loud and clear. The whole ship creaks, clatters and rustles as they lurch to their posts. The gangplank lifts, the sails unfurl, and off the

Dreamer glides, pushed along by a stiff breeze that none of us can feel.

The cloying quiet be ripped apart by a piercing shriek. I spin about and see that it be Rumguts, shivering and pointing at the biggest damned tentacle I ever seen. Her second shriek heralds a second tentacle. Then cries go up all over me ship as a dozen more of them looming limbs burst out of the water on all sides. Rumguts dives to one side as the first one thumps down onto our deck. Me ship's timbers groan in protest as the tentacle's sucker takes hold and the sinuous thing begins to contract.

"Captain! What do we do?!" There be panic in that voice that I ain't heard before.

It be Inkman, his lips curled back, his eyes wide, and his whole body rigid with terror. I can't look at him, not when he be like this. Ain't the Inkman I know. Ain't the Inkman *he* knows neither. I turn away and I run.

"Captain?!"

Three strides, four strides, five…

"Captain!!"

…ten strides, eleven, twelve, thirteen…

Onto a barrel with me left boot, onto the gunwale with me right, and then I be sailing through the air. I pass between two more tentacles as they descend upon me stricken Albatross.

Me 30 Perception points have told me true. Nine and a half meters from the Albatross to the Dreamer. Had I waited a moment longer, I'd have plunged into that misty water, and Bathala-knows what be waiting for me down there.

Since me Read the Brine ability still be on cooldown, it's me Wits of 27 what have calculated the Speed and trajectory of me target. And it be all 28 Sand what's made me take this Leap of Faith with neither trepidation nor hesitation.

When I land on the Dreamer's main deck, me weapons already be drawn. Stormshot in me left and me Seahawk Saber in me right.

Before I take me first step, I activate Daring Dash and throw meself toward the object of me aching desires. Sandwich.

I hit him hard and we sprawl onto the boards. Through the blood rushing in me ears, I hear the whine of the ghast's pistol shot as it passes over our heads. Seems Daring Dash be too quick even for the ghast captain. Bet it be the first shot he's missed in a very long time.

With me fresh-minted Kinesthete coordination, I've kept me left arm free, even though the rest of me body be tangled up with me erstwhile lover, and Stormshot be a comforting weight in me palm.

"Crack!" says Stormshot and "Crackle" says both ghast captain and gale lich as they go down thrashing and sparking with lightning.

Your pistol Damage = 300
Level 10 Dreamer Captain
HP: 900/1200

Your lightning Damage = 50
Level 9 Gale Lich
HP: 950/1000

I knew I wouldn't have a hope in hell of killing them. I just wanted to distract them for a moment or two. Just enough time to shove me squirming Sandwich away. Just enough time to sweep me Seahawk down on his wrist, freeing hand and Star from his treacherous flesh.

True to form, he be a well-mannered lad and has the good grace to scream. While something dark and vengeful in me could listen to that scream all day long, I ain't got the time right now. But what I *do* have time for is a little closure. Me former bunkmate deserves as much, and frankly, so the bloody hell do I.

Touch of Fate shimmers into place a fraction of a moment before a dozen pistol shots try to burst me bubble.

Touch of Fate Aura: 1400/2000

If a dead man could look bemused, those what have just fired on me be looking damn well bamboozled. And I ain't waiting around for them to recover their rotten Wits.

Reaver Rage sends me over the edge, overcoming any faint bit of feeling I might have had for James Montagu of Sandwich. One fierce stroke, that's all it takes to slice right through that lying toff's throat. I look into his baby blues one last time, all wide and innocent like a frightened child, as the bastard gurgles his last. Ain't more false words coming out of that mouth, and it be them otherwords what get the final say.

You have killed James Montagu of Sandwich, a Level 6 English Captain.
Your XP Reward = 600XP
Progress to Pirate Captain Level 10 = 81575/90000

Then I cut through the ranks of them ghouls, reaping me a path to the closest falconet, ignoring them otherwords now as they flash past me eyes.

And it be right kind of the posted gunner to have lined up me Albatross with practiced precision. Seems he were planning to cut Jonesy down with grapeshot should the necessity arise. The barrel be aligned perfectly with the helm.

I slice him down while trying to ignore the barrage of shots me aura be shrugging off.

Touch of Fate Aura: 500/2000

I sheath me Seahawk and use Hasty Hands to help me haul the grapeshot out of that swivel gun quicksmart. I drop them shots into the sea before replacing them with the Star. Meanwhile, the ghouls be hacking with earnest at me aura, desperate to slice me into schnitzel and reclaim their precious Star.

Touch of Fate Aura: 100/2000

I grab the gunner's flint and tinder, light the fuse, and pray to Bathala that this here ghoul be half the cannoneer that Powderfinger be. The aim looks about right, but since I traded in me Gunner 1st Class skill, I just don't know.

The falconet roars, the diamond flies through the air, a shooting star like no other, and smacks into the railing of me quarterdeck. Me pounding heart skips a beat as I will that bloody rock to stay put, be stuck fast and in that wood, to refrain from toppling into the sea where it won't do anyone no good but clammy old Cthulhu.

Touch of Fate Aura: 50/2000

I see Jonesy, her dreadlocks flying as she rolls under the swipe of a tentacle on her way to fetching the Star. I see Silverback and North, boarding axes in hand, chopping at a tentacle what's wrapped itself around the main mast. I see Inkman, come to his senses now, jabbing and hacking at a tentacle with his taiaha, his tattooed face splattered with gore and his eyes wide and wild. I see Rumguts and Powderfinger defending that Irish soak's grog barrels with a falconet, blasting any tentacle what dare comes close to her pride and joy. I see Black and White Russian, side by side, fighting off them tentacular advances, repelling them borders with every ounce of ferocity and courage they have left. I see Doc the Croc rushing from one fallen sailor to the next, his caring hands belying the cruelty of his eyes. I see all of me pirates, fighting for their sorry, salty lives.

Touch of Fate Aura: 0/2000

Jonesy wrenches the Star of Atlantis from the splintered rail and looks up at me. Our eyes meet over the mist-bound sea. I smile at her, letting her know that all be well, even as the first shot passes through me flesh.

You have taken 50 Damage from a pistol shot!
Grace "Deadeye" Cortez
Level 9 Pirate Captain
HP: 358/408

In all me days of pirating, I ain't never be shot before. Stabbed, sliced, battered and bruised, aye. But for all the lead balls I be dealing out, I ain't never received one in return. Not until this very moment.

There ain't no pain. Not yet. So I fill me lungs with air and send me Rallying Cry across the watery abyss between us.

"This place be R'lyeh, Jonesy! It be all the Star needs. A thought and a spoken word."

You have taken 75 Damage from a cutlass slice!
Grace "Deadeye" Cortez
Level 9 Pirate Captain
HP: 283/408

I grit me teeth against the pain, point at the helm behind her and mouth a single word. "Freeport".

I see the pleading in Jonesy's eyes. I shake me head.

You have taken 150 Damage from pistol shots!
Grace "Deadeye" Cortez
Level 9 Pirate Captain
HP: 133/408

The falconet before me be splattered in blood. Me own blood.

You have taken 75 Damage from a cutlass strike!
Grace "Deadeye" Cortez
Level 9 Pirate Captain
HP: 58/408

There be blood on me hands, blood all over me body, blood in me mouth. The sea-sky takes on a scarlet pallor, like the setting of the sun, but I know it just be the blood weeping from me eyes.

And out there in that bloody sea, Jonesy cradles the Star in her hands, presses it to the wheel, and mouths a word I recognize, even from here.

"Port Royal."

Even better, I reckon to meself. Me navigator be going home, and she be taking me crew with her.

I blink and they be gone, only tentacles and splinters of timber to mark their passing. Me friends be safe and sound, with the Albatross at their disposal and all the riches of an ancient empire in their hold. Jonesy will make a fine captain, and Inkman will be a rock at her side, just like he was for me. They be a fine crew. The finest a captain could ever hope for. And I be wishing them all the best.

Congratulations!
You have committed an act of True Heroism
You are now a Hero: 1st Class
The legend of Captain "Deadeye" Cortez will be remembered and spoken of across all of the seven seas.

The water churns and swells beneath us. A sound like no other erupts from the Drowning Dark, a call so drenched in wretched despair that it nearly breaks me heart to hear it.

Then me heart does break, blasted in half by a dead man's shot.

The Dreamer Captain has scored a *Critical Hit* against you!
You have taken 150 Damage from a pistol shot!
Grace "Deadeye" Cortez
Level 9 Pirate Captain
HP: -92/408

And so I fall.
And so I sink.
And so I feel the Drowning Dark embrace me.
And so...

AFTERWORD

Thank you so much for picking up and reading *Skulls of Atlantis*! I hope you enjoyed it.

Please take a moment to leave a review and/or rating on your favorite platform. Reader feedback is a vital part of the Indie author business. The more reviews and ratings we get, the more chance we have of getting noticed by other readers and the more likely we can get the financial support needed to write more books.

I'm always working to better understand the fields of science fiction, fantasy and gaming, and I collect those realizations into a monthly Lorekeeper newsletter which I'd be happy to send you.

As an added bonus, you will receive a FREE dark yet humorous Gamelit Novella featuring an equally ass-kicking female MC.

Sign up here >> https://www.edmcrae.com/free-stormbane

ACKNOWLEDGMENTS

Special thanks to all the readers on Royal Road. Your enthusiastic support has played a massive part in getting this book done!

ABOUT THE AUTHOR

Edwin McRae has been a screenwriter and narrative designer for over 12 years now. After four years of writing for television, he started with Grinding Gear Games in 2010. He became lead writer on the creative team that took their online ARPG, Path of Exile, from 80,000 players to 20 million players and a 100 million dollar buyout from Tencent. During the last eight years he's worked with numerous Indie game developers, helping them turn their ideas into stories that players can experience and enjoy.

For Edwin, the Gamelit genre has beautifully combined his twin passions of video games and science fiction.

You can find links to Edwin's other books and interactive stories over at www.edmcrae.com/books

If you're on Facebook, check out Edwin's author page which he updates regularly with thoughts about gaming, science-fiction and snippets about his writing life.

Please do drop in for a look!

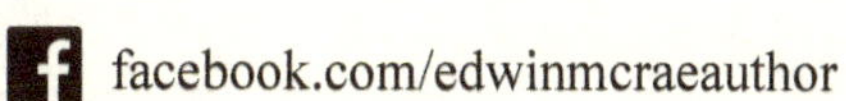
facebook.com/edwinmcraeauthor